The
Proud Sinner

Books by Priscilla Royal

The Medieval Mysteries
Wine of Violence
Tyrant of the Mind
Sorrow Without End
Justice for the Damned
Forsaken Soul
Chambers of Death
Valley of Dry Bones
A Killing Season
The Sanctity of Hate
Covenant with Hell
Satan's Lullaby
Land of Shadows
The Proud Sinner

The Proud Sinner

A Medieval Mystery

Priscilla Royal

Poisoned Pen Press

Copyright © 2017 by Priscilla Royal

First Edition 2017

10 9 8 7 6 5 4 3 2 1

Library of Congress Catalog Card Number: 2016952018

ISBN: 9781464207259   Hardcover
         9781464207273   Trade Paperback

Poisoned Pen Press
6962 E. First Ave., Ste. 103
Scottsdale, AZ 85251
www.poisonedpenpress.com
info@poisonedpenpress.com

Printed in the United States of America

*To Paula Mildenhall, my Australian friend,
who owns a heart as big as her wonderful country.*

Acknowledgments

Patrick Hoi Yan Cheung, Christine and Peter Goodhugh, Maddee James, Henie Lentz, Dianne Levy, Paula Mildenhall, Sharon Kay Penman, Barbara Peters (Poisoned Pen Bookstore in Scottsdale, Arizona), Robert Rosenwald and all the staff of Poisoned Pen Press, Marianne and Sharon Silva, Lyn and Michael Speakman, the staff of the University Press Bookstore (Berkeley, California).

Fair is foul, and foul is fair,
Hover through the fog and filthy air.
　　　　—Witches, *Macbeth*, Act 1, Scene 1, 1.10-11

Chapter One

Two women knelt in silence before Prioress Eleanor, heads bowed. One wore a diaphanous veil that obscured her face. The other suffered a ragged scar that cut through her lips.

The prioress gave her blessing and bid them rise.

"To what do we owe the honor of this visit, my lady?" Anchoress Juliana raised her veil as she stood. Although her cheeks were hollowed by habitual fasting, the wounds from the time when she beat her head against the stones of her enclosure walls were long healed.

The other woman remained kneeling while a heavily pregnant cat rubbed against her legs. Reaching out, she stroked the purring creature.

"I see that my Arthur has visited once again," Eleanor said, looking at the cat's rounded belly.

"Or one of his sons," the anchoress replied. "The females come here so Eda can ease their birthing." She turned and gently touched the woman's shoulder.

Eda blushed but said nothing.

"I have come to seek your advice," the prioress said to the anchoress, a woman whom many called holy.

Juliana tilted her head and waited, her expression warm with affection. Although their journeys to their chosen vocations had taken very different paths, she and Prioress Eleanor had been friends since childhood.

"It is about Gracia. The time has come for her to decide whether to stay in our priory and take vows, or to seek the secular life. She has not yet spoken to me of her choice, or requested my advice, but the moment for either will come soon."

The anchoress concurred.

"Before it arrives, I need your counsel and beg for wisdom to guide me in helping Gracia make the best decision. You would have a better understanding of her needs and wishes, for I can think only with my selfish heart in this matter."

Eda glanced up, first at the prioress and next at the woman she served. Her eyes asked a question she otherwise left unspoken.

Eleanor saw her expression and read its meaning.

Sitting back on her heels, Eda waited and held the rumbling cat close to her chest.

"I have no wish to pry into confidences between friends," Eleanor said to the anchoress' maid. "I only seek to understand what Gracia truly longs for. It is her happiness I care most about and not my own desires."

Gazing with fondness on her servant, Juliana's eyes asked permission to share some of what she had told her about Gracia.

Eda hesitated, then nodded and rose, releasing the cat from her arms. Walking a short distance, she stood by the heavy wooden door that opened into a world she still visited but which her mistress had utterly rejected.

The cat saw a fleeing shadow on the floor and with a rumble of joy gave awkward chase into the shadows of the simple altar.

"Come with me," Juliana said to the prioress and gestured toward a smaller door that led beyond the small quarters in which she and Eda lived.

Eleanor followed.

The garden outside was surrounded by a high stone wall, glistening with rills of ice. The ground was covered with fresh snow. Although the plot grew many vegetables and herbs in the warm seasons, the wintering earth was as hard as a devil's heart. The soft whiteness masked its current barrenness; a few mounds suggested that the garden was simply hiding while it patiently waited for its imminent resurrection.

In the far corner, there was a small stone bench, but the two women chose to walk.

The air was bitter cold.

Eleanor looked up. The grey sky was fading into a mist that threatened to shatter into snowflakes. Although the late afternoon light was growing pale, it shone with weak determination on a tiny part of the wall and gave a fragile beauty to those rivulets frozen in place before they could escape the chill.

"Does Eda ever speak?" Eleanor asked.

"Once or twice she has tried, and I welcome it when she does. The effort shows a regained trust, but I never demand she speak." Juliana scowled with a rare anger. "I pray daily to God that He will forgive her parents for the agony they inflicted on their daughter. In truth, I believe they did so out of love and sought only to cure her of her faltering speech."

Eleanor winced. How could a child endure the pain of a burning iron pressed against her lips? A respected physician advised that remedy for Eda's stuttering, but her parents could only bear her screams so long before her father snatched the iron from the doctor's hands and flung both it and the tormenter from the house. After that day, however, Eda refused to utter any words.

"I pray for her cure as well, but until God chooses the time for that mercy, she and I converse in gestures. For other needs that suit our life in the anchorage, we continue to develop special signs."

"And Gracia has learned this hand speech," Eleanor said. "She told me."

"Each loves the other with the devotion of a sister, my lady." Juliana looked up at the vanishing sky and held out a hand to catch any tiny flakes.

There were no harbingers.

"Gracia and Eda have suffered profoundly from the cruelty of life," the anchoress added softly, "but have found comfort for their pain in each other and at the priory."

Eleanor did not question her observation or conclusion. Anchoress Juliana had had come to her vocation suffering deep wounds inflicted by the world and understood the anguish well.

In silence, they continued on their circular path, now blackened where their pacing had melted the snow and exposed the soil beneath. The earth remained unyielding and crunched in protest under their light weight. The sharp air had whipped their faces into a pink glow, even the anchoress' sallow cheeks.

"You say that Eda has found peace at Tyndal, yet she has not taken vows." Might Gytha follow that path? Eleanor wondered.

"She has no wish to go back to her family," Juliana replied. "I remain patient and trust God to guide her."

"Her family aside, has she ever expressed a desire to leave our priory for a worldly life?"

The anchoress shook her head. "What has the world to offer her? No man would marry her. The fearful have always mocked her. She has no siblings or other kin. After her parents die, she would be alone, reduced to begging on the road to Norwich or even whoring."

The prioress shivered, but the cold was not the reason. "After Gracia's family died of a fever, she was left to beg in Walsingham and raped before she had even reached womanhood. Eda must know this tale and have learned from it. Do you think the two have discussed the future and their choices?"

"I do not know, my lady, but it is likely. Indeed, I wonder if they could bear to be parted. Perhaps their mutual confidences and experiences are leading them..." Juliana stopped and looked toward the door to the anchorage.

Eda stepped into the garden and raised a hand to catch the anchoress' attention. Lifting both hands over her head, she acted as if she were ringing a church bell, then put one hand to her mouth. With the other, she extended her hand, palm up, toward the prioress as if begging a mercy.

"Eda says that a messenger has come for you and waits in the chapel outside the anchorage door," Juliana said. "I fear it is a matter of some urgency."

Concerned, Eleanor hurried inside. When she reached the solid oaken door that was the only entrance from the world to the walled-in anchorage, she waited for the maid to unlock the barrier. As Prioress of Tyndal, she had a key to this place but chose to honor the terms of Juliana's entombment and never used it. Only Eda possessed the other key to allow her entrance and egress so she might provide whatever was needed to serve her holy mistress.

The maid inserted the key and opened the door.

Eleanor quickly slipped through and into the Lady Chapel outside.

The door slammed shut behind her with a purposeful thud and a loud click as the key was turned.

Brother Beorn, a lay brother, stepped into sight, his face pale with worry. "My lady, you must come immediately! A party of seven abbots has arrived, and one is gravely ill. Prior Andrew is with them."

Seven abbots, one sick? Eleanor felt a foreboding, an unease she had not suffered in a long time. "Summon Sister Anne and one of the healing brothers from the hospital to attend the sick man," she said. "Next, gather some of the lay brothers and swiftly prepare the new guest quarters for our visitors. Since the attached kitchen must also be made ready to serve its first meal, send word to Sister Matilda that she will be required to perform one of her miracles and increase the amount of our own supper tonight to feed the abbots and their servants."

Brother Beorn inclined his head, then swiftly left to do her bidding.

As she hurried to the courtyard, Prioress Eleanor prayed for the sick abbot's recovery and caught herself begging God not to bring her priory more than it could bear. But an ominous chill had settled into her soul, and she feared her plea would be denied.

Chapter Two

Sister Anne watched two lay brothers ease Abbot Ilbert onto the bed. Dire though his illness seemed, she would not touch him nor stand too close. God must take a hand in healing, she thought, for she had no choice but to honor the spirit of the vows both the abbot and she had taken.

He moaned.

She dared to step nearer.

His eyes were wide with terror, or so she first concluded, but then she saw that his pupils were extremely dilated. A white froth coated his lips.

Ordering one of the lay brothers to the sick man's side, she told him to place one hand on the abbot's forehead and another on his chest.

"He has no fever," the lay brother said. "His heart is pounding rapidly."

Sister Anne was perplexed and prayed the abbot could answer questions. "Are you able to describe your suffering?" she asked gently while fearing any explanation was beyond his strength.

"A priest. I want a priest," Ilbert mumbled and twisted his head to stare at the wall. "Get thee hence, Whore of Babylon!"

The sub-infirmarian stepped back, saying to the lay brother, "There must be a priest in the party of abbots but send for Brother Thomas as well. I need his keen observations."

The young man hurried away.

She motioned to the thin man who had followed Abbot Ilbert to this room after helping him down from his horse. If he is the abbot's servant, she thought, perhaps he can give me vital details. If I am to treat this man properly, I must quickly determine the nature of this troubling sickness. "You came to Tyndal Priory because your master was ill. Please describe his symptoms. When did he first appear unwell?"

The man glanced anxiously at his prone master as if hoping for guidance in how he should reply. Realizing nothing would be forthcoming, he clutched his hands nervously. "I fear I can tell you little enough, Sister. Soon after we left the inn, where we spent last night, he complained of feeling weak." He lowered his voice. "Twice along the road, we were obliged to stop because he suffered an urgent need to urinate. But he could not do so and groaned as if in pain, although he refused to speak of it. When we approached the village of Tyndal, he announced he was too sick to ride further. We were most fortunate that the Abbot of Caldwell knew of your priory hospital and led us to your gate."

Sister Anne was not pleased when she heard the abbot could not pass water, and she prayed he did not have a blockage. The man was skeletally thin, but that could be caused by fasting and not a cancer. "Had he been unable to urinate before this journey?"

The man again looked to the abbot, his eyes begging for orders and direction. "Not to my knowledge," he whispered, "but I have not been long in his service."

"You mentioned he seemed in pain on the journey. Do you know if the pain came in waves? Did he indicate by any means where he felt it? "

If the cause was stones, they might still pass, or so she hoped. If not, treatment might require a procedure she could not perform. Although some swore by black cumin to dissolve the stones, she had never known that to work. Physicians often inserted fingers into the rectum to feel for the stone and try to squeeze it out. Surgery was the last resort, as men often died from it. Yet stones were preferable to a growth that blocked the urine. For that, there was no cure.

The thin man waved his hand vaguely around his own abdomen but denied being aware of anything more specific.

"Is there anyone in your party in whom he confides? I am not asking to learn about the man's sins but rather the details of his mortal ills."

The man squared his shoulders. "As Abbot Ilbert often proclaims, he looks only to God for comfort and advice. Mortals might lead him to sin rather than salvation. His faith is his only companion, and his confidences are solely for God."

Loyally spoken, she thought, but most unhelpful. Shutting her eyes to hide her frustration, she asked if the abbot had recently vomited or complained of nausea. She was not surprised when the servant said he did not know.

Noticing that the abbot's eyes were shut, Sister Anne walked away from the servant and slowly approached the bed until she was close enough to observe Ilbert more clearly.

The servant gasped as if terrified that she might do something to sully his master's chastity, but he also seemed reluctant to criticize a nun.

Taking pity on the frightened man, Sister Anne assured him that she had taken the same vows as the abbot and understood how far she must stand away from the bed to honor both words and intent.

He gulped and commenced sweating.

She did not move from her spot and began to study the abbot for clues to his illness.

Ilbert's hands were swollen, she noted, which would suggest kidney disease. But she needed to know if there had been a history of his complaints. If he had vomited or ever complained of pain specific to a part of his body, for instance, she might find a clue to the illness. Although this servant had not been with Abbot Ilbert long, he should have noticed something if this onset of illness was not sudden. Surely another servant would have mentioned ongoing sufferings to this unhelpful man? If the condition was sudden, these symptoms were even more troubling, as was the foam now bubbling around his mouth.

Not daring to step closer to the patient, she spoke to the lay brother who had come with her from the hospital. "Examine him as best you can, Brother, and note anything that suggests how his humors might have become unbalanced."

The lay brother walked toward the bed.

As if startled by the movement, Abbot Ilbert's eyes flew open, and he shook his head back and forth with frightening violence. His eyes were glazed, and his pupils were almost completely black.

In fear, the lay brother jumped away.

Ilbert began to howl, and his body arched and fell with powerful convulsions. As if he were fighting off a band of demons, he beat his arms against the bed.

The abbot's servant screamed and ran from the room.

Shaking off her own surprise, Sister Anne ran forward but instantly realized she could do nothing to help the man.

As quickly as the convulsions had started, they were over. His body still, Ilbert lay on the bed like a heap of discarded clothes.

Looking down at him, the sub-infirmarian knew without question that Abbot Ilbert was dead.

◇◇◇

"Dead? He is really dead?" Odo, the rotund Abbot of Caldwell, ran his tongue around his plump lips while his thick-skinned brow attempted to furrow in dismay. "How unfortunate for us all."

Prior Andrew said nothing. Bending his painful leg, he shifted his weight to the stick he often used now to help him walk.

Prioress Eleanor had been prepared to offer the abbot sympathy over the tragic death of a brother servant of God. She had not been ready for his reaction that expressed more annoyance than sorrow. Fearing she might reveal her surprise, she bowed her head and murmured something incomprehensible.

It did not matter what she said. The Abbot of Caldwell was not listening.

Abbot Odo gazed over their heads and around the courtyard with the fervor of a pilgrim seeking a holy site. Then his eyes settled with evident joy on the newly constructed guest quarters a short distance from where they all stood. "A gift to Tyndal Priory from Queen Eleanor, or so I have been told."

As he waved in the direction of the new building and smiled, Eleanor found his expression had an unexpected charm and seemed oddly familiar. That observation unsettled her even more than she had been over his callousness.

"Our queen possesses a deep faith," she said, keeping any excess of both humility and pride out of her voice. "We were grateful she honored our priory with one of her many benevolent acts."

He nodded with a twinkle of amusement in his eyes.

This man might easily be dismissed as one too obsessed with the carnal pleasures of food and drink to offer any threat, she thought, but she concluded that the sparkle suggested a perceptive intelligence and cunning wit. Perhaps he takes pleasure in playing with the foolish who, because of his corpulence, underestimate him. She resolved not to be one of that number.

"I assume we shall be housed there soon? The air is icy, and our journey has been a tiring one. I am sure your hospitable charity includes a hot meal sufficient to revive us." A slight mockery lurked behind his otherwise genuine and openly joyful anticipation of supper.

Dangerously clever or not, Eleanor thought, Abbot Odo was still a man who divided his day, not by the hours of prayerful Office, but by the arrival of meals. Perhaps she was being unkind, but surely God would forgive her. As for penance, she was certain it would be appropriate to the magnitude of her sin.

"The lay brothers are preparing your rooms now. As soon as you are settled, the kitchen will serve a supper for you. Because we were unable to plan for your visit, this meal must be a simple one, prepared in accordance with the Rule of Saint Benedict and shared by those of us who live and pray here. I promise, however, that it will be sustaining." The prioress' smile was calculated to answer the abbot's mockery with scorn.

The abbot looked troubled.

Ignoring him, the prioress asked Prior Andrew to go to the warming room and confirm that the lay brothers were preparing the guest quarters, not sitting idly around the fire. The request was unnecessary, but she knew his leg ached badly from the cold. By greeting the new visitors to Tyndal, her prior had sufficiently honored his obligation under the rules of monastic hospitality and need not suffer any longer.

Glancing at her with gratitude for the escape she offered, the prior hastily limped away.

Abbot Odo cleared his throat. "Supper is always a cold meal in, ah, smaller monasteries. Surely not here!" As if reminding her that he was an abbot while she was a mere woman, whatever her rank and birth, his eyes bored into the tiny prioress standing before him.

Eleanor, her staff of office held firmly in hand, boldly met his gaze. "A hot one is always prepared here in winter." She quickly softened her voice. "Although it will be a humble stew, Sister Matilda will make sure the quantity is sufficient even for those few in your party who are not accustomed to the meager diets we chose when we vow ourselves to God's service." As a woman, the prioress was skilled in the art of issuing a barbed retort properly wrapped in a humble tone.

He blinked.

She had won that contest.

"Wine? I assume you have decent wine?"

"We and our gracious King Edward share the same wine merchant."

"Ah." Odo sounded like a man who had just been serviced by an especially skillful prostitute and was much relieved. "I should have remembered," he added with that familiar and troubling smile.

"You seem quite knowledgeable about Tyndal Priory," Eleanor said, growing more curious than she knew she ought to be. Yet why would he know so much about an obscure little priory near the coast of East Anglia? "I thought Caldwell Abbey was far to the south of here."

Odo glowed with the delight of a chess player about to checkmate his opponent's king. "You do not know?"

"I am an ignorant woman," Eleanor replied.

"My younger brother is Crowner Ralf. I grew up in this boggy land, although God was kind enough to spare me too many years of suffering here."

To stop herself from betraying her total loss of composure, Eleanor clutched her staff of office until her fingers hurt. If the crowner had ever mentioned his second brother's name, she had forgotten it. "We shall immediately send word to him that you have arrived," she said in a steady enough voice.

"Do not rush to summon him," Odo muttered. "I would not grieve if I never saw the foul reprobate again."

Eleanor knew that Ralf, the king's man and her friend, felt the same about Odo, servant of God and Abbot of Caldwell.

Chapter Three

Odo stabbed his knife into his bowl of stew. Broth splattered the immaculate white tablecloth, dotting it with brown spots.

Sitting beside him, Abbot Gifre stopped eating long enough to glare at the wanton stains. "Were you never taught manners? Your family rank may not be as high as mine, but surely they were not villeins."

"This is a wretched meal." The Abbot of Caldwell glowered at his table companions. "Where is the meat? Has anyone found a single morsel?"

Two chose to shake their heads. The others ignored him.

"Is it too much to ask for a little venison to be served to honored guests? This broth would be meager fare for a Lenten stew." Odo wiped his knife carefully on a piece of bread, popped the flavored lump into his mouth, and slammed the knife down next to the bowl before shoving the spoon to one side. "This prioress is favored by King Edward and his queen. Surely royal beneficence extends to gifts of fresh meat from the king's forests."

"Meat heats the blood," Didier replied, his expression conveying the proper look of disapproval.

"Drink your wine, Abbot Odo," Abbot Mordredus said after a final sip of the stew. "Perhaps it will blunt your foul mood even if the meal cannot fill your capacious stomach." He leaned over and let his eyes gaze on Odo's rounded belly with undisguised scorn. "If you imbibe your usual quantity, you will soon believe the bits of chicken are the finest venison."

"Chicken? You had chicken in your supper?" Odo glared into his bowl. "I found only parsnips." He grunted. "I hate parsnips."

"There is a turnip." Abbot Tristram raised his spoon with the pale root vegetable visible. Then he seemed to lose interest in his meal, dropped the item back into his bowl and began to slowly twirl his spoon in the partially eaten stew.

"Hush, all of you!" Abbot Ancell carefully placed his spoon beside his bowl and looked around at the party of abbots. "Have you each forgotten that one of our brothers in Christ has just died?"

"Not a man known for his sanctity." Abbot Mordredus tore off a piece of bread from the loaf he shared with Didier and rubbed it around his bowl.

Ancell put a finger to his lips. "I advise discretion, lest we encourage wicked gossip among those less able than we to distinguish virtuous criticism from the vice of idle talk." He bent his head toward the table of their servants not far removed from their own.

Silence fell.

Two Tyndal lay brothers arrived with more loaves of bread and an ewer of wine.

Despite his complaints, Odo reached for the large earthenware container of stew he shared with Gifre. Before he added more to his bowl, he first stood and hunted for chunks of chicken hidden with the root vegetables, serving himself all the bits of meat he found.

Gifre waited for his companion to display good manners and offer to serve him. When Odo chose instead to ladle spoonfuls from his bowl into his mouth with a dedicated celerity, Gifre called to one of the Tyndal lay brothers and asked to be given the remaining broth, now significantly bereft of chicken. Although he did not speak, his narrowed eyes expressed very clearly the depth of his contempt for the uncouth Abbot of Caldwell.

"This stew was quite hot," Abbot Didier remarked with evident pleasure as he looked up at the lay brother who placed another barley loaf between him and the abbot who shared portions with him.

"Prioress Eleanor not only ordered a new kitchen to be built adjacent to these guest quarters," the young lay brother said, "but an enclosed passageway from there so the food is not chilled by winter winds."

"If she is that clever," Odo growled, "she could have gotten decent meat to serve us instead of these wretched vegetables. Surely, her infirmarian has told her that vegetables are not good for a man's health."

"The seasoning of the dish is pleasant," Gifre muttered.

Odo chewed thoughtfully on a piece of fowl. "A parsnip is a parsnip, no matter how a cook tries to disguise it. Even mutton would be an improvement."

Ancell opened his mouth to say something but evidently thought better of it and went back to his wine. He waved aside more of the dark bread.

A priory lay brother bent to whisper in Abbot Gifre's ear.

The abbot glanced over at the servants' table and pursed his lips as he pondered his decision. "They have eaten enough, Brother." He glanced around at his companions. "Shall we agree to dismiss them from the table so they might prepare our bedding for the night?"

Most nodded. Ancell failed to respond. He had folded his hands and shut his eyes.

Gifre waved the lay brother off in the direction of the servants who had already assumed their meal was over and had risen to attend their tasks. A couple of them whisked chunks of bread into their sleeves.

Another priory lay brother asked the abbots if they wished a man to lead them to the church for the Offices.

Abbot Tristram politely refused the offer. "Each of us has brought his own prie-dieu on this journey. For the Offices, we shall gather here for evening and morning prayers."

"As it pleases you," the lay brother replied, carefully keeping even the mildest censure out of his voice. "But the choir of monks at our priory is renowned for beautiful singing, and you may wish to hear them. Many have claimed that their voices, raised to God in praise, are like a joyous blessing." The lay brother's eyes twinkled, although it was unclear whether he was express- ing delight over the singing or amusement over the hesitancy of these abbots to suffer a walk through the chill winter air to experience the wonder.

"The denial of such pleasure shall be one of our penances," Tristram replied and looked at his unfinished meal. His face was pale enough to suggest he alone might have cause to avoid the cold night walk.

Once told there was no further need for them to remain, the Tyndal lay brothers disappeared from the dining room.

As soon as they were alone, Abbot Didier sighed. "I suppose we shall all pray tonight for Abbot Ilbert's soul."

"As we must for all sinners," Ancell replied. "He was also one of our most revered brothers in Christ or he would not have shared this arduous journey to Norwich."

Odo had found a chicken bone in his stew and was sucking on it. "I did not understand why he came. Surely Rome knew of his inequities and would have found his presence offensive at this meeting."

"It was the special papal legate who requested his attendance in Norwich." Ancell waved his hand in front of his face and began to rub his reddening eyes. Because supper had begun later than usual, and darkness had fallen, a lay brother had found only two common tallow candles to provide light. Unlike waxen ones, these emitted a thick, reeking smoke. "Ilbert was known for his ability to command donations from many wealthy nobles for the desired crusade, if not men willing enough to take vows and fight." The abbot coughed.

Didier sat back in his chair. "Surely he was misinformed about Ilbert's character or he would not have summoned him just for the coin he might bring."

Ancell did not reply and continued to massage his now- tearing eyes.

"I doubt that," Mordredus said. "His sins were infamous. Even I had heard he was a man suffering from violent wrath, and our abbeys lie at some distance from each other. But I should not condemn on hearsay. All mortals suffer from the weakness of the flesh and fall into sin. Some are contrite and struggle daily with Satan." His glance rested on Didier for a long moment. "Others do not. Perhaps our dead brother had repented, served his penance, and become a man of gentler wisdom."

"Many praised Ilbert for his righteous anger and saw God's purifying fire blazing in his eyes when he lashed out with his whip at the wicked." Tristram clutched his hands in a prayerful manner.

Didier slammed his fist on the table. "And many did not see anything virtuous in his anger. I never did! My nephew was one of his clerks. Ilbert beat him until the lad almost died."

"What was your nephew's sin?" Mordredus leaned forward, eyes wide with interest.

"It was Lent. He had been fasting and collapsed, spilling ink on a good piece of parchment. Ilbert ordered him tied to a pillar and then whipped him himself."

No one said a word.

Ancell broke the silence. Although his voice was hushed, it rang with piercing sharpness in that room of speechless abbots. "Did your nephew remain in Ilbert's service?"

Didier's lips twisted into a sneer. "He went back to his parents who cared for his wounds. When he healed, he bid farewell to them, barricaded himself in his old room, and has never emerged. He still lives, for the servants swear they hear him praying."

Mordredus squeezed his chin with his fingers before saying, "Yet that suffering may have led him to a holier life."

"Without doubt, his suffering will lead him directly to God," Didier replied, "for my nephew will surely starve himself to death soon. Is a marred piece of sheep's flesh worthy of such cruelty by a man sworn to God? I pray daily that the boy will find peace and return to the loving arms of his family."

Odo saw that Gifre had left some stew in his bowl, reached over, and pulled it toward him. Raising the bowl, he gulped the little left and burped.

Gifre closed his eyes and did not open them until he faced the other side of the table where he did not have to gaze upon his fellow abbot's ample jowls.

"Perhaps," Odo said, "Ilbert's death was punishment for his sins." He ran a fingernail between the gaps in his front teeth. "As I heard the tale, the convulsions preceding his death were violent. Lay brothers had to hold him lest his fits caused him to fly off the bed. His eyes darkened and bulged. He repeatedly struck his head and howled." The abbot looked around the table. "Might we not conclude that this death was a proper one for a man of wrath?"

The priory bells began to ring for Compline.

Chapter Four

The next morning, grey mist covered the white earth with soft melancholy. A thin winding sheet of snow had fallen overnight.

The mood of the gathered abbots, their servants, and the priory leaders, who had come to wish them a safe journey to Norwich, was minimally brighter.

Prioress Eleanor looked with anticipation toward the open priory entrance gate. She had sent Brother Thomas to remind Crowner Ralf that his brother had not only arrived but would soon leave. There might be little love between them, but Ralf was loyal to his family and his absence was odd.

"Where is Abbot Tristram?" Gifre was already seated on his horse. His tone suggested impatience to be on his way.

Abbot Didier pointed toward the hospital. "I see him coming."

The missing abbot was slowly wending his way toward the party. Two lay brothers were assisting him.

"He was taken ill in the night," Sister Anne said, bending close to her prioress so others would not hear her. "I advised him to stay in our care until he was well, but he rejected my counsel. Either he has improved significantly or has reason not to let his companions travel on without him."

Eleanor knew that tone of voice well. Her friend and sub-infirmarian was annoyed that the patient had rejected her guidance. When she looked at the expression on Abbot Tristram's face, however, she immediately concluded that the man should have taken it.

"You have caused us to delay," Abbot Mordredus said, his voice as cutting as the winter air. "The special papal legate awaits our arrival!"

Tristram stiffened and waved aside his assistants. "I am ready to leave now."

"Is he?" Eleanor whispered to Anne. "He seems too weak."

"Last night, he began to vomit and suffered diarrhea. His servant ran to the hospital to seek aid. We were able to stop those ailments, but the abbot's pallor is now tinged with a yellow cast. I believe he is growing worse, but he chose to ignore my fears, saying he must travel on." Her expression was sad. "As soon as one of his problems improves, another takes its place."

"What has caused this illness?" Eleanor was watching Tristram's listless progress to the horse held for him to mount. The death of the first abbot yesterday and the current illness of the second were disturbing coincidences, even though each man had exhibited different symptoms. This might not be a common plague, yet the situation concerned her.

"The signs point to food poisoning, but the root vegetable and chicken stew was given to everyone last night, including our own religious. No one else is ill, and Sister Matilda does not tolerate carelessness in her kitchen."

"But the kitchen serving the guest quarters is new. Our dear sister cannot oversee it as she is accustomed to doing for the priory meals. The meal may have had the same ingredients, but the preparation might have been different."

"Supper was prepared under Sister Matilda's eye. When she learned of the abbots' arrival, she had another old chicken killed and found more onions, turnips, and parsnips to add from our stores so there would be enough for the entire party. This stew was cooked in the original kitchen, then brought over to the new one. The only thing done there was to heat it all again so it would be hot for the guests."

Eleanor frowned. "You are certain that none of the other abbots got sick?"

"None. I am convinced that Abbot Tristram is not suffering from anything rotten in the stew that he ate."

Eleanor shared her sub-infirmarian's frustration. If blame were due, she would take the responsibility on herself. As prioress, it was her duty to guarantee the comfort and safety of any guests to which Tyndal offered the grace of hospitality.

Looking over her shoulder, she saw Abbot Odo talking with Prior Andrew. It was evident from the words she overheard that they were discussing how to prepare Abbot Ilbert's corpse so it could be sent back to his abbey for burial. Odo seemed to have strong opinions on the matter for his face was red while her prior looked like a chastened boy.

She sighed and glanced again toward the entry gate. Still no crowner was in sight. What a mismatched trio of brothers, she thought. The eldest was sheriff here but spent all his time at court. He and Ralf looked alike, but their natures lacked any kinship. The only outward resemblance the abbot bore to his brothers was that smile which mirrored Ralf's.

Yet Odo did share other traits with Ralf, Eleanor thought, and some of those mutual qualities might have fueled the intense dislike each felt for the other. Despite her brief acquaintance with the rotund abbot, she had learned that neither was a patient man, both held strong opinions, and each viewed the vocation chosen by the other with contempt. They also shared a passion for food. At least Ralf led an active life and had a wife who learned from Sister Anne that moderation in eating and drinking was important to health. Odo, on the other hand, had clearly never embraced moderation when it came to the pleasures of the table.

A horse neighed with impatience. Another snorted in agreement.

Slow moving though Odo was due to his impressive weight, there was nothing sluggish about his wits, Eleanor thought, and, like the younger brother he loathed, the abbot's eyes never stopped moving lest he miss some important or useful detail. Ralf might condemn his brother for hypocrisy, arrogance, and rampant ambition, but Eleanor suspected that one dismissed the Abbot of Caldwell at one's peril, a fact equally true of the rough-hewn crowner.

Whether or not Ralf did come in time to see his brother, Abbot Odo would be leaving soon, the prioress decided with relief. He was a man who might be easily offended and was not an enemy she cared to have.

A squeal of pain ended all her musing, and she spun around to see the cause.

Two men were holding Abbot Tristram, who had failed to mount his horse and was doubled over with unmistakable agony.

Sister Anne hurried to his side, calling for the assistance of the hospital lay brothers who had remained nearby.

Odo turned his attention away from the prior to the commotion and folded his arms into his sleeves. His expression was inscrutable.

"He should either mount his horse or remain behind," Abbot Ancell muttered. "Daylight flees, and we must reach Norwich before Satan's hour arrives."

Odo walked over to the sick abbot, laid a surprisingly gentle hand on his shoulder, and spoke quietly to him.

Tristram was visibly trembling.

Odo then looked at Sister Anne and asked a question.

Knowing her sub-infirmarian well, Eleanor assumed she was telling the Abbot of Caldwell that his brother in faith was not able to sit on a horse nor was he well enough to continue on this journey, even if he were carried in a litter.

The hospital brothers were awaiting instructions. At the sub-infirmarian's direction, they carried the ailing abbot away, supporting his weight between them.

Tristram offered no protest.

Odo faced the other abbots and called out for their attention. "We have a choice. Our beloved brother, Abbot Tristram, is unable to ride. He is in much pain, and this good sister says he should stay here until the weather and his health allow him to travel." He stopped to look each abbot in the eye. "We can linger here until our brother heals or we can travel on to Norwich without him. What is your decision?"

"Abbot Tristram is surrounded by many prayers at Tyndal. If we remained, our few would mean little more to God, especially since they can be offered as effectively on the road," Gifre said. "I am ready to leave before darkness falls. Another night in an inn would be insufferable." His horse briefly pawed the ground with approval.

"We dare not offend the legate who waits for us in Norwich. Rome would not be pleased if we failed to answer his call." Abbot Mordredus signaled for assistance in mounting his horse.

Odo waited for the other abbots to speak. When none did, he muttered about the likelihood that a papal legate might have secured a haunch of venison from the king to serve them and looked about for men to lift him into the saddle.

Didier and Ancell glanced at each other, nodded agreement, and started toward their horses.

"We shall leave Abbot Tristram in your care and travel on," Odo said to Sister Anne. "On our journey back…" The Abbot of Caldwell turned to the prioress, but his eyes grew large and his words froze in his mouth before they could be uttered.

Eleanor became aware that someone stood behind her. Looking over her shoulder, she saw Ralf had arrived with Brother Thomas by his side.

"We came through the mill gate," the monk murmured.

Ralf strode toward Odo and did not stop until he stood only a foot away from the bulge of his brother's stomach. Gazing with pointed interest at the paunch, the crowner chuckled. "Dear brother in flesh and sin! What a joy to see you in such abundant health!"

Odo stepped back as if the Devil had just opened his arms to embrace him with terrifying fondness.

"I see the typically austere abbey life suits you well."

"And you still bear the scars of your wickedness," Odo hissed, "along with your usual stench of hellfire's smoke."

"These scars and my sword paid for your position at Caldwell, my increasingly weighty brother, or does your deliberate forgetfulness of my largesse mean that the padded cushion, used to protect your knees from cold stone floors during prayer, needs replacing?" He raised his hand as if swearing an oath. "Never fear. I shall pay for another. Heaven forbid that your knees should suffer."

"When I am a bishop, you will regret your impiety and lack of respect for a man of God. Fear the bell, book, and candle, Ralf."

"Tell that to Fulke and see if he agrees with your threat. I keep the family name honorable in East Anglia so our eldest brother can keep his position, rank, and increase his wealth under a king who demands honesty, not empty phrases. If our eldest loses influence and the family loses honor, where will you be? Certainly not a bishop and possibly not an abbot of anything."

"Although I am a loyal subject of the king, God has my ultimate allegiance. I trust in His protection no matter what you and Fulke do."

Ralf spat near his brother's feet.

"Blasphemous wretch! We are going to Norwich to meet with the special papal legate. You may worship the talents the world admires, but my proven skills in promoting the faith, and improving adherence by all believers in tithing and other worthy gifts to the Church, will win me that bishopric." Realizing others might hear him, Odo quickly bowed his head and steepled his hands. "But only if God finds my service acceptable, for I am one of His lowliest servants. My greatest desire is to gain wisdom in our faith before any advancement." His tone was almost believably meek.

Ralf snorted.

Eleanor glanced at Sister Anne. "So their journey to Norwich was not just about their longing to assure the Pope that he had their financial support for the preached crusade," she whispered. "That was the tale told to Prior Andrew."

"We should have known better," the sub-infirmarian replied, her eyes sparkling with humor.

Ralf slapped his brother on his shoulder. "Well said, Odo, and God has granted your prayers for wisdom. He has decided you need time for reflection in this holy place of faith." He watched with evident pleasure as his brother's eyes started to blaze with ire, then flickered with puzzlement. "Perhaps it was due to your mewling prayers that He has decided you must stay longer at Tyndal Priory. The legate, it seems, must wait in Norwich without your company, or else find others nearby who will impress him with their devotion to the crusading cause."

"How dare you speak of holy places of faith and reflection, venomous liegeman of Satan?" Odo roared, brushing his shoulder as if cleansing it of Hell's ash. But as he studied his brother's face more closely, he asked in a quieter tone, "We must stay here? Why?"

"Yes, sweet brother, you must remain in the priory guest quarters, unless you wish to mingle with the wicked at the local inn or raise tents and bed down in a nearby snow-filled forest. I have just received word that the road to Norwich is impassable. The last snow and high winds further on have buried it in deep drifts. A bridge has collapsed from the weight. No one can walk or ride through to your desired destination."

Eleanor may not have been any more pleased with this news than Odo or his fellow abbots, but she quickly stepped forward to offer hospitality. "The quarters will be prepared for your longer stay," she said, "and the adjacent kitchen staffed to prepare hot meals for your comfort until you are able to travel on."

To Odo's credit, the abbot thanked the prioress for her charity and failed to voice any allegation that his hated brother was lying about the condition of the road just to thwart him. But his expression, as he gave Ralf one last glance, suggested that the strength of his rage might cause even Satan to tremble.

Chapter Five

Gracia warmed the mulled cider with an iron heated in the crackling fire. The scent of ginger, cinnamon, and cloves softened the air and raised the spirits of those assembled in Prioress Eleanor's chambers.

Ralf, very pleased with himself after spoiling his brother's plans to meet with the man from Rome, was recounting his verbal jousting with Odo. "He has always been insufferable," he laughed. "A little pricking momentarily stops him from trying to elbow aside a few angels and assuming a place closer to God than he deserves."

Sister Anne and Brother Thomas smiled.

"Your brother should be grateful you warned him before he left and became stranded in the forest at nightfall." Eleanor was amused, but she noted that her other two friends had been quiet and their usual enjoyment of the crowner's wit was muted.

"He is fat enough to survive a night in the snow," Ralf replied, "and he most likely has a good supply of fine wine with him as well. My brother has never lacked for ways to produce a fine meal."

Eleanor shook her head. "I doubt he liked the one he and the other abbots were given last night. We were not prepared for special guests, and they had to eat what we were served."

Ralf grunted. "Tyndal Priory is one of the few monasteries that actually follows the Benedictine Rule on diet. That is one of the many reasons I respect your leadership, my lady. At

Caldwell Abbey, my brother insists that meat be served daily, except during Lent." He drank his cider and sighed with content over the fragrant warmth. "My brother hates Lent, although he would never admit it."

"I, too, am glad you warned him about the fallen bridge and blocked road," Sister Anne said. "Two sick men, one dead, is enough tragedy."

"One has died of those two?" The crowner looked at Brother Thomas.

The monk blinked as if his thoughts had taken him a long distance away. "I failed to mention that the one died. Abbot Ilbert's illness brought the party here, but he was so unwell he died shortly after arrival."

"Ilbert? I've heard tales of him," the crowner grunted. "He loved to beat his monks when they offended him and claimed his edicts were God's law, so disobedience was akin to heresy."

"Ralf!" Sister Anne shook an admonishing finger at her former suitor and now beloved friend. "You are accusing the abbot of terrible transgressions. No man is the same as God, and such pride would qualify as one of the seven deadliest sins."

"I doubt God cares if one small weed is not pulled in the abbey vegetable garden, yet Ilbert whipped a lay brother for missing it." He looked sheepish. "Forgive me, Annie. Despite my brother's opinion of me, my dear wife is laboring to change me into a less impious man."

She chuckled. "I will acknowledge that Gytha has made a little progress. A saint could do no better."

"Yet I still cannot abide men who claim to have God's ear while sinning grievously against the intent of His commandments." Leaning back with a more serious look, he took a deep breath. "From what did Abbot Ilbert die?"

"That is what troubles me," Sister Anne said. "I do not know. His symptoms could have been caused by any number of illnesses. Although I do not pretend to have perfect knowledge, and God does not always enlighten me to the cause of mortal ills, I am familiar enough with the usual ailments."

"You have greater skill than most who treat illness." Eleanor reached over and patted her friend's arm. "Do not condemn yourself for this one death you could not understand."

"The convulsions were strange, as were the dilated eyes." The sub-infirmarian continued in a troubled voice. "After the abbot's death, I even asked his servant if his master suffered from the falling sickness. I only thought of that because of the convulsions. None of the other symptoms matched what I have observed in others suffering the condition. I was told he did not. As for pain, Abbot Ilbert did not complain of it except on the day he died. The combination of the quick onset and specific symptoms does not point to anything I know well."

Thomas leaned forward. "What about Abbot Tristram? Do his symptoms match the early ones suffered by Abbot Ilbert?"

"Not that I have discovered."

"Is Abbot Tristram in danger of dying?" The monk's expression was grave.

Anne hesitated. "No more than we all are, or so I hope. He is comfortable. His abdominal pains have lessened, and his vomiting and diarrhea have ceased. He is weak, and his face is a yellow color. That last symptom worries me, but he could heal. Since a man may not wish to tell a woman about many complaints, I have sent a lay brother to ask Abbot Tristram's servant further questions. If God wills it, we may yet discover that the abbot has a recognizable illness."

"Do not trouble yourself too much, Annie. If these men are like my brother, they all suffer from self-indulgence. Odo's fat will one day suffocate him."

"Both Abbot Ilbert and Abbot Tristram are lean men, Ralf. They show no signs that they have feasted with regularity at a bountiful abbatial table." Sister Anne may have meant to jest, but her sharply expressed reply betrayed her uneasiness.

Eleanor was watching Brother Thomas who had retreated back into a pensive mood. "You seem most deep in thought, Brother. I would hear what you have to say."

"I share Sister Anne's concern, my lady. If this is some strange new plague attacking our land, the death of Abbot Ilbert and illness of Abbot Tristram are important to evaluate. If not, why have two abbots fallen ill, at least one fatally, within such a short period of time? Does this plague have different manifestations? Has Abbot Tristram sickened with another illness, or is there a third cause which we have yet to discover?"

"It is winter," Ralf said. "They are not young men, and making a journey in the cold is one most men of sense and of all ages avoid for reasons of health and safety."

"They were summoned to Norwich by the special papal legate. Would you refuse to obey the king's command if he ordered you to come to him today?" Sister Anne's tone suggested a rare impatience with the crowner.

"King Edward would not do so unless the reason was a dire one."

"Nor would the papal legate," Eleanor said. "As I have heard the story, his visit with the king took longer than hoped, and winter stranded him on our shores. The need to recover Jerusalem is a pressing one and a sacred cause. Since the legate cannot return to Rome, is he not right to call on those men of influence to confer on the best way to successfully preach the crusade and gather the funds needed for the effort?"

Eleanor saw Ralf's eyes flash and quickly changed the subject back to the discomfort Brother Thomas and Sister Anne felt over the oddity of the illnesses. She did not want to enter into an unwinnable and fraught debate with the crowner, nor was she in the mood to admit to her friend that this visit was darkly stained with the abbots' ambition.

"With your permission," Thomas said, "I would like to accompany our sub-infirmarian and examine Abbot Ilbert's corpse to discover what it might teach us."

The prioress hesitated. If this were a new and virulent plague, she did not want her beloved nun and monk to breathe any more contaminated air from the stench of the corpse and become the next victims. Yet she must give approval. It was their duty to the village and priory to learn what had killed the abbot and decide if others were in danger of contagion.

"You have it, but please exercise caution," she said. "God may wish more angels, but I would prefer that He not take the two I have on Earth with me."

Blushing from her compliment, the two religious bowed their thanks and left to seek any knowledge that might be gained from the corpse.

Crowner Ralf put down his mazer and refused the offer from Gracia of more cider. "Fear not," he said to the prioress, "the death of one abbot and the illness of the other are hardly surprising in winter. Does Death not take more souls in the darker seasons?"

Eleanor dutifully concurred.

"Annie is a skilled healer, and Brother Thomas is an observant man. If this quandary is solvable, they will discover the secret and do so quickly. But I doubt you have any reason to fear that a new pestilence has come to England. We are no more sinful a race than any other. Why should God send a new and potent scourge solely to us?"

Eleanor nodded as if convinced by his argument. Although appreciative of Ralf's attempt to calm her fears, she trusted the instincts of her two religious more, and knew they believed something more dangerous than common winter ills might be involved here. "You are kind, Ralf, and I shall take your words to heart." Smiling, she moved on to a happier topic. "How are your three children?"

"Rosy-cheeked and happy," he replied with evident pride. "Our second son is a sweet-natured lad like his mother, while our eldest is very adventurous. He's a good boy, overall, but he must be watched lest he unwittingly find himself in trouble!"

Eleanor laughed. "He sounds very much like his father must have been at the same age."

"I was a boisterous one," he admitted.

"And Sibley?" This daughter was the child of a prior marriage, but Ralf's current wife adored her. The crowner often joked that Gytha had only wed him because of the little girl.

He grinned. "She rules the boys like a second mother."

"My blessing upon your family, Ralf. Please tell Gytha that I long for a visit when the weather and her duties permit."

He stood and bowed. "I will go to them now, my lady, but please be at peace. There is nothing of concern in this matter of one death and another illness. Annie may not know the causes at this moment, but she will."

"You read my apprehension well, dear friend, and I take comfort in your assurances."

As he left her audience chamber, Prioress Eleanor's expression of false confidence faded. Despite her words to the contrary, Prioress Eleanor was gravely worried.

Chapter Six

To distract herself until Sister Anne and Brother Thomas came back, Prioress Eleanor had chosen to study her accounting rolls.

At least, she thought as she pressed her hands against her aching eyes, the work of reviewing the economic health of her priory was done for a while. Many found such work tedious. She often found it refreshing.

Had she been possessed of a more arrogant nature, she might have been proud of her accomplishments in the twelve years of her stewardship. When she first arrived, the coffers were empty, the few priory assets suffering from incompetent management and embezzlement. After the election of a new prior, a man skilled in land management and the one whom she had prayed would be chosen, she slowly made her priory self-sustaining. Truth be told, she admitted in silence, Tyndal Priory had become prosperous.

Not wealthy like the abbeys of her visitors but affluent enough to provide her high-ranking guests with fresh linen and comfortable bedding devoid of fleas, wines purchased from the king's vintner, the occasional wheaten loaf of bread, earthenware serving bowls, pewter cups, and sturdy wooden trenchers.

She and her religious still used bread trenchers so the poor might receive the greater nourishment they provided, but her desire to adhere to a more austere life, as one appropriate to God's servants, did not mean deliberately unpalatable food. The skills of Sister Matilda, ruler of pots, baking oven, and kitchen hearth, made even Lenten meals pleasurable—Abbot Odo's dismissal of Tyndal's simpler fare aside.

Thus she dragged her mind reluctantly back to the troubling problems at hand.

Sister Matilda's cooking talent was why she doubted Abbot Tristram had fallen ill from tainted food last night. But she knew the addition of the second kitchen to serve guests in the newly finished quarters needed oversight. This was a duty an ordinary nun could not perform on the monk's side of the priory, but the choice of a talented lay brother could have fallen to a sub-prioress, if Eleanor had had one. Although she respected Sister Ruth's decision to remove herself from the position, and did not miss the frequent quarrels with a woman who had never ceased to resent her, Eleanor also regretted the loss of the woman's administrative skills and ardent attention to detail.

"Would you like more wood in the fire, my lady?"

Eleanor looked up in surprise to see Gracia, broom in hand, looking worried. "No, my child, I am content. You were thought-ful to ask."

Gracia murmured a reply and went back to sweeping, stopping only to pet Arthur, the prioress' cat, who was curled into a round ball of orange fur near the fire.

After rolling up the accounts, Eleanor walked over to the window and opened the shutter just enough to peer out at the priory land.

Few were on the paths leading to the mill on one side and the hospital on the other. The great thick walls that kept the world back from those who had rejected it rose high above the snow-softened landscape. Although made of grey stone, they were black with damp and might have looked menacing to anyone not aware that only the gentle lived within, men and women who devoted their lives to praying for souls in Purgatory.

But invasions sometimes did breach walls built to withstand all common weaponry and protect the innocent. Might the Evil One have slipped in with the party of abbots and brought her the tragedy of some nameless plague? Remembering Brother

Thomas' frown, she shivered. Or had the Devil brought violent death to her once again after a long and welcome hiatus?

She looked over her shoulder and watched Gracia finish the sweeping.

And then there was this question of whether her beloved maid would choose to leave or stay, the answer to which might break her heart.

The girl was healthy but had never gotten much taller in the years since Eleanor and Brother Thomas had rescued her from the streets of Walsingham. Yet the child had grown into a bright, observant young woman, always quiet and keeping her own counsel.

In the tradition of the prioress' maternal family, who had come with Queen Eleanor from the Aquitaine, the prioress had made sure Gracia was well-educated. At the end of her work today, the girl would take up a book she had borrowed from the priory library and read to Eleanor. It was a shared time they both especially cherished.

What will be Gracia's future, she wondered. Instinctively, she hugged herself to keep from shivering, not from the cold air slipping in from the window, but from nervous dread.

In the background, the flames in the fireplace snapped loudly, punctuating her fears.

In the beginning, Gracia had been interested in taking vows, but Eleanor discouraged her, insisting she wait until she was older. Growing up at Amesbury Priory, the prioress remembered young women who rushed themselves, or were hurried by others, into a religious life for which they had no true longing. They suffered. Many claimed such agonies cleansed the soul and made it more acceptable to God.

Eleanor doubted that.

And so she had insisted Gracia wait until she was able to understand what both God and the world had to offer. She also swore that the choice must be Gracia's alone. The latter had been one of the hardest oaths she had ever sworn.

Five years had since passed. The time was nigh for the decision.

She closed the shutter and walked toward the fireplace. Picking up the large orange cat, she eased herself into the chair and waited for Arthur to comfortably reposition himself. He was showing no signs of age, she concluded with relief, and the priory was almost entirely unburdened with rodents, thanks to his efforts and those of his many descendants. Although his favored female had died, he had found others to satisfy his needs.

Perhaps this borders on the sacrilegious, the prioress thought with amusement she feared was wicked, but I doubt my cat cares whether his carnal relations are within any prohibited range of kinship.

The warmth of the room and the study of the accounting rolls made her eyes ache and feel heavy. She hoped she was not starting one of her migraines. For a moment, she closed her eyes. With the soothing sound of the whisking broom in her ears, she sent her thanks to God for His benevolence to her priory and for the joy she had had from Gracia's companionship during the past few years.

"Are you asleep, my lady?" The voice was soft. Had Eleanor truly been asleep, she would not have been awakened, but she did wonder why she had not heard Gracia stop her work.

"Nay," she said, opening her eyes.

Gracia looked so grave. The expression reminded Eleanor of the early days when the child feared accepting enough food to nourish her and a comfortable place to sleep, lest all be wrenched from her as swiftly as her family when they all died of a fever.

"Come, child," she said. "Draw that stool over and sit by me."

Gracia hesitated. "I beg permission to speak with you, my lady, on a matter troubling my heart."

Eleanor froze. There was something unsettling in the tone of the young woman's voice and her choice of words. Did she just say her heart was troubled? Had the girl fallen in love?

There were lay brothers of the same age as Gracia in the priory, lads who might find the young woman appealing and try to dally with her. Gracia rarely went out to the market as her predecessor had, so the prioress doubted she had met a young man from the village. Eleanor did feel confident that Gracia was not likely to have lain with any of them. The rape had taught her to be wary of coupling.

She dragged herself back from these fears. "Confide in me, my child," she said gently. "There is nothing you cannot tell me." Eleanor reached out to take Gracia's hand.

The young woman began to extend hers.

Suddenly, from outside the door, they heard voices in the prioress' audience chamber.

Arthur jumped off Eleanor's lap and hurried out of the room. One of the voices was that of Brother Thomas, a monk whom the cat favored highly.

Eleanor reluctantly rose as well.

"Shall I bring refreshment, my lady?"

Sighing, Eleanor asked her to fetch and heat more spiced cider to ward off the chill that Sister Anne and Brother Thomas had suffered when they went to examine the abbot's corpse.

Although she was eager to hear the news the two religious brought, she resented that her duty demanded she lose that precious moment of confidence Gracia had requested.

Chapter Seven

Brother Thomas smiled at Gracia when she hurried through the door, and she responded with her usual playful look. Before he followed Sister Anne inside, he watched the maid for a brief moment as she rushed to whatever task she had been given.

He felt a kinship with her, one she seemed to sense. Even though Gracia had become a young woman, she would always be to him that cleverly minded, thin waif who balked at trusting anyone. It was a caution he understood. He had never told her how much pain they shared, including rape and the loss of everyone each had ever loved.

Sister Anne and their prioress were talking in low tones, and Thomas let his mind shift from the death of Abbot Ilbert to Gracia's future. Like their prioress, he knew the maid had reached the age when she must decide whether to take vows or seek a life in the secular world.

Why would she take vows? Could one who had been abused as a child ever truly believe in the existence of a caring God? Could she serve a God she was convinced was not benevolent, even if she must worship and obey Him out of fear for her soul? Or might she choose vows to escape the world outside the priory walls, a world that was filled with a cruelty she knew far too well?

The prioress' orange cat put a paw on his leg and began to purr loudly. Thomas crouched and began to pet the creature.

But what might he say if Gracia came to him for counsel on whether to stay or leave? What, indeed, dare he say? Although he had come to Tyndal with no vocation, and endured hellish dreams for years that destroyed sleep, he had at last discovered more tranquility here than he had imagined possible. Perhaps she might as well.

Perhaps.

Repeating the word, he found it had a sour taste.

Ought he to give her such hope? Sometimes he had doubts about God's essential nature, especially when he saw how the world took unrestrained pleasure in salting the wounds of those who erred so little while rewarding those most in the Devil's thrall. But he was a man who had long fought with God and discovered He never punished him for it. Over time, he had found Him willing to listen. On occasion, He gave answers. Thomas had had no choice but to receive the tonsure and take the vows, but he had slowly learned to live with an ultimately unknowable God.

Thomas found a mat in the cat's fur and gently began pulling it apart. There was a small twig caught there, and he eased it out.

Arthur purred.

Smiling at the cat's patience, the monk shook his head. This was also not the time he should be giving advice to a young girl who had options. Just as he had loosened the bonds of one grief, and hoped he might find comfort in ways he dared express only to God, he was pushed to the edge of Satan's pit of despondency once again. Maybe, he thought with bitterness, he should take solace in knowing he had not yet fallen in.

At this moment, his faith was too brittle to give any wisdom to Gracia. He had not yet found the right answers himself. Wincing, he silently cursed.

"Brother Thomas?"

He rose. Prioress Eleanor was studying him with eyes that missed nothing. Uneasy, he looked at the floor and said, "You seek to know what Sister Anne and I have learned."

"And she has forewarned me to expect news that is disturbing." The prioress tilted her head as she continued to gaze at her monk.

From her concerned expression, Thomas feared that she had seen too much of his unhappy soul through his eyes. Was she worried more about that than any suggestion that untoward death had once again set foot in Tyndal Priory? He prayed not.

"When Sister Anne described the symptoms Abbot Ilbert exhibited just before he died," he said quickly, "I was reminded of the death of a high-ranking cleric I once served in my youth."

The prioress raised an eyebrow. Thomas rarely referred to his days before coming here. She begged him to explain.

"The man fell ill several hours after eating a meal he complained tasted bitter. When he was unable to produce urine for the physician to interpret, his body began to swell. He died with eyes dilated, mouth frothing, and severe convulsions. Rumor was rife that he had been poisoned, but no one could prove it. He was not a man well-loved, however. When I sought to learn more, I was told by the secretary to a bishop that I would serve God far better by praying for the man's soul than discovering the reason that soul had fled so soon to Him."

"And from that you concluded that his death was unnatural and the result of a human hand?" Eleanor saw Gracia hesitating at the door with a jug of the spiced cider and told her to enter. There was little she did not allow or trust the young woman to hear. "What was the man's crime, Brother?"

"He had sent word to Rome that one man in line for a bishopric had two mistresses and several children."

"Who was awarded the position?" Sister Anne thanked Gracia when she served the mazer of cider.

"Not the man with the mistresses."

"And this party of abbots is traveling to Norwich, in part, because each one hopes to impress the papal legate with his administrative skills and ability to channel gold to Rome. Should a position open up for advancement within the Church, every one of them longs to have an influential friend close to the ear of Pope Martin." Eleanor took the warm cup of cider from Gracia and held it close to her breast for a moment. "Your description of the similarity in symptoms and death is interesting."

"Indeed, my lady. The corpse of this abbot looked much the same as the one in the tale I just told. The symptoms described by Sister Anne most certainly are."

"Did you ever discover the poison used in that early death?" Eleanor looked optimistic, but her hope quickly faded. The monk would have said if he had known.

As expected, Brother Thomas replied that he had not.

"I wonder if Abbot Ilbert had also sent Rome news that might have displeased one of his fellows," the prioress said.

"We still have the illness of Abbot Tristram," Sister Anne added. "His symptoms are quite different."

"And perhaps not fatal?" Eleanor looked at her friend. "You thought he might have suffered from food turned putrid."

Brother Thomas held out his cup for Gracia to refill it. "Rotten food served in this priory? Sister Matilda is too exacting in her kitchen fiefdom."

"Not many have ever gotten sick from her cooking, and some have since discovered that they suffer distress whenever they eat certain foods, no matter how well prepared, while others remain in good health." Sister Anne's face betrayed her vexation. "I agree that two men falling ill at the same time raises questions, but I must repeat: they each suffered different, albeit severe symptoms."

"We have fish from our ponds, honey made by our own bees, ale from our respected brewery, birds from our flocks, and vegetables or fruit grown in our own earth," Eleanor said. "Other than portions sufficient to help the sick regain strength, I have refused gifts of venison and boar from the king, citing our steadfast adherence to the dietary rule dictated by Saint Benedict. Our spices do come from a reputable merchant, but we are otherwise self-sufficient in our food supply. Even our grain is grown on nearby priory land."

"And so we do not suffer from the temptations of merchants to cut corners on the quality of our food in order to make greater profit," Thomas added.

Eleanor concurred. "Any contamination of priory food is highly unlikely."

"We must still talk to Sister Matilda," Anne said.

"And we shall," the prioress replied, "but the food served last night was no different from what we all ate here. Nothing was done in the new kitchen except heat the stew after it was delivered to the monks' side of our priory."

"Something might have happened during the journey between the kitchens," Anne said.

"No other abbot got sick, nor did any of their servants," Thomas replied.

"I must still make sure we are not guilty of any fault in causing Abbot Tristram's illness. The guest quarters and adjacent kitchen have just been completed. The lay brothers working in the new kitchen are unaccustomed to their duties, although Brother Beorn swears they know the difference between a roasting spit and a cleaver."

Thomas laughed. "Does he, himself?"

Sister Anne noted that their prioress did not share the levity and gave the monk a warning look.

"Prior Andrew is in charge of them," Eleanor continued, "but confesses his knowledge of cooking is that of a former soldier who might once have cooked a small bird over an open fire beside the battlefield. As is justified, he planned to fall back on the rule requiring monks and lay brothers to rotate through the kitchen. He recognizes that some may have more talent than others, and could be retained in the kitchen longer, but these abbots are our first guests. He has not yet had the opportunity to find anyone to match the skills of Sister Matilda among the men under his rule. He has done his best and is not the one to blame." She pointed to herself instead.

"You are condemning yourself in this," Sister Anne said. "No one else would."

"I am still prioress here and have grown careless in some areas that need greater oversight. This new kitchen is one of them."

"Prior Andrew…" Brother Thomas stopped when he saw his prioress' solemn expression.

"He is a good man of wisdom and talent, but his skills lie in the breeding of sheep, judicious use of rents, and the purchase of lands for our benefit."

"This is not laxity on your part," Anne said, reaching over to grasp her prioress' hand. "You cannot do everything. The affluence of the priory, and the burdens that royal favor have occasionally placed upon us, make your duties more onerous than they were in the past."

"Then my fault lies in not appointing a sub-prioress." Eleanor smiled at her two friends. "You are kind to find excuses for me, but I fear we will all agree when I say that the reputation of Tyndal Priory, and even our hospital, will be sullied if word spreads that we might have poisoned our guests, no matter how unwillingly."

With reluctance the two monastics nodded.

"So let us finish our cider and send word that Prior Andrew must meet us in the old priory kitchen. Sister Matilda will be grieved to hear her cooking questioned, even condemned, but she will answer honestly and confess if there was any way she might have erred."

"If I may have your permission, I would like to talk with the abbots to see if they remember some detail about the meal that would point to a cause for Abbot Tristram's illness." Thomas grinned. "Sister Matilda's kitchen is too dangerous a place for me. I fear I would suffer the sin of gluttony were I to join you. The smell of her baking is far too tempting to mortals like me who feel all resolve weaken when faced with her elderflower pie."

Eleanor laughed. "Go, Brother! But I fear we may more quickly succumb to temptation ourselves without you. Even if she is not baking fruit tarts or making custards, we shall miss your greater strength and restraining counsel. Pray give us a gentle penance for our frailty!"

Once he gave his solemn promise, she rose and spoke briefly to Gracia, who needed few words to understand what her mistress required.

As the others left the prioress' quarters, the young woman ran to seek the prior.

Chapter Eight

Sister Matilda was a round woman of middle years, her fingers already knotted with the joint disease, but her indignation so inflamed her humors that she hopped from foot to foot like an outraged child of two summers.

"Have I ever been careless with food cooked for other notable guests? Why should I suddenly become so, my lady?"

"Calm yourself, Sister." Prioress Eleanor laid a gentle hand on the woman's plump shoulder and held her down. "No one is accusing you of anything."

Sister Anne added her concurrence. "We only want to make sure nothing happened by accident and that no blame can be placed on the priory."

"I have never approved of building this new kitchen." Righteous irritation dripped like fresh vinegar from Sister Matilda's every word. "As I asked at the time it was planned, how can I make sure the food retains the purity God gave it if I cannot oversee the lay brothers who prepare it, and taste what they cook to make sure the seasonings are right?" She took a deep breath. "Brother Beorn, good man though he is, wouldn't know a loaf of bread from a pile of cow dung. How could he choose men to prepare meals as they should be done in that...?" She waved her hand in the general direction of the offending structure.

Prior Andrew blushed and addressed his prioress. "I must defend Brother Beorn. He did the best he could in choosing the first lay brothers to work there, but it is my responsibility to approve his choices and make sure all is done properly in the kitchen. I have failed."

"Not one of you has failed," Eleanor replied. Although she had managed not to laugh at Sister Matilda's description of Brother Beorn's ignorance about food—a man who would forget to eat were he not forced to the common table twice a day—she knew the nun was right. Good food required the oversight of someone who knew how to prepare dishes, the skill to create new ones, and had the ability to taste each item as it cooked to adjust the seasonings to perfection. The elder lay brother was definitely not the right person for that. As for Prior Andrew, he was too busy with his stewardship of priory wealth to spend time with those lay brothers assigned to the new cooking tasks, nor did he have the knowledge required to choose a lay brother with Sister Matilda's skilled palate.

Eleanor swallowed a bitter sigh. Blame was due, indeed, but she was utterly convinced it lay solely with her. Why had she been so remiss in her failure to appoint a sub-prioress? Was it wayward pride in thinking she could do everything?

Slowly, the bright red color in Sister Matilda's face faded, and she bowed her head. "My lady, I beg pardon for my choler. It was unseemly. I can only tell you that, when I received word we had an unannounced party of seven abbots to feed, plus their servants, I was hard-pressed to increase the stew with enough chicken. The root vegetables were easily found. But this was not the first time we have had to do this. God blessed us with a miracle akin to the loaves and fishes, and one of the lay sisters discovered another old chicken to help feed the increased number."

"Your anger is justified and forgiven, Sister," Eleanor replied. "I was certain that all was properly done here. My questions are only about the process after the meal left this kitchen. How was that done?"

"I sent word that lay brothers must be summoned to meet the lay sisters at the opening in the stone wall that divides the monks from the nuns. It is the one we always use to deliver meals to the men on the monks' side of the priory. This is our common practice, and we did not deviate from it." She raised her head and added, with a hint of pride, "Nor did it take longer to deliver that stew."

Eleanor turned to her prior and asked for an explanation of what happened next.

"When the lay brothers received the food through the window, they rushed it to the new kitchen where it was heated again in a pot that was new. The men may be less skilled in kitchen craft than desired, but Brother Beorn would only choose responsible people." He raised a hand. "I questioned them. They admitted they were uneasy considering the high rank of these guests and longed not to fail in this first test of their duties. But all they had to do was keep the food hot until the abbots were at their table. I did confirm that one of the lay brothers tasted the stew first to make sure it was warm enough."

"But was it overcooked?" Sister Matilda muttered under her breath and quickly lowered her gaze to hide her scorn. Her lips moved as if she prayed to be forgiven for thoughts that might verge on the sinful.

"And the lay brother remains in good health?" Sister Anne knew he must, but wanted the fact confirmed.

Prior Andrew verified it.

"That means there is no fault in our cooking here," Sister Matilda said, straightening her back, and then added in a charitable tone, "nor in the reheating of the dish."

"We did not doubt it," Eleanor replied, "but it was my duty to make sure nothing questionable occurred after the stew left your well-run kitchen."

Now that Sister Matilda was mollified, the prioress thanked her for her precise description of events. Dismissed with her honor intact, the nun walked over to a table and took out her remaining anger by pummeling a rising loaf of bread.

The trio of religious retreated to the prioress' chambers.

◇◇◇

Sister Anne paced the room. "Of course, I do not pretend to have the skills of a trained physician!" Her expression tempered her denial. Although she was always humble about her learning, she had also been trained by her father, a well-respected physician, and thus expected more competence from herself than she had shown with these abbots. "Yet I fear I have not observed what I should, or else my knowledge is far more limited than even I had thought."

"At least the death of Abbot Ilbert may not have been caused by a common sickness," Eleanor said. "Do not forget what Brother Thomas said about his past experience. The abbot might have suffered more from the hand of an enemy than from a mortal illness. You were in agreement after you both examined the corpse."

"Does that suggest a similar attack was made against Abbot Tristram?" Prior Andrew lowered himself into a chair. He was always allowed to sit without Eleanor's permission. His old battle wound especially pained his leg in the winter months, despite the relief from one of Sister Anne's potions made with the milky juice of the Oriental poppy.

When the prior spoke, the sub-infirmarian stopped and seemed to relax. "He did mention that he had fallen ill at the inn the night before arriving here. By that next morning he felt better but became ill again the morning after sleeping here."

"The problem might lie in something that happened at that inn, not anything he encountered in our priory," Eleanor replied. "Brother Thomas is currently talking with the abbots. If he learns something of value, the cause of the illnesses may soon be resolved."

But Eleanor feared otherwise. If Ilbert had been murdered, and one of the abbots was a killer, she hardly thought any details would be confessed that would reveal the slayer.

But she was not a naïve child. After twelve years of ruling this priory, she knew full well that these abbots were ambitious men, each eager to advance in the ranks of Church hierarchy. Murder, as a way to remove a competitor, was not limited to the courts of kings. It also occurred among those who claimed God as their liege lord, including, it was rumored, two or three popes.

"And if he learns nothing to help us discover the reasons?" As she often did, Sister Anne chose to voice the least desirable, but equally likely, outcome.

"Then I shall beg Crowner Ralf to grant us a great kindness," the prioress said. "I hate asking him to leave his family to travel in this weather, but only he can ride to the inn and ask the questions for which we all desperately need answers."

Chapter Nine

The abbots were seated, backs rigid, in the large dining hall which was encircled by their individual quarters. Knowing that a plain monk dare not sit in the presence of an abbot without permission, they had shown their displeasure with Brother Thomas' commission from Prioress Eleanor by deliberately making him stand.

The monk found humor in the insult. Bastard though he was, the rank of his paternal family far exceeded that of any man before him. Had they known it, they might have trembled in fear, contemplating the possible consequences of their insolence. In fact, there would be none. His father, now dead, had never spoken to Thomas since his son's arrest for sodomy years ago, and his cousins either chose to ignore his kinship with them or quickly forgot that he had ever existed.

"Speak, Brother, and ask your questions." Abbot Odo shifted in his chair with a hefty show of impatience.

Or else his back is troubling him, the monk decided with a flash of charity. According to Sister Anne, men of such great weight often suffered severe pain in their backs and knees that could become unbearable. It was a punishment for the sin of gluttony.

"I do not understand why Prior Andrew did not come to speak to us instead of you," Abbot Ancell said.

Abbot Didier sat in silence and with such a distant expression that it was clear his thoughts were far removed from this or possibly any other cloister.

"Sister Anne is concerned about the death of Abbot Ilbert and the illness of Abbot Tristram. Although the former is in God's care, she had hoped to hasten the latter's healing by asking some questions. Because I sometimes assist her at the hospital, she asked our prior for permission to send me on her behalf. She, as a woman vowed to God, should not do so out of respect for the vows all have taken. Prior Andrew was in agreement, and I have come at his request."

Abbot Mordredus snorted. "The answer to all her questions is that she is a poorly educated woman and suffers from pride if she thinks to emulate the healing skills of a physician."

Blinking, Didier suddenly opted to join the discussion. "She is unnaturally tall," he remarked, "which suggests she is abnormal for her sex. Perhaps that is why she believes she can treat illness as well as a man? I hope she is not possessed by Satan."

Thomas bowed his head to hide his anger. "Our Infirmarian, Sister Christina, is respected by all as a saintly woman. It is her opinion that Sister Anne has been blessed by God with unique skills so that her healing of wicked men might bring them to repentance and a renewed commitment to virtue."

To that, the abbots chose not to reply, although two of them murmured something that sounded as if they were sending a brief protest over this matter to God.

"Very well, Brother," Gifre said, flinging a sharp glare in the direction of Odo, as if the man had done something offensive. "Ask your questions."

Odo smirked at him and shifted again in his chair.

"I shall be as brief as possible," Thomas replied with suitable humility. "If you will, think back to the inn where you spent the night before you traveled on to Tyndal Priory."

Didier licked his lips.

"Wine? I need wine for my dry throat if I am to reply," Odo said, looking over his shoulder for his servant to bring what he requested.

A man disappeared into the abbot's chambers and quickly returned with a large pewter cup. Odo drained it and shoved the cup back in the servant's hands for more.

The other abbots showed no interest in similar refreshment.

Thomas waited for the servant to replenish Odo's restorative drink. "What happened that night at the inn?" he asked after the Abbot of Caldwell had sighed with apparent satisfaction.

"What happened every night we had to stay with impious men because there was no monastery nearby." Odo sipped before continuing. "We arrived. Our horses were stabled. We were given beds together because separate rooms were not possible."

"Unlike the fine quarters here," Ancell added. He smiled at Thomas.

"We required a table for eating apart from the women, many of whom were whores, and located in a quiet part of the inn so the raucous laughter of drunken men would not infect our souls with wantonness. The food was dreadful and sleep impossible. We found it difficult to honor the hours of prayer. In the morning, we left as soon as the sun rose."

"You said the food was appalling. What was wrong with it?"

Odo shivered.

"Our brother prefers fine wines and dishes served only in the king's court," Gifre said, his lips curling with scorn. "The inn food was the fare of common men. An elderly ox had been slaughtered, roasted, and added to a stew of vegetables grown pallid from months of storage. The meat was tough, but men of our vocation should thank God for any bounty and not complain. Does the sparrow ever curse God for the sustenance He provides? As for the drink, it was ale made by the innkeeper's wife. Thin, flavorless, but not sour."

"No one sickened?" Thomas was secretly pleased that the other abbots seemed to feel the same disdain for Odo as did Crowner Ralf. Yet he had also noticed that they allowed the Abbot of Caldwell some authority over them. However begrudging, that was a sign of respect. Perhaps the man did possess more ability than his brother wished to acknowledge.

Mordredus winced at the memory. "Tristram was sleeping in the middle of our bed and clambered over me to run to the garderobe, or whatever served as such in that place, just as I had fallen asleep. I followed to protect him from any temptation to sin." He glanced at Didier. "Our brother Odo is right. There were whores at the inn."

"He was the only one who sickened after supper?"

"He moaned with pain in his gut and suffered diarrhea so foul the stench overcame the reek of the jakes. I sickened at the smell and had to leave him there lest I vomit."

Ancell shrugged. "But Abbot Tristram was well enough to ride when we were ready to leave, unlike this morning."

"You all ate the same food and drank the same ale prepared by the inn?"

Gifre nodded.

"And our meal was served by our servants, Brother, with our special plate," Ancell said, then blinked as he noticed a quizzical look in the monk's eyes. "Those were simple dishes. Nothing that might tempt a thief."

Or so lavish as to shock even a papal legate, Thomas thought, then cast the irreverent thought aside. Listening to these men, he feared he was beginning to think too much like Ralf. "I only meant to ask if it had been prepared by your men or the cooks at the inn."

"It was cooked in a common pot and roasted on a common spit at the inn, but no profane hand touched our food after it was cooked." Odo looked around at his fellow abbots. "I inquired."

Thomas wondered if any of the other customers who ate at the inn had sickened. He doubted the abbots would have noticed, but he asked anyway.

"We would not know, Brother. We left as soon as the sun appeared the next morning," Ancell said.

The others concurred.

"When did Abbot Ilbert become unwell?"

"Just as we arrived at the fork of the road, one of which led to the village and the other to your priory," Odo said. "He complained of faintness and a racing heart. Next he began to foam at the mouth. Since I knew of the hospital here, I insisted we make haste to the priory and led the way."

Didier raised his hand. "I recall he made us stop because he wanted to relieve himself. Twice, perhaps? He took so long that light was failing when we reached your priory."

"Did anything unusual occur at the inn that you can remember?"

"Nothing," Odo said at once.

Didier quickly agreed.

Gifre looked thoughtful. "There was one odd thing. Abbot Ilbert complained that he suffered attacks of the wind. At the time, I was surprised because it seemed remarkable that a man who ate so little would be stricken by that."

"Was he taking anything to ease his suffering?" Thomas felt a spark of hope.

Gifre's lips twisted into a disagreeable grimace as he gestured toward Odo. "He told me that he had sought Abbot Odo's advice, knowing our brother suffered greatly from the condition, and that our beloved brother had suggested a remedy by which he swore."

Odo's face flushed scarlet. "He did not, and I do not! Either he lied to you or you are lying. You have gotten into a habit of spreading malicious tales about me. This is yet another of your attempts to shame me."

"I cannot imagine what you mean," Gifre replied with a brief wave of his hand. "I grieved when I learned that you might be in such pain and wondered if a change in diet would ease your distress."

Odo leapt to his feet with greater speed than most men of his bulk.

Abbot Ancell pulled at the man's robe to remind him that this was neither the time nor the place for an unseemly altercation between men of God.

Sighing with the force of released steam, Odo sat down.

Thomas might have laughed if the circumstances had been less dire. "Did Abbot Ilbert tell you what the remedy was?"

"He did not mention what Abbot Odo had suggested." Gifre smirked. "Nor did I ask."

"He could not because he never approached me." Odo sneered.

"Does anyone know if Abbot Ilbert found a cure for his discomfort or what it was?" Thomas looked at each man.

They all shook their heads.

"Do any of you take a potion or herb to treat some ailment? Did Abbots Ilbert and Tristram?" If they did, and they took the wrong dose, that might explain the illnesses.

"We all have, on occasion, taken something for a mortal complaint," Ancell said. "I know of nothing unusual or new that any of us took on this journey."

All agreed.

Unable to think of further questions, Brother Thomas thanked the abbots for their kindness in answering him. Then he bowed and left them to continue in private whatever quarrels they had among themselves.

Chapter Ten

The wind was icy sharp, but Ralf barely felt it. During this journey, his thoughts had remained behind at his manor near Tyndal village. The sweet smile of his wife as she made sure he was warmly dressed and the laughter of his three children brought him indescribable joy. "It is more than this wicked man deserves," he murmured to the wind and his horse.

In that murky part of his soul, where sorrow and anger had festered over the years, terror still lurked that something malign would steal all this happiness from him. He grimaced and reminded himself that every moment God gave him with the family he adored must be treasured without the foul contamination of dread.

He shivered uncomfortably. Perhaps it tempted the Evil One to even think this, but he had become a man of greater faith after his marriage. Although his beloved Gytha had never said a word to him about his carelessness in matters of religious practice, he felt easy with her by his side on those occasions when they attended Mass together. He had even made his confessions once a year as was obligatory, a deed that surely made Brother Thomas as glad as it did his wife. On occasion, he caught himself praying to God out of gratitude. Shutting his eyes, he did so now and begged Him to keep his family safe during his absence.

Taking in a deep breath that hurt his lungs, he forced his thoughts back to the world of murder and evil men.

The road curved and as he rode around the bend he saw the inn he sought just ahead. It looked prosperous enough from the outside, he concluded, with extensive stables, sturdy walls, and a fine roof.

For good reason, most inns were in cities and villages. The protection of the king's law did not always extend to lonely places where outlaws hid. Ralf wondered if this place either welcomed the lawless or paid them a fee to be left in peace.

The moment the crowner rode up to the door, a groomsman raced to meet him. Although the man's long hair almost hid the disfigurement, Ralf noted that at least one ear was missing, a sign that he had been caught in some crime. Did the man look familiar or was the vague resemblance only an illusion?

Dismounting, the crowner asked to see the innkeeper. The groom described his master and said he would be inside jesting with the inn's guests as was his wont. Then he quickly led Ralf's horse away, perhaps sensing that the man with a sword might not treat a one-time felon with any kindness.

Ralf found the innkeeper easily enough. He was a giant of a man with hair as black as an imp's heart but cheeks ruddy as a fresh apple. Slapping a customer on the back, he roared with laughter that cut through the clamor from other guests.

Sniffing like a hungry dog, the crowner decided that he might have some of whatever was being cooked. Maybe it had poisoned an abbot, Ralf thought, but his stomach had never borne any similarity to one possessed by a monastic claiming temperance. Perhaps it did to his gluttonous brother's, one with whom he had always fought over portions at the table as a boy, but Odo could never be confused with a man enamored of denial.

When he sat at a table in the corner where he could get a sense of the place, a serving wench took only a moment to arrive at his side. Her warm greeting suggested that she was willing to serve any need, whether food, drink, or intimate companionship.

Ralf grinned in response, ordered ale and whatever was roasting in the kitchen. The woman looked slightly disappointed but promptly left to bring him what he wished.

A jug of ale arrived first.

The innkeeper was not far behind and now loomed over the crowner. "The groom said you were looking for me." His eyes narrowed with caution, but his lips were ready to smile if the man with the sword had come with good coin and no wish to trouble him.

"Sit, if you will, and share some ale with me." Ralf motioned to another serving maid, and she brought the extra cup.

"Tell me your business, and I shall decide if we can be friends."

Laughing, Ralf poured the ale. "We can. I wish information but nothing that would suggest you bear any fault in what happened." He gestured at the inn. "You have much business and therefore have a fine reputation. Why should I think any ill of you?"

"I have heard of you, Crowner Ralf. You are not here to spend the night on a journey elsewhere or because you heard that we serve a fine and very legal roasted meat."

"I am flattered that you know my name."

"My groom had cause to remember when you once stood by the side of your brother, the sheriff."

Ralf began to recall the incident. "I repeat. I have no wish to cause you grief, any more than I have any interest in your groom. He was caught, tried, and justice was rendered. I saw the missing ear."

"Be brief and tell me what you need from me." The innkeeper drank the cup of ale and refilled it.

"A few days ago, a group of abbots arrived with their servants."

"How could I forget them? They wanted to send their mewling clerks to clear my inn of customers, all of whom they suspected of wickedness, and dared to require separate rooms and a large, private table acceptable to them for their evening meal. There were seven of them, not including their servants. I was glad to see their backs the next day."

"Tell me about their stay here."

"Why?"

Ralf bent forward. "No honest man hesitates to answer the legitimate questions of a king's man."

The innkeeper shrugged. "And honest men have been hanged, Crowner. I know the tricks of those like you. You will try to trap me into saying something which could be interpreted one way or the other. Perhaps you hope I will accidentally omit a detail so you can arrest me for a wrongdoing I never committed because you cannot be bothered discovering the truth."

"If you know my name, Innkeeper, you should also know that I value justice over expediency. Ask your groom who may be grateful that I urged clemency and thus saved him from hanging. I don't care how many whores you have, how many felons you employ, or how you manage to stay safe in this lonely place without armed men to protect you against outlaws. I could delve more deeply into any of those things, and perhaps find crimes, but I won't unless you lie to me about what I need to learn."

The man started to say something but noted Ralf's sword and the scars he bore from prior battles. He chose to pour himself another drink.

"I refused to cast my guests out," he said, "and told the abbots that they must all share a room. My inn is not on any route favored by King Edward so I am not a rich man and cannot afford the luxury of providing separate chambers." He snorted. "The abbots thought I should impoverish myself out of Christian charity, but I know that they have coin enough for comforts in their abbeys yet always lack it when it comes to paying men like me. They were not pleased but had no choice. It was getting dark, and Tyndal village was too far to reach before the woods come alive with outlaws."

"So they settled into one room. With their servants?"

"Those slept in the stables. The abbots wished to be no more crowded than they were."

Ralf looked around and noted the number of large-breasted serving wenches who bent low to hear a guest's order. The pleasure on those men's faces as they murmured their wishes into so much soft flesh certainly suggested a thriving business in serving more than food and drink. "Few men of God are ignorant of the sins they might witness here." He raised a hand to stop any protest. "You could not remove all mortal wickedness from their sight. How were they able to sup publicly and protect their claimed virtue while they did?"

The innkeeper pointed to a corner near the passageway to the kitchen. "I cleared a large table there. It was quiet enough, and, grumbling all the while, they ate heartily enough."

"How were they served?"

"By their servants. They would have no women near them nor allow their supper to be touched by a woman's hand." He snorted. "Or at least six of them had issue with that."

Ralf was not surprised at the suggestion that at least one of the seven was willing to be led into temptation.

"There were six thin ones and one so fat I was surprised he could ride a horse. The abbot I saw thrusting away at Betsy in the stable straw was not the fat one. I never learned his name, nor did she. Ask her if you like, but it was dark and she cares nothing about faces or the length of a cock. She has even learned to squeal at the right moments, but she does love the feel of coin and could confirm how much of that she took."

The crowner decided the identity of the fornicating abbot would be easily discovered should it become pertinent. His brother might even tell him, if he saw any profit in doing so. He continued his questions. "How was the food collected from the kitchen and served to the abbots?"

"The cook complained to me about that. The fat abbot pushed his way into the kitchen, dragging one of their servants by the arm. He informed the cook that this person would take charge of the meals for the religious. No one else was to be served before they got their supper, he said. Then the other abbatial servants lined up to draw pitchers of ale and returned for the bowls of stew ladled out by this chosen servant. He even sliced extra meat from the roast on the spit. These holy men were locusts and left little for my other guests to eat."

"Could you describe this special servant?"

"Nay, Crowner. He looked like all the others, except his head was covered with a hood. I could not tell if he was tonsured, but that mattered not to me."

"He wore a hood in a hot kitchen? Didn't you think that strange?"

"Perhaps, but I paid little heed. The entire party was odd, to my thinking."

"So no one from the kitchen or any other person hired by you touched the food served the abbots, other than to roast the meat, simmer the stew, and brew your ale?" All this would have been started long before the abbots arrived. There was no reason to suspect contamination of food until the party was ready to eat.

The innkeeper glared. "I have answered your questions freely, Crowner, but now I fear the cause of them. If I am to continue my willing participation, I must know why you are asking for these troubling details."

Ralf drank another cup to think before replying. "One of the abbots fell ill the next day and has died. One more claims he was sickened the night he was here, felt better the next day, yet currently lies in the priory hospital with a recurrence of his illness."

The innkeeper leapt to his feet. "You seek some fault with me, Crowner? I knew you lied when you said you had no problem with me or my inn. This conversation is over!"

"Sit. The priory sub-infirmarian does not think the cause was bad food eaten here. I am trying to find out if it is possible for anyone to have deliberately tainted the food with an herb or even poison. I want to discover when that could have happened, as well as whether any stranger hovered about the party. I need your help, not your arrest."

Slowly sitting back down, the innkeeper seemed to relax. "And if my information helps you discover the cause, what shall be my reward?"

"My blindness to what may help your inn prosper, apart from drinkable enough ale, clean beds, and succulent meat. At least none of the abbots complained of fleas." His grin resembled that of a wolf contemplating a dinner of rabbit.

"If they were bitten by fleas, they brought their own virginal ones, Crowner. None of mine would have been holy enough to bite their pious flesh. As for any hint that the meat served once wandered in a forbidden forest, I have witnesses to swear that the meat we spitted was from an old ox whose service to a nearby farmer had come to an end but nourished my guests for a pittance."

Ralf ignored the last remark. "So was there any time at all that the food served the abbots was left unattended? Did anyone else, besides the abbots and their servants, complain of illness? I ask the latter, not because I question the honesty of your cook, but because these things happen everywhere."

For a moment, the man seemed to truly ponder his response. "The kitchen is too small and busy for any stranger to slip in without being noticed. He'd be chased away with a ladle to the head. My cook was angry about the servants taking over her stew and what was left of her roast. I took her complaint to the fat abbot who almost spat in my face with his contempt. He was lucky I did not send him to the cook. He was fat enough to make a tastier roast than an aged ox."

Ralf laughed. The image of his despised brother being turned on a roasting spit by a sweating kitchen brat delighted him.

The innkeeper blinked at the reaction, then misinterpreted it and relaxed. "These men claim to be vowed to God, Crowner, but they eat, drink, and whore like those of us who are honest sinners."

"Indeed, they do," Ralf said as the serving wench plopped a slice of steaming meat on a trencher in front of him. It smelled wonderful, and the crowner took a moment to cut and eat a few bites. "If this is an old ox, your cook has recreated the miracle at Cana and turned tough meat into a delicious thing."

The innkeeper paled.

Ralf winked. "I know miracles can happen. My wife is adept at such culinary wonders."

"To answer your question further," the innkeeper hastily added, "there was no grievance about the quality of the food from anyone who spent the night here. Quantity, perhaps." He glared. "When the abbots left the next day, a few other travelers joined them. I know nothing of their health. Most here were local men and would have sent word of any illness with a demand for the repayment of coin. A few strangers, stranded by the weather, remained, but had no complaints about my inn."

"Was anyone aware that an abbot was ill?"

The man shook his head. "I certainly did not know of it. None of the abbots spoke much to me the next day, other than to give me a thin pouch of even thinner coin. The godly ones took hot barley loaves with them to eat on the road to break their fasts. I don't think the fare here was of the quality they were accustomed to in their abbeys." He snorted. "If an abbot was poisoned, it was done by someone in his service. Other than Betsy and the groom, my people avoided these religious. Was it the fat abbot who fell ill? He seemed most likely to suffer from over-indulgence at table. More of the extra slices of ox probably ended up in his belly."

"It was not him." Ralf hesitated. "You mentioned that one of the abbots took his ease with that serving woman." The crowner decided that the groom with his cropped ear would have spent little time with the abbots, preferring to stay closer to the horses.

"Lest you think Betsy poisoned him, Crowner, she is not stupid. Even if she hated the man, she'd let him lift her skirt for enough coin. If he tried to beat her, she was just as likely to bite him in his manhood." He rubbed at his nose. "Almost gelded a man once."

Finishing his ale and sopping up the last of the meat juices with bread, Ralf rose and thanked the innkeeper. When he tried to pay, however, the man pushed his hand aside.

"Your word that you shall leave me in peace for my cooperation is sufficient, Crowner."

Ralf gave his oath, although he said he might have to come back for further details if the investigation warranted it.

"Not too often," the man replied. "Your face is known here and spoils the appetites of good men."

With that, the crowner left, well-contented with his meal and the information gathered. The ale might have lacked the robust taste of Tyndal's, he decided, but the bread was better than the sour rye of the poor. The meat, suspiciously similar to venison, was good. Had his stomach been a cat, it would have purred. As he collected his horse from the nervous groom, his mood was sufficiently good that he flipped the man a small coin and grinned.

As he rode back to Tyndal, pondering all he had learned, his mood changed. He should have known that Brother Thomas rarely grew suspicious without cause. His own conclusion that the abbots had suffered only from their sinful indulgences was too simple. Some malign force was at work here.

Chapter Eleven

The daylight was growing dim. So was the life of Abbot Tristram.

Sister Anne slipped as close as she dared and watched him. His breathing was shallow, but that was a mercy after the delirium that caused him to scream and the painful seizures he suffered.

At least they had decided he would be more comfortable in his own chamber in the guest quarters. Had he remained in the hospital, his howls of agony, as he imagined devils tearing his entrails out of his body, would have alarmed the fragile sick nearby. As a man approaches death, he must consider his sins and how to placate God, but each must look into his own fiery pit of Hell and not be confused by others and their special fears of damnation.

The abbot's breathing grew slower, and then he gasped, open-mouthed, with a short rasping sound deep in his throat.

Unable to touch him, Anne asked the lay brother to put his hand with care just above Tristram's lips and nose. He next put his hand on the abbot's chest but quickly looked up at her with unmistakable sorrow.

The body of Abbot Tristram lay silent and hollow. Death had taken his soul to his meeting with God.

At least his earthly torment is over, Sister Anne thought.

What most grieved her was the failure to cure or even ease the abbot's final suffering. When she had first spoken to him after he was taken from the courtyard to the special bed in the hospital, she concluded that he had a gentle enough soul for a mortal. Perhaps he did expect the attending lay brother to do more for him than other men might have required, but he'd had no quarrel with her questions about his condition and let her try remedies she hoped would help.

That was better than being cursed as the Whore of Babylon and ordered away, although she knew there was likely little she could have done for Abbot Ilbert even if he had permitted it. At least he had died in the comfort of knowing he had rejected any contamination by a daughter of Eve, but she regretted he never told her, or one of the hospital brothers, if he was taking anything as a remedy against some ailment. That might have helped her identify or reject the cause of his illness.

Sister Anne slipped to her knees near Abbot Tristram's bed and prayed. Brother Thomas, who had arrived just in time to give the man the last rites, bowed his head in silence. The attendant lay brother murmured softly.

There is nothing quite so still as death, Anne thought. Her breath caught and tears stung. The face of her young son came to mind, as it often did when she stepped aside to let Death take away a soul. Her boy might have died many years ago, but the memory of his lifeless body remained fresh. She longed to reach out for the comforting touch of her husband's hand, a man now known as Brother John. But he had chosen God to console him in his grief and never touched her hand again.

"Let us look at him," Brother Thomas said in a hushed voice.

She was grateful he had not seen her reaction to this death and rose quickly to her feet. "You are right, Brother. If he could not give us answers when he was alive, perhaps his body will in death," she said and quickly sent the lay brother to the hospital to prepare a place by the altar for this corpse to rest until burial arrangements could be made.

But any hope of revelation quickly dimmed. Brother Thomas was thorough in his examination of the corpse, but, apart from the yellowed color of the man's skin and eyes, there were no other untoward signs present. The only thing of interest he noted was that the abbot, although thin, was flabby compared to most men his age. He pointed that out.

"As knowledgeable medical men say, we should eat, drink, and exercise in moderation." Anne said. "Perhaps he exercised less than was advisable."

"His yellow coloring. Might that have been caused by a poison?"

"Men die with that hue, and there is no question of murder, Brother." Her tone was flat. "I cannot dismiss your concern, but I cannot confirm that his death was hastened by someone who hated him."

Gracia appeared at the door to the room. "Crowner Ralf has arrived back safely from the inn," she said, "and Prioress Eleanor asks you both to join her in her chambers to hear his news." Her gaze suddenly fell on the motionless man lying on the bed but realized there was no need to ask questions. Murmuring a prayer for the abbot's soul, the maid left with Brother Thomas close behind.

Sister Anne remained just long enough to take a final look at the corpse. At least, she thought, the other abbots had not been nigh to hear his screams. They had fled the guest quarters to pray in the church for their companion's soul. Or else, she thought with less charity, they did not want to be reminded of Death when the man from Rome awaited them and brought hope of future earthly rewards.

She hurried to catch up with Gracia and Brother Thomas.

As she approached them on the path, the sub-infirmarian forced her mind from her treatment failures to consider Prioress Eleanor's worries over Gracia's future.

The maid has never lost her wariness of others, even if she has learned to laugh, Anne thought. Perhaps she would be wise to remain at the priory and take vows. The world had never been kind to her.

Anne knew that Gracia did not have the dowry needed to allow her to become a nun, yet she was also too well-educated to enter as a lay sister. The sub-infirmarian shook her head and then realized that she had fallen further behind the maid and monk.

She began to run.

Gracia looked over her shoulder and stopped to wait for her. As if realizing what Sister Anne was thinking, her bright expression dimmed into something inscrutable.

Ralf threw out his arms in irritation. "I think the innkeeper was telling the truth, my lady. He knew I could easily find out if I came back with enough men to question everyone. And, no, he could not pay everyone off to lie to me before I did."

Eleanor smiled.

"If the one abbot was poisoned, it must have been done cleverly and by one of the servants. No one else at the inn has sickened, nor, except for Abbot Tristram, have any others in the party of religious." He looked at Sister Anne and Brother Thomas. "And the second abbot has since died? Were there any signs that matched those you noted on the first one's body?"

"They both suffered convulsions and frothing," Anne replied. "Other symptoms were quite different, but we know little enough about their prior conditions or anything else that might help."

"Yet the coincidence of illness remains troublesome," Thomas added.

"I concur, but is that truly questionable by itself without symptoms that are more alike? A poisoning seems unlikely to be the cause of Abbot Tristram's death. He had been ill, then recovered, and yet later began to exhibit more dire afflictions before he gave up his soul in agony." Sister Anne frowned. "But because the facts suggest nothing was ill-prepared at the inn..." She rubbed at her eyes in frustration. "I am missing something or lack the knowledge to identify the cause!"

Ralf murmured sympathy and reached out for her hand, but remembered her vocation and drew back.

"My father was the physician, not I," she continued. "He had the education I so profoundly lack, as well as the skill to read medical treatises in languages I cannot."

"But he taught you from the manuscripts he had. No son could have learned any more."

"You are kind, Ralf," Sister Anne replied, but his words did not comfort. She often grieved that her father was left with only a daughter to whom he might pass on his great learning. He never once said he would have preferred a son, and never stinted in his lessons to her, but conventional wisdom was adamant that women remained inferior creatures even when a father chose to be indulgent. When she later failed to save her own son's life, she felt the full weight of her inadequacy and ignored the truth that her apothecary husband had also failed to keep their boy alive.

"It is almost as if God has struck these men with some new plague," Eleanor said, shivering at the thought. "May He have mercy on the innocent, if such is the case."

The thought did cross Ralf's mind that God might have had good reason to strike these two abbots down if they were anything like his hypocritical brother. And well they could have been, he thought. Another had broken his vow of celibacy at the inn, apparently with a practiced vigor. That was one sin he never thought festered in his brother's benighted soul, even if there were other evils which probably lay rotting there.

"Although I did not think it true before," he chose to say, "I now side with Brother Thomas in the belief that at least the first death was murder. And if the first, then we must consider the second to be suspect."

"Poisons are hard to identify if they are not common ones," Anne said. "The symptoms exhibited by Abbot Tristram could be caused by any number of ailments. If his body was weak, as his corpse suggests he might have been, a lesser disease could have overcome him, even if it might not a stronger man."

Eleanor looked at the two monastics. "Do you both concur with Ralf that the two deaths might be unnatural?"

"I do," said Brother Thomas and glanced at the sub-infirmarian.

"It is possible," she added, "although I am not convinced about Abbot Tristram's."

"Your questioning of the abbots did not produce enlightenment?" Ralf's tone suggested no hint of criticism.

"Much jesting about flatulence in which your brother was judged an expert, yet I learned nothing that struck me as relevant except that not one of the abbots liked any of his fellows. But since you have talked to the innkeeper, I should question the abbots' servants," Thomas replied. "One of them might have noticed something untoward. One of them apparently took responsibility to act as a shield against the secular world."

"Or, if God is merciful to us, one will exhibit a murderous dislike of the two dead men," Ralf said. "We can only hope that a guilty soul might tremble before a monk who speaks with God, and confess."

"It is too late tonight to talk to the men, but I shall tomorrow after I take the medicines to those who need them in the village," Thomas said.

"How is Signy's girl? And are there many others suffering there?" Eleanor had long ago approved Sister Anne's suggestion that Thomas carry some remedies to the sick who were unable to travel to the hospital. It had become a popular charity, not only because it allowed the frail to receive treatment without the hardship of moving from their beds, but because Brother Thomas was loved for his kindness and wise counseling.

"Signy's daughter is almost well. There are only two others: an elderly man, who may not last the winter, and a woman who still suffers pain after her seventh birthing."

"Then I shall send word to the abbots that you will be talking to their servants before the midday meal." Eleanor needed only to look at Gracia for the maid to begin serving ale.

For once, Ralf refused refreshment and said he longed to return to his family instead.

Prioress Eleanor said he must do so and sent her love and a blessing to Gytha and the children.

The others, who remained with the prioress in her chamber, chose, in the growing darkness of that winter night, to talk about anything except murder.

Chapter Twelve

Two young women walked in companionable silence and then laughed like innocent children when the crisp snow gave way under their feet with a crackling sound. A fresh layer had fallen overnight, covering their route from the hospital apothecary hut to the anchorage attached to the Lady Chapel. The air was brisk, but the morning sun shone with a bold light as if celebrating its arrival after banishment by mists as sharp as dagger-points on mortal flesh.

Gracia tried to take shallow breaths because the cold hurt her chest and throat, but she reveled in the warmth of her thick cloak and snug winter gloves. Others might choose to forget the time when they suffered from ice and hunger, but she refused to do so. Instead, she greeted each new day as a blessing from God that put the grief of her sad days further behind.

From time to time, she still had nightmares in which her parents gasped for breath before they died, their eyes wide with panic as they suffocated. And she had other moments when the smell of food from the priory kitchen revived her terror of hunger and her certainty that the time of starvation must come again. But all that could be set aside when her prioress sat her down, held her hand, and taught her the lessons of kindness, or when Brother Thomas looked at her with his astonishing understanding and proved to her that men could be gentle.

A hand tapped her shoulder, and Gracia looked up at her companion.

Eda, Anchoress Juliana's maid, smiled and pointed toward the path that led to the mill.

A line of young lay brothers was being led to the assigned work for the day. At their head marched Brother Beorn, a man of grim demeanor and strict rules, who was respected and hated in equal measure by his charges.

Gracia remembered her mistress telling her that the youths might, after they grew older, appreciate that he understood mercy and was always fair. In that moment, they would learn to love him. Now they only saw his intolerance of any laxity in the labor of serving God, and they winced under his sharp rebukes. Gracia kept that lesson her prioress taught firmly in mind.

Eda pointed with her fingers as if counting the ones in the line until she reached the one she wanted to indicate for her friend. Then she put her hand over her heart, fluttered her eyelashes, and grinned.

"I see Brother Anthony," Gracia said with an uncomfortable laugh and knowing that her face was turning red. The young lay brother was often at the apothecary when she came for things needed by her prioress or with Eda. When he shyly looked into her eyes, a bewildering warmth crept through her body.

Was this lust?

Her emotions confused her. He was gentle and appealing, but she also drew back from him, honoring his vocation. But if she could desire to lie with him, might she feel the same for another man?

The world outside Tyndal Priory did not tempt her. Unlike the woman who first served Prioress Eleanor, she never went beyond the walls unless sent on an errand. Here she felt safe with food, warmth, and love that never threatened to hurt her. Why, then, had her own body chosen to attack her? Was God telling her she was too wicked to remain on His holy ground?

Eda touched her friend's shoulder again and began to move her hands rapidly, her expression more serious. She pointed toward the guest quarters and raised her steepled hands to heaven.

After a few more gestures, Gracia indicated she needed more information to properly reply. She might have given voice to her question but spoke with her hands as much as she was able. Although Eda understood speech, the prioress' maid chose to respect her manner of communication as proof of their loving friendship.

Eda had seldom alluded to the torment that left the horrific scar that cut through her mouth and a subsequent infection that almost killed her. Gracia had only briefly mentioned her parents' deaths or the man who had violated her. Their individual experiences of the world's cruelty had initially drawn each to the other, but the bond between them strengthened as Gracia and Eda became like sisters, a kinship neither had enjoyed before.

Eda was now asking Gracia about the illnesses of the abbots and explained that she had over overheard two lay brothers discussing this while she was waiting for the soothing medicine needed by the anchoress.

Gracia realized she did not have the facility in hand language to explain and told Eda in words what she knew and how Sister Anne was confused by the symptoms.

Eda took a moment to think and began to make more signs. Her hands outlined a window and next mimed a man speaking with great remorse.

As the maid continued, Gracia suddenly stopped her. "Anchoress Juliana must be told about this matter of the abbots! Let us hurry, and I shall explain it fully to you both."

◇◇◇

The Anchoress Juliana sipped the remedy, cleared her sore throat of phlegm, and listened to Gracia's tale of the dying abbots.

"You have spoken of the possibility that at least one abbot was murdered." She swallowed and winced. "Eda was right to mention the man who came to my window, and you were wise to want to hear more. Not knowing the tale of the abbots, I assumed the man was only a troubled soul seeking advice. Now,

I see that Prioress Eleanor should hear the tale and decide if his visit relates to the abbots' deaths. It is the timing of the two events that suggests a connection. Otherwise, I confess that many suffer the same torments of ignorance that this man did."

Eda pointed to the cup, then at the small fire and her mouth to ask if her mistress wanted the potion warmed.

Juliana shook her head. "Unless God wills otherwise, Sister Oliva's cure will soothe my throat soon enough."

Eda nodded, pointed to the entry door to the anchorage, made eating motions, and signaled for permission to leave.

The anchoress chuckled. "You may go to Sister Matilda for our noon meal, but please wait a moment longer until I finish with Gracia or she will be locked in the anchorage until your return. She did not ask for entombment here!"

Eda grinned at the prioress' maid.

Juliana swallowed more of the soothing drink. "Please relay to Prioress Eleanor what I shall quickly tell you and convey my regret that I delayed to do so out of ignorance. I beg her forgiveness if I have erred."

Gracia swore to do so, although she was certain that the prioress would find no fault.

Juliana thought for a moment before beginning her tale. "The man came to seek my humble counsel after the sun had set, although that is not unusual in the dark seasons. He longed to understand how a mortal can know whether or not something is truly God's intention. Did a man sin if he abetted an act that might be a sin but, on the other hand, might be God's will? How could one comprehend what was sin and what was not? At first, I thought he wanted me to address the scope of what a priest could advise, but he soon made it clear that he was troubled most over something he had done, or perhaps failed to have done. He grew agitated, and he began to weep. He seemed unable to explain exactly what he meant, but he said he feared the fires of Hell."

"Did he give you any other details?" Gracia was memorizing the story and leaned closer with her intense desire to recall every word spoken.

"Although I asked for that, he refused to say anything more specific. At one point, he pounded on the wall outside my window and groaned, but he could not bring himself to utter more than the questions he asked. I fear I erred in some way, although I told him, as I must, that he should seek a priest if he wanted absolution for any sin or explanation of whether any act in a given situation is a transgression. He fled without another word to me. As a simple woman, I may never take the place of a priest. He was obliged to seek one." She bowed her head.

Gracia knew that no woman could ever forgive sins, but she also knew that God often conveyed His wisdom and will through the human tongues of holy anchoresses.

After a moment, Anchoress Juliana raised her eyes. Her expression was now vague, as if her soul had started on a journey in another direction and longed to continue it.

The meeting with the anchoress was done. Gracia rose, followed Eda from the anchorage, and hurried to take the news to Prioress Eleanor.

Chapter Thirteen

Brother Thomas cheerfully bade farewell to the young girl lying in the bed.

She smiled bashfully and cuddled her cloth poppet. It may have been made from worn rags and tied to roughly form the appropriate arms, legs, and head, but she had lovingly draped it with a piece of wool to make a dress. Pulling her covers up, she carefully made sure her doll was warm as well.

Signy took a deep breath and put a gentle hand on the lad standing beside her. "Keep watch on your sister, Nute, and don't let her out of bed for long. Keep the fire…"

The lanky boy, who was taller than she, laughed. "Have I ever failed you or my sister, Mother?" He winked at the monk.

The woman he called *mother* pulled his head down and kissed him on his still-smooth cheek, then left for the entry door with Brother Thomas following. Once outside, she shut the door firmly to keep out any hint of chill. "Nute is a good boy," she said with obvious pride.

"Almost a man, I would say," Thomas replied, glancing back at the innkeeper's new house.

"He is, Brother, but I have a little time yet before I must admit to him that I know it." Her laugh was rich and melodically deep.

As they walked toward the nearby inn, Thomas watched this woman who dressed like a widow, although she had never married, and who raised two orphans, but had never borne a child of her own. Despite her plain dress and middle years, she possessed a body of rare perfection in an imperfect world. Even men who had known her for years stopped to admire when she passed by. Women did as well, gazing with awe at her hair sparkling red-gold in the sun and bright, even on the greyest days.

Yet she had not, for many years, bestowed a promising smile on any man who longed for her to share his bed, even those who wished to marry her. Her charity was vast but anonymous. Had she not been an innkeeper with a clever head for honest profits, she might have been called saintly in the daily speech of the villagers. Among those who received her charity, however, many whispered that she was one of the blessed.

"You are busy despite the snows," Thomas said, entering just after her into the warmth of the inn.

"The timing of the storms was a godsend to me." Signy called to a serving maid. "Bring a flavored ale for Brother Thomas. He needs the warmth for both body and spirit."

With gratitude, he thanked her.

"A few have tried to go back to their homes after they learned that drifts had buried roads and heavy snow caused bridges to crumble on the road to Norwich. Others stay on, hoping for a warm day when their particular route might become passable once again."

The innkeeper and monk sat down.

The table had been rubbed spotless. No rotting scraps of food were ground into the rushes under their feet. A burly red cat, seeking foolishly bold rodents, edged his way along the wall toward the kitchen. Meticulous about the state of her inn, Signy had worked hard to gain a well-earned reputation for providing decent lodging at a fair price.

"I see a few pilgrims." Thomas indicated a table of solemn folk. Each was dressed in somber robes with a leather travel bag around the waist and a stout walking stick placed carefully on the floor. "Some travel in winter because they believe the great hardships are especially good for their souls. Perhaps they are ones waiting for the road to Norwich to clear?"

He looked around at others huddled at tables. A few men

sat on the floor, playing a game of dice. The pilgrims looked at the ceiling or each other and ignored them.

The serving woman brought the warmed ale and shyly put the cup in front of Brother Thomas, then begged a blessing.

Signy smiled approval, although she was well aware that requests for blessings often hid a woman's more worldly desire to spend a moment longer near this handsome monk. But everyone in the village knew that Brother Thomas remained strong in his vows and had never succumbed to feminine wiles. His virtue might be regretted from time to time, but women also knew their own chastity would never be questioned when they needed to confide a secret to him in more private settings.

After the woman left, Thomas sipped the warm ale. He had not realized quite how much he needed it after walking here through the cold breeze. "You have heard that a party of abbots has come to Tyndal?"

"I have."

"Perhaps you have not yet learned that one was ill and died soon after he arrived. Another fell ill, and he, too, has died."

Signy's expression suggested a growing concern. "What was the cause of these deaths, Brother? I assume that Prioress Eleanor would have sent word if there was danger of contagion."

"Sister Anne has no reason to fear there is, or the village would have been warned, but she is puzzled by the causes of both deaths. Each man died in different ways. Their symptoms match many illnesses, yet possess some that match none."

"That is a rare failure for our talented sub-infirmarian. Many ills are beyond mortal aid, but she is swift to know what she can treat and what is solely within God's grace to cure."

"I am looking for any others who traveled with the party of abbots. Perhaps they can give me details that might help Sister Anne find the reasons for the two deaths." He looked hopeful. "The religious came to our priory three days ago."

"A few arrived here for lodging at that time," she replied, glancing over the inn inhabitants, "but I am unsure which of these were members of that party. Some, I recall, but not everyone." Her eyes twinkled with gentle humor. "I also do not know why they sought my inn instead of the priory if they had traveled in the company of God's servants. I have heard Tyndal's new guest quarters are comfortable, and surely most would seize the opportunity for ongoing conversation with those dedicated to God as good for their souls."

"Not all men like the monastic diet," Thomas said with a laugh. "And, perhaps, they had had enough of the company of abbots."

Surprised, the innkeeper asked why.

"One of them is Ralf's brother, Odo, who is Abbot of Caldwell."

"Odo?" She slapped the table with her hand and laughed until her cheeks became a spring flower pink. "Him? Truly? I hope you do not jest!"

This was one of the few times in many years Thomas had ever seen her possessed of such unabashed merriment.

She glanced around, and then bent her head closer so she might keep her voice low. "Of course, our Ralf has always hated him for being a sanctimonious ninny, but Odo never had more than one or two friends in the village. Shall I tell you a scandalous tale about him?"

Now Thomas leaned closer.

"It is said that Odo found his vocation in God's service when a girl saw him emerging naked from swimming. She proclaimed in a loud voice for all to hear that he must be a lass for she saw no evidence of manhood."

"Even Ralf has never told that story," Thomas chuckled.

"I tell you the tale, and swear I shall add the wickedness to my next confession, only to illustrate how despised he was by many here, not just his brother. As to the truth of the story, I was not the girl, I do not know her name, and have no knowledge of whether it occurred or not. It is true that Odo never lusted after women as a boy. Food was his passion, and it is a mistress to whom he has reputedly remained faithful. We might have forgiven a bastard seeded by him in a willing lass, or lauded his choice of God over mortal flesh, but we could never forgive his scorn for us all as if he had been God's finest creation and we were His mistakes. From boyhood, he judged anyone living in Tyndal or even Norwich to be contemptible."

Thomas nodded thoughtfully. "I wonder why Ralf paid for his brother's entry to the great Caldwell Abbey and eased his way into the rank he currently holds if he loathes Odo so much? Our crowner could have found an abbey or priory of lesser status in which to place his detested brother. Family honor would have been satisfied."

"For all his roughness of manner, Ralf is both kind and generous. He may hate Odo, but he is still his brother. He would never deny the man the right to be in a place where he could best serve the liege lord he chose with the skill even our crowner knew his brother possessed." Signy turned her face away.

Thomas saw her flushed cheeks and felt a deep sadness on her behalf. Her words about Ralf were charitable. Years ago, she had deeply loved the crowner but soon discovered that he had taken her into his bed only because he needed the comfort of a woman's body. Until he married this last time, his great love had been Sister Anne who, before she took vows, had wed another.

Signy looked at Thomas again with a calm look and dry eyes. "Gytha is still too good for him," she said and laughed. Despite the innkeeper's regret over Ralf, she and his wife were loving friends.

"A statement with which he would agree."

They fell silent and let the cheerfulness of the warm inn surround them for awhile. The great red cat returned, trotting jauntily by with a grey object in his teeth.

Thomas put down his cup and refused more. Gazing around the inn again, he asked, "Have any here suffered from fevers or agues, loose bowels, or nausea?"

She thought a moment before shaking her head. "Yet there are other ills. The young man and his wife near the fire seem troubled. She is quite pale, and he hovers over her with evident uneasiness. In that corner over there, the man sitting alone has a rash on his hands. I assumed it was chilblains, but he has not been outside since his arrival and the condition does not seem to trouble him any less. Both he and the young couple came here about the time your abbots arrived at the priory." She briefly shut her eyes and frowned. "Others may have done so as well, but my memory fails me. Will you need a more accurate answer to your question?"

"I may," Thomas said as he rose.

"Tomorrow I will be able to provide it."

"At the moment, I should talk to those you have pointed out. Perhaps I can alleviate their ills, and they may tell me something that could be helpful to our sub-infirmarian." He read her growing look of concern well. "As for your daughter, fear not. She is on the mend."

"Her poppet is healing, you mean." Signy's good humor restored, she exhaled with relief. "You cleverly got her to take the medicine you brought and to feel easier about her illness. I tried not to laugh when you explained that my little girl must serve as an example to the sick doll by replicating her treatment. The wile was successful, even though a little medicine was wasted!"

"Then repeat my advice that her poppet is almost well but must not overdo. They both must obey you about eating and resting."

The innkeeper swore to do as he recommended and left to oversee the kitchen.

The monk went to talk to the young couple.

◇◇◇

They looked up at him, and the man hastily put his arm around the ashen-faced woman.

Sliding onto the bench across from them, Thomas noted a faint scent of blood and a suspicion began to form about the cause of their dismay. "I am from the nearby priory and bring cures from the hospital to those who cannot travel there. If I am not wrong, you are ill," he said gently to the young woman.

She looked away, and Thomas was now convinced he knew the ailment, although the cause might be one of two. He prayed it was not the more grievous one.

"It is nothing worthy of your kind attention, Brother," the man said.

Thomas bent closer to them. "I think it is," he said. "Your wife bleeds, does she not? It is not the normal courses, and she needs a cure."

The young woman began to weep softly.

"What did you take?" Thomas whispered. "Confess your sin and be forgiven first, but also let me help your body heal so you may live to perform your penance."

"She took nothing!" The man hissed with outrage and more firmly clutched her to him. "She began to bleed just before we arrived here, and it has not stopped."

"But she was with child?"

The man said nothing. The woman whispered in the affirmative.

"Is the discharge a heavy one?"

The young man looked nervously at the pale woman.

She glanced at the monk, her blue eyes watery with fear. Slowly, she looked down and refused to speak further.

Yet, as she did, Thomas thought she might have murmured, "I have sinned," but he was unsure. He asked further questions but got few answers from the husband. All he learned was that the bleeding would not stop but was not a steady stream.

"There is snow outside," he said to the young man. "Take your wife to a private place and have her sit in a drift as long as she can bear the cold. I shall come tomorrow with lady's mantle. The herb will give her relief. In addition, I will consult with our sub-infirmarian for any other efficacious treatment." If this was a self-induced abortion, there was nothing else that might be used. At least the blood flow was minimal and might even have stopped by the time he returned.

The couple bent their heads and murmured nervous gratitude.

Thomas gave them the comfort of a blessing and left to attend the man in the corner.

◇◇◇

He was not a pilgrim, the monk thought, but his shabby dress suggested he was not a merchant either. Why, if neither faith nor necessity demanded it, had this man decided to travel in inclement weather and on dangerous roads when the wise would not?

As Thomas approached, he saw the man trying to flex his hands as if they hurt him. "I might be able to ease your discomfort," he said. "I bring medicines from the hospital at Tyndal Priory and have a little knowledge of ailments."

The man's eyes widened in shock as if the monk had awakened him suddenly from a deep sleep.

"Forgive me if I startled you."

"You only surprised me, Brother. I was just thinking how I longed to go back home. I have been here too long."

"Your hands pain you." Thomas reached out for them.

After a moment's hesitation, the man let the monk examine them. The skin was scaly and thick with tiny red lumps and a few blisters. The man winced.

"Did that hurt?" Thomas had been gentle with his touch, but he also noted that the hands felt unusually warm. This could be chilblains, but the scaly skin argued against that conclusion.

"They have gotten more sensitive as the blisters break." The man shrugged with attempted indifference.

"Our healers might have a salve that would soothe the discomfort."

He drew back his hands. "I have heard of your hospital's renown, Brother, but I have no desire to go into the cold to go there. Surely these hands will heal if God wills it."

"There is no need to leave the inn. I can explain to our sub-infirmarian what the rash looks like and how it feels. Barring a snowstorm, I will bring the remedy to you tomorrow."

The man's dark eyes brightened. "I confess that would be a true charity," he replied.

Thomas stood. "Are you far from home?"

"Very far." The man truly looked too weary to even contemplate the distance of the needed journey. He bowed his head as if longing for sleep.

Thomas wanted to ask if he had traveled with the abbots, but there was something in the man's eyes that made him hesitate.

He seemed exhausted and was most likely not sleeping because of the pain in his hands.

Tomorrow would be soon enough to further question this man as well as the young couple, the monk decided. They were all suffering, and he chose not to add a hard interrogation to their pains before bringing some relief.

It was not a decision Ralf would necessarily approve, but Thomas saw no reason to forego mercy. Signy would identify others who had joined the abbots on their journey. As for this young couple, neither was likely to have noticed much after the wife began to bleed. The man with the blistered hands probably had little to offer either.

With courtesy, he wished the man the mercy of God's grace and left the inn to hurry back to the priory.

Chapter Fourteen

Eda served Prioress Eleanor a cup of ale and quietly left the anchorage to gather firewood.

The thick door thudded shut, and they heard the lock turned from the outside. This time, Eleanor had brought her key to allow exit, but she shuddered at the irrevocable sound of that closing door.

I do not have the great faith needed to become an anchoress, she thought. I could not bear entombment. Aloud, she remarked, "She could have remained. I have nothing to say to you that she may not hear."

Juliana glanced at the formidable door with a fond look. "She is humble beyond any need. When Gytha suggested she become my maid, I fought your decision to accept the offer, but you were far wiser than I. Even now, I am shamed by my benightedness. Eda's virtue and kindness remind me daily of my imperfections and teach me how to strive to be a better servant to God. I shall always be grateful to you and Gytha, as well as Eda for her willingness to join me in this place."

Eleanor was also grateful for another reason. Eda had calmed the anchoress, a woman whom many had always considered holy but one who had long warred against the torments of violent internal demons. Juliana still bore physical scars on her body of those battles.

"She is also sharp-witted," the prioress said. "I am grateful she mentioned your visitor to Gracia."

"I would not have thought to tell you otherwise. On further reflection, I confess that the visitor struck me as more troubled than most who come to me seeking advice." She bowed her head and shut her eyes. "Before I can explain further, let me think back on the moment when he knelt outside my window. I must recall everything."

Eleanor waited and prayed that the anchoress held a clue that might bring an answer to these sad deaths.

Juliana looked up. "His voice was not familiar, his accent was not local, and his speech suggested a man of low birth. It was growing dark, but I could not have seen his face anyway. He kept it hidden by a hood. Not an aged man, from the strength and tenor of his voice."

"His hands? The cloth of his hood?"

"As I said, the light had fled, and I could see little. He did not show his hands. I think the cloth of his hood was coarse, but the impression might be based on his rough speech more than the hood I could barely see." She gazed upward as if begging for brighter memory, then shook her head. "The air was cold, and I did not lean forward to hear him as I do in summer. My weak flesh longed for warmth, a transgression that will be included in my next shriving."

"Gracia has repeated the words he spoke at your window. Have you remembered anything more? You said his grief was vague but sharp."

"Little else, I fear, but the deep pain in his voice still catches at my heart. Many say they have sinned, and truly grieve, but this man sounded as if he were clinging by his fingertips over the maw of Hell."

"He told you nothing about his particular sin?"

"I hoped he would. All he said, and he repeated this, was that he feared he had committed a terrible act but also wondered if it had been God's will and thus no sin. When I asked what it was, he refused to tell me. I suspect he knew it must be confessed to a priest, yet I urged him to say more to bring balm to his heart. Although a sinner must seek a priest to gain forgiveness, even a

woman might learn from God if the sin was at least pardonable."
The anchoress bowed her head. "His distress was so intense and
his longing for tranquility so sincere that I wanted to give him
a little peace until he could gain a priest's solace."

"Brother Thomas could hear his confession."

"I was about to suggest this when the man jumped back from
my window and fled into the night. I could not see where he
went. Then another came to speak with me, a woman who was
worried that her husband was unfaithful."

"She did not say anything about this prior suppliant?"

"I doubt she noticed anything, my lady. Her voice was familiar, as was her complaint. Villagers are used to seeing others in
front of them at the window and approach only when the space
is vacant. No one pays attention to those kneeling there. They
may love gossip, but they honor the need for secrecy with a
penitent." A brief smile of humor mellowed her sharp features.
"I often wonder if their virtue lies more in the hope that their
own sins not be distributed like seed around the village than any
wish to honor another's secrets in such moments."

With the anchoress unable to provide further details, Eleanor
followed her usual practice of blessing Juliana before leaving her
to the prayers she had dedicated her life to performing. Should
the man come back, or the anchoress remember anything more,
Eleanor knew she would be informed.

A priest might be forbidden to divulge the secrets of confessions, but an anchoress was under no such obligation to remain
silent about what she heard in confidence. Juliana never spoke of
village sins, or the transgressions committed by strangers, but the
suspicious deaths of two abbots required her to break that custom.

After the prioress had escaped the narrow walls of the anchorage and dutifully locked the door behind her, Eleanor walked
slowly through the silence of the church. Perhaps, she thought, I
should have taken the opportunity to talk to Juliana about Gracia.

But she quickly dismissed the regret. When this matter of
the abbots was done, she would concentrate again on how to
prepare herself for the frightening moment when Gracia chose

to speak about her future. Murder always seems to take precedence over other human problems, she thought, and allowed herself a flash of resentment before concentrating again on the crime she must solve.

Going over all the anchoress had told her, Eleanor wondered about the man's hood. It was a detail mentioned by the innkeeper to Ralf. But most men wore hoods in the cold and wet. It may have been odd for a man to keep his hood on in the kitchen of an inn. It would have been equally strange if the visitor to the anchorage had not worn one in the raw cold.

Perhaps this man who had visited Juliana had nothing to do with murder. Yet a stranger at this time of the year who suffered such agonies over a possible sin when a poisoner lurked nearby? She sighed. She could not dismiss this tale even if its significance was unclear.

Emerging into the cloister garth, she looked up. The light was dull. Was another snowstorm coming? The question turned her mood as dreary as the light.

She hoped Brother Thomas would hurry back from the village before snow began to fall and felt anxious for his safety. Of late, he had appeared more pensive than usual, and Prior Andrew mentioned that the good monk had been seen pacing the monks' cloister long after Compline.

In the early days of his life here, he had often slept badly and reports came to her that he frequently remained awake between the night and morning Offices, shaking his fist at the moon during Satan's hours. In recent years, he had rarely done this, and even Sister Anne had commented that his soul seemed more at peace.

What had happened to disquiet him so deeply again? The change troubled her.

Yet this investigation into the abbots' deaths seemed to have refreshed his spirit. She wondered if murder was a challenge he enjoyed tilting against since he could not fight in battle as other men did. A secret worldly pleasure for this good servant of God?

She smiled as she climbed the stairs to her chambers. Although her beloved monk was revered by all who knew him for his gentleness and wisdom, she was secretly glad he might have one tiny flaw. It was a possibility she would put in a hidden part of her heart and cherish. If anything, it made her love him more.

Chapter Fifteen

Prior Andrew sat with the five living abbots and tried to encourage a reverential discourse during the midday dinner.

Now he wished he had brought a monk to read from a holy work and forced the usual mealtime silence on these men. His choice to allow these monastic guests the worldly habit of conversation was not only a common practice of priory hospitality but was meant to soften the grimness of the recent deaths.

The prior's decision turned out to be a regrettable one.

Instead of remembering the godly works of their dead brothers in faith, or musing on the transitory nature of mortal life, these men were determined to criticize all the perceived deficiencies of the dead abbots, especially those possessed by Abbot Tristram.

Prior Andrew abandoned all hope, fell silent, and let them talk.

"How he managed to rise to the position of abbot fills me with amazement." Gifre had made a small pile of roasted root vegetables in the middle of the bread slice sitting atop his wooden trencher. With great care, he began to mash down the sides of the mound with a crust as if he were erecting an unassailable castle.

With fascination, Prior Andrew watched this exercise in construction. If Gifre did not eat his vegetarian fortification, the prior decided, the poor would at least benefit from the food.

"His family has served the local baron well," Odo replied, half opening his eyes. He had been leaning back with eyes shut. Except for bits of parsnip, his trencher was empty.

"I thought you were asleep," Mordredus said with derision. He looked around for a lay brother and then pointed to his own empty cup.

"His prior did all the work." Didier had devoured his portion of the first cooked dish and gazed over his shoulder as if anticipating the next course. When none seemed imminent, he shrugged, placed his elbows on the table, and leaned forward. "His most recent subordinate was heard to complain that he was so burdened with the abbot's work that he lacked time to take care of his own responsibilities."

"That was true, Abbot." Mordredus sipped the fresh ale, sighed with appreciation over the quality of the second serving, and eagerly drank more. "I learned of the problem from a reliable source."

"And made good use of it, no doubt." Odo reached out for his cup and glared at his empty trencher. "I am weary of this Lenten food when the season is not even upon us."

"What are you implying about me?" Mordredus glared at him. "I do not like your tone."

The Abbot of Caldwell belched.

"Hush, good men." Abbot Ancell wagged a skeletal finger at the men surrounding him. "Prior Andrew will think we care more about a man's weaknesses, from which all mortals suffer, than the state of his soul when it must face God."

"The state of Tristram's soul was the responsibility of his confessor. His laziness was a burden to us all," Mordredus replied. "Even on this journey I had to lend my servant to help Tristram's man load the abbot's prie-dieu. His master had delayed the effort with belated tasks. His servant had to mend a small tear in Abbot Tristram's sleeve. That could not wait until we arrived at our destination? A spot of mud on his boot? The servant must stop everything and clean it off."

Odo looked around with surprise. "In order to allow us more time to serve God, servants should mend and clean everything for us. I see no sin in letting men of lesser rank serve Him in the ways He intended them to do. My servants take my boots off. Am I not weary from many hours of laboring to the glory of the Lord?"

"You are too fat to take your boots off, let alone bend to clean away a mud stain," Didier muttered but winced as if hoping he had not been overheard.

Ancell shut his eyes, bemused by whatever he was privately thinking.

"Surely the papal envoy would not be so unwise as to have considered the man worthy of a bishopric—were one to fall open, of course." Mordredus looked for the expected agreement from his companions. "In truth, Tristram never did any task that he could not find another to perform."

There were nods enough, and silence fell for a few moments while lay brothers refreshed cups and offered second servings of well-seasoned roasted parsnips, some soft beans, succulent onions, and turnips. Only Didier accepted another small portion.

Odo laid his fist on the table and looked at Prior Andrew. "Will you explain why we have been served no meat? And do not tell me that your priory is too poor. These guest quarters are new, as are the stables where our beasts are tended. Perhaps you find our rank insufficient to warrant the courtesy of a proper diet?"

Prior Andrew tried not to stare in disdain at the abbot's massive hand. With great effort he lifted his eyes to gaze at the deep furrows of discontent in Odo's forehead. "Our prioress requires all to adhere strictly to the Benedictine diet. Fowl and fish are served, but our kitchen does not prepare meat as it heats the blood which leads to lust-filled thoughts."

Odo snorted. "Meat gives men strength to fight the wiles of Satan. Prioress Eleanor should be educated in these matters. The Rule has been modified to include the consumption of meat, Prior Andrew."

"Only for the weak, aged, and ill," Andrew replied, belatedly realizing he had rudely contradicted this man who outranked him.

The Abbot of Caldwell did not respond to the insult, or else chose to ignore it. "We are no longer young men," he said, "and may therefore eat meat to maintain our strength as we valiantly do battle in God's service against all evil."

Andrew bowed his head in what he hoped was a sufficient display of humility in the face of greater wisdom. "Indeed, my lord," he murmured, "but I think you shall find that the next course, although lacking in red flesh, is most pleasing. Others have praised it to Queen Eleanor with such fervor that she sent a cook to learn how to prepare it. Later, we received word that the queen was greatly pleased with the dish."

Odo brightened.

"Where is this marvel of kitchen perfection, Prior?" Gifre waved at a lay brother to remove from his wooden trencher the vegetarian citadel.

Prior Andrew turned to the server standing behind him and gave the order to bring the promised delight.

After a short interval, a lay brother arrived with a small, steaming mushroom tart which was quickly sliced for serving.

The dish was first presented to Abbot Ancell, who looked at the rising steam with amazement and spread his hands over it to feel the surprising heat. Looking at the prior with awe, he expressed appreciation for the unusually hot dish. "But I am not worthy to be served first," he said, gesturing at the others around the table. "Let…" He hesitated, then bowed his head to Abbot Gifre. "Let he who has served God longest be the first to receive this special bounty."

As the tart was carried to the abbot, Mordredus stopped the lay brother and stared for a moment at the tart before also reaching out to test the warmth. "Even in my abbey, we have been unable to serve food this hot. You have created a miracle, Prior Andrew, and must reveal your secret!"

Gifre also held his hand over the tart to enjoy the heat but paused before accepting the honor of being the first served. The others, struck with the need to emulate Ancell's act of humility, urged him to do so.

"Have mercy, Abbot, and take it. The food is getting cold,"

Odo muttered. "We acknowledge your virtuous reluctance. Accept your portion and pass it on."

"More is on the way," Prior Andrew said. "Eat all you wish."

Gifre took him at his word, asked for most of the dish to be served on a fresh slice on bread over his wooden trencher, and immediately took a large bite. His eyebrows arched in amazement. "It is most certainly a dish worthy of a queen," he said. "Although I have eaten many mushrooms, these must have special seasonings for I have never tasted a finer creation! Was a local cheese added? And mustard?"

Odo looked at the little that was left for him and grumbled. He took a couple of bites. "It is ice-cold," he complained and waved at a lay brother to take it away as the second hot tart had just arrived. "Give me some of that," he shouted to the servers and immediately cut into the fresh one, devouring it at a happy pace. Soon, Sister Matilda's fungal marvel gained the high praise from all, even Didier, who found mushrooms distasteful.

At least it did until Abbot Gifre grabbed at his throat.

"My mouth is on fire!" he screamed. A rank odor of sweat emanated from him as he swiftly bent to one side and vomited.

Prior Andrew leapt up and rushed to help, but the abbot fell to the floor in convulsions, screaming in agony.

"Send for Sister Anne!" the prior shouted to a lay brother who raced from the room.

From across the table, Odo rose from his seat, one hand pressed to his cheek. "I am dying! I cannot feel my face!" The abbot swayed perilously. "May God have mercy on us all," he murmured, then rolled his eyes heavenward and collapsed on the ground.

The other abbots jumped up and ran to the wall, as far as possible from their afflicted brothers.

Only Abbot Ancell recovered sufficiently to come and kneel by Prior Andrew's side. "Abbot Gifre's soul is in danger," he whispered to the prior who had his hand pressed to the prone man's chest. "He must confess his sins."

Andrew moved back to give Ancell room. "Quickly utter forgiveness in his ear, my lord. Abbot Gifre is dead."

Chapter Sixteen

In a small room near the apothecary hut, Sister Anne watched as Brother Thomas finished studying Gifre's cadaver. As she had with Ilbert and Tristram, the sub-infirmarian did not touch this abbot's body out of respect for his vows, and turned her back when Thomas uncovered the man's genitals.

The monk looked over his shoulder at her. "From the symptoms we have been told, I agree with you that he was killed by some poison. But I have found nothing of note other than a slight foam around the mouth."

"I have ordered a testing of the remains of the tarts served to them. Sister Oliva has captured some mice and will feed them the crumbs. We should know soon what happens."

"What of Ralf's brother?" Thomas had delayed sending word to the crowner about Odo's exact condition. Unlike Gifre, he was alive, although deathly ill, and had been carried to his room to be placed under the care of a knowledgeable lay brother from the hospital. Considering the great weight of the abbot, the man chosen to care for him was also possessed of a particularly robust build.

"If God shows mercy on him, he will not die as this man did," Anne replied. "I will go to him later. He was suffering chills and nausea, but he spoke to me as he was carried away. That was a good sign."

"Sister Anne?" Sister Oliva, the sub-infirmarian's young assistant, was standing at the door. "If you are ready for them, I have the results of the tests for you to see."

The sub-infirmarian and the monk followed her the short distance into the apothecary hut. As they entered, they saw a lay brother guarding the carefully separated tart bits. On the table were also two cages. One held dead mice. In the other, three mice turned their wary eyes to watch the looming creatures who had come to study them.

"The dead mice ate the first tart," Sister Oliva pointed to the mostly eaten food. Without being asked, she described the manner of death the mice had suffered.

"And the others ate this?" Sister Anne pointed to those tart remnants.

"The live ones feasted well on them but have suffered no consequences. Other than showing their displeasure with our presence, they seem quite pleased with their meal." The nun fell silent as she watched the sub-infirmarian first carefully examine the deadly tart, and then the other.

"Monkshood," Sister Anne said, pointing to the first tart. "If you look carefully at that small remaining piece, you will see sharp-pointed bits of leaf on it. The symptoms are consistent with its poisonous nature."

Thomas bent close to look. "I agree. It might also be taken for a seasoning herb."

"Yet there is no evidence of it on the others," Sister Anne said.

"If I may have permission to speak?" The young nun moved forward to stand in front of the poisoned food.

"I welcome your observations, Sister." Anne smiled with pleased encouragement. Her young assistant had shown great talent in learning the apothecary art.

"The bits lie on top and do not look any different from the fresh cuttings we mix in oil and keep for treating joint pain."

"Well noted!" Anne looked at Brother Thomas with some excitement. "That suggests they were not cooked with the tart but added to the top after."

"Sister Matilda will be relieved," the monk replied. "She cannot be blamed for this."

"That does not mean that the poison was not sprinkled on top by a servant or even a lay brother who brought it from the kitchen."

A gasp from behind them caused the monastics to spin around.

Abbot Ancell stood near the door, gape-mouthed. "I could have eaten that," he croaked.

"God protected you from harm," Thomas said with a look he hoped was gentle. How long had the abbot been standing there, and how much had he overheard? Perhaps it did not matter, other than causing the man greater apprehension than any of them wished him to suffer. According to Prior Andrew, Ancell had been the only one who cared enough about Abbot Gifre's soul to set terror aside, kneel by the corpse, and whisper forgiveness before the dead man's spirit fled. That thought lent greater kindness to the monk's reply.

"I have just come from Abbot Odo's bedside," Ancell said. "He suffers pain and sees the world as yellowish-green, but he remains alive."

Sister Anne sighed with relief. "Then he may live," she said.

Abbot Ancell murmured a brief prayer.

"What happened at dinner?" Thomas subtly edged the abbot away from the sight of the dead mice.

Ancell had spied them, however, and his face paled. "I fear the shock of this event has chased all memory from me. I cannot recall what we spoke about at dinner or even who sat where."

"Prior Andrew said the tarts were brought as the second course. Can you recall anything unusual about them? Taste? Smell? How they were served?"

The Abbot of Jayden eased himself down on a bench and put his head in his hands. "A little is coming back to me." He looked up at the monk with sorrow. "Since I was closest to the dining hall entry, the lay brother initially offered me the food. As is the common practice in my abbey, I refused the first piece and said that the man who has served God longest should have the honor. That was Abbot Gifre." He gulped. "My decision brought about his death!" He raised his hands to plead with Heaven. "May God forgive me!"

Thomas put a hand on his shoulder. "You were unaware that death was hidden in the mushroom tart, my lord. Your intention was a gesture of pious humility. God would not condemn when you could not know the food was lethal." He waited until color slipped back into the man's cheeks. "What happened next?"

"Abbot Gifre also refused and pointed to another abbot." Ancell rubbed his eyes. "I do not recall which one it was." He scowled as he tried to think. "Perhaps it was Abbot Odo, but, before he could reply, the others proclaimed that Abbot Gifre must be served first. I did notice that he took most of it, leaving only a little for Abbot Odo, who accepted the remaining small portion."

"How much did Abbot Odo eat?" Sister Anne tucked her hands into her sleeves as a cold draft blew through the hut.

"Very little." His cheeks flushed despite the chill. "I fear he complained that the debate had continued so long the tart was too cold for his taste. He does not love mushrooms, but his stomach was growling. Another arrived, to his relief, and others soon after that one." He shuddered but quickly brightened. "I do remember how amazed we all were because the other dishes were so hot, as was the first. They were steaming! Might that signify anything?"

"That is because the new kitchen was built next to the guest quarters," Sister Anne replied. "The short serving time allows for hotter food."

Ancell looked disappointed that his observation had served no useful purpose.

Sister Anne reassured him that his memory of the dinner had been helpful.

Thomas took in a deep breath. Despite not liking Ralf's brother, he was grateful this one time that the man suffered from epicurean gluttony. Had he been less obsessed with the quality of his food, he might have finished the poisoned tart, no matter how cold, and died like Gifre.

"Did you notice anything in particular about either tart?" Sister Anne gestured to Sister Oliva who began to remove the cages of mice.

Ancell considered the question for a long moment. "Yes," he said. "The first one was sprinkled with herbs. The second served to me was plain. I wondered why only one had been decorated. When we were given ale instead of wine with this meal, we were pleasantly surprised that the second servings of the drink were of the same quality as the first. Why should the second tarts be lacking in the finer presentation?"

Anne and Thomas denied any such discourtesy and murmured some innocuous reason. Neither wanted to reveal that the ornamentation had been lethal.

Chapter Seventeen

Thomas watched the abbots' servants gather around him.

The deaths had frightened them, and each showed alarm in a different way. One twitched as if besieged by fleas. Another looked around as if expecting the Devil's arrival. All looked guilty, as innocent men often do when faced with questioning. The monk felt pity, but he refused to reveal that. After all, one of these men might be a ruthless murderer.

Some of the men were tonsured, were mostly of middle or later years, and appeared by their dress to be lay brothers. One was an elderly priest, the monk noted. Two were young men in secular attire, perhaps from families local to the specific abbey. What surprised Thomas most was the small number of servants who had accompanied these abbots, all of whom had surely hoped to impress the papal envoy with their worthiness to advance to a bishopric.

Did each abbot wish to appear especially humble or was there another reason? Thomas was curious and phrased his query more diplomatically than he had thought it.

The untonsured servant of Abbot Didier spoke first. "I was chosen to come because I could handle a horse as well as provide for any of my master's other needs." He was a black-bearded man whose plainness of robe proclaimed his low rank while the finer quality of wool suggested otherwise.

"And I was brought because I made fewer mistakes than others who served Abbot Ilbert. He feared the unbalancing of his humors on the journey and did not wish to suffer choler at such a crucial time." Even with his master dead, the skeletally thin lay brother looked behind him before he answered Thomas' question.

As others replied, Thomas wondered at the presumed innocence of the papal envoy. To bring so few servants was hardly a believable act of humility when the abbeys these men ran were known for fine plate, rich sources of income, and regal guest quarters. All the abbots were recognized for their skills in political maneuvering and occasional visits to court. He had to assume they knew what they were doing.

"Where were each of you during today's noon meal?" Thomas knew none of the servants had been with the abbots.

An elderly lay brother spoke first. One of his hands shook with a mild palsy. "Ask us individually for specific details, Brother, but we all had been ordered to clean and organize the room of our respective abbot." He glanced around at his fellows. They each nodded. "Once our masters realized they would be staying here for longer than one night, they wanted the rooms prepared to their specific needs."

Thomas asked for more information.

"Abbot Didier likes a softer bed. He brings pillows with him on his journeys." The black-bearded servant tilted his head as if waiting for a particular reaction from the monk.

Thomas looked to the next servant.

"Abbot Odo cannot sleep unless he has a cup of his preferred wine set by his bed before he sleeps." The man with the palsy hesitated. "And a plate of sliced beef, lest he awaken and feel weak."

"And mine has a prie-dieu designed to ease his painful knees." Abbot Ancell's bald servant immediately lowered his gaze.

Didier's man muttered something to the muscular village man who stood next to him and served Mordredus.

"I did not hear you," Thomas said.

"My comment was a private jest, and I swear it had nothing to do with this tragedy," the man replied. "I beg your forgiveness for the impropriety." But his lips betrayed his lack of repentance with a twitch of amusement.

The monk almost insisted on a better answer but chose to let the matter pass. As Thomas had learned, Didier liked to share his bed with female company when he could. If the servant thought he could find a woman at Tyndal Priory who would lie with his master, he would find out soon enough that none existed.

Thomas turned to the two men who had served Abbots Ilbert and Tristram. "Where were you?"

Ilbert's thin lay brother looked around again before replying. "Since my lord had died, Abbot Mordredus took me into his service, saying he was weary from the effort of doing things that he was not accustomed to performing for himself. His own servant was most grateful." He glanced at a muscular man who winked with presumed concurrence.

"Abbot Gifre said his familial rank and the fame of his abbey allowed him an extra servant and ordered me to attend him." Tristram's man had the same down-curled mouth as his dead master. "He was worried that his silken robes might be stolen, so I was helping to bring in a chest containing them from the cart and was in the company of his usual man."

"Each of you can therefore vouch for the whereabouts of the others at any time during the hour the abbots dined?"

Most agreed.

Thomas looked for a reply from those who had not.

"We all helped others where we could, Brother," said Gifre's lay brother. "But I cannot give my oath that I saw everyone at all times."

Mordredus' servant looked at the man with evident disapproval, scratched his chin through his beard, and then added, "We had formed a special brotherhood on this journey, no matter whether we had taken vows or not. If one of us was not done with his work when the abbots finished a meal, that servant was not allowed to eat until his allotted tasks were completed. And we were given very little time for our own dinner as it was. None of us wanted his fellow servant to miss any meal."

"Aye," Gifre's man muttered with ill-disguised annoyance.

What Christian charity shown by the abbots, the monk thought, but quickly set his disgust aside. "Did any of you notice the kitchen brothers delivering the meal to the abbots?"

They all shook their heads. "We did not have time," Didier's servant said.

"And the first night you arrived? Were you all together?"

"We ate our suppers at a table separate from our masters but at the same time. After the guest chambers were examined by each abbot, we were given our orders."

The grim-visaged former servant of Tristram said, "My master was ill in the night, Brother. I helped him to the garderobe when he called out for help. He was quite sick but initially refused my offer to seek aid from the hospital. He had been stricken in a similar way at the inn before we arrived here and believed he would recover just as quickly again." The man looked pale as if he feared he would be blamed for not saving his master's life. "This attack became far more severe, and he finally allowed me to call for hospital brothers."

"God had called for his soul," Thomas murmured. "Abbot Tristram was beyond mortal help."

The man looked away, but the expression in his eyes suggested relief as if he had been afraid his master might have condemned him from the afterlife.

"Tell me about that night you stayed in the inn." Thomas cast a glance at the secular men, who cared for Didier and Mordredus, but all levity had fled. Their faces were now cloaked in identically grave demeanors.

The others turned their gaze to the elder lay brother, as if begging him to become their spokesman.

He answered with a thin smile. "Our journey was difficult from the start. The roads were so bad we had to travel slowly for the safety of our horses. Our carts broke down. One wheel took too long to repair. By nightfall, we had no choice but to stay at this inn. It is dangerous to travel in darkness."

The others murmured concurrence.

"When we arrived, my master, Abbot Odo, spoke with the innkeeper and demanded that each of the abbots be given a single room and the inn be rid of current guests so we might not be troubled with wicked talk. The raucous noise of Satan's minions would destroy the peace in which we all longed to pray." He hesitated.

Thomas urged him to continue.

"The innkeeper swore he had no private rooms and would not throw good customers into the snow for our sakes. He arranged for our masters to sleep together in one room on straw pallets which, he claimed, were clean. The rest of us slept in the stables."

Didier's servant chuckled.

"For supper, the innkeeper agreed to set up separate tables for us, abbots at the largest and servants at a smaller one, so we might eat apart from the others at the inn. We relieved him of the worry about serving us. We all went to the kitchen and brought food directly to our individual masters. The serving women there were not allowed to approach us."

Mordredus' servant waved his hand. "Forgive me, Brother, but there was one inn servant, a man, who helped us."

The elder lay brother's eyes widened. "You are correct! I had forgotten him. While we poured the ale, he took the bowls we carried and filled them with stew, demanding that he be allowed to slice more bits of the ox from the spit to add to the portions. The kitchen was as hot as the outside air was cold. It was not pleasant to come that close to the blazing fire or wait there long. We were grateful to him for his efficient help."

Thomas imagined that Odo's servant with the palsied hand might have especially appreciated the assistance and wondered why Ralf's brother had particularly chosen him for this journey. "He apportioned out all the food to you and the abbots?" the monk chose to ask instead. "Other than the ale, you did not seek food that he did not help you with?" This is promising, he thought.

"He did it all," Mordredus' servant said, "although we did not eat until after the abbots had their meals. He did ask a few questions about the preferences of some of our masters." He grinned at Odo's man. "Yours got extra meat while mine got a little less, being more temperate."

The lay brother seemed oblivious to the hint of mockery and pursed his lips in thought before continuing. "After we had settled our masters into their narrow beds that night, some of us came back to the table and stayed quite late, considering the early hour we were expected to rise."

"While some of us went to the stables as soon as we could," Gifre's man said with a hint of disapproval.

Thomas turned to Odo's servant and asked what he had done.

"I found a quiet place to pray, Brother, and then sought rest. It has been many years since I had a young man's bladder. I cannot withstand much ale."

"The man who had helped with the meal joined us at the table later," Didier's servant said.

Thomas, trying not to betray his eagerness to learn more about this man, kept his tone casual. "Are you sure he was an inn servant?"

"We assumed that to be the case. Just as we arrived, he came out to greet us," Mordredus' man said. "Yet none of the inn's serving women or cook seemed familiar with him. At the time, I wondered if he was new there." The man hesitated. "The innkeeper did not acknowledge him, either, but he did not seem to pay attention to any who served the inn as long as they did their jobs. The man did return to the kitchen after the meals. I think he slept there. Why would he do so if he had not been hired by the innkeeper?"

"Why did he help you?" Thomas asked.

"I thought he was asked to do so by Abbot Mordredus," Gifre's servant said. "I saw him talking to the abbot."

Mordredus' man scratched his chin as he struggled to remember. "I know nothing of that. I was talking to the groom about my master's horse," he said, "but it is possible."

"Could you describe him?" Thomas was growing more hopeful that something important might be revealed.

The servants looked at each other. No one spoke. Finally, the elder lay brother said, "He was not memorable, Brother. I, for one, could not even tell you the color of his hair, which was mostly hidden by a hood." He looked apologetic. "I might have seen him clearer in the light of the kitchen fires, but, as God is my witness, we do not concern ourselves with the forms of mortal men. Our minds remain on God."

Even the two secular servants agreed, although they refused to meet Thomas' gaze. The monk suspected their thoughts that evening might have been far less on prayer and more on those daughters of Eve who served a variety of men's wishes at the inn.

Odo's servant grasped his ailing hand to tame the trembling. "He did leave the inn the next day with those who joined us for the journey to Norwich. Most of them were pilgrims waiting for a large number of other travelers to guarantee safety from outlaws."

"Did he say anything to any of you about his background or purpose in traveling? Did he seem familiar with any of the others in the group?"

Mordredus' servant looked around at his fellows, but none had anything to add. "To your first question, he said nothing, nor did he talk to us again once we left the inn. I paid little enough attention to him myself, but I did not notice that he spent any time with the others who traveled with us either."

There was a low rumble of agreement.

"He did not come to this priory with you," Thomas said. "Does anyone recall if he stayed with the rest of the party who went into the village or if he disappeared along the route?"

This time, the dead abbot's servant did not look over his shoulder. "For my sake, I could not tell you if he left our party before Abbot Ilbert fell mortally ill. I truly did not pay any attention to him."

Others confirmed that no one knew when he parted company with the abbatial party, although Gifre's servant said he thought the man must have gone with the pilgrims to stay at Tyndal's village inn. There was no side road or habitation between the inn they had stayed at the night before and the village after which this priory was named.

Thomas suspected the man had gone on to the village with the others because he was well aware that there was little else between the first inn and here. If so, the mysterious servant could still be at Signy's inn. But he might also have turned back the way he had come when he learned the road to Norwich was impassable. Others must have done so by now.

"If any of you remembers something not mentioned, no matter how minor, please send for me. The smallest detail may be important."

When Thomas dismissed them, the men rose and quickly vanished to attend what duties their masters demanded.

Yet one did linger behind. It was Abbot Didier's servant.

"I had no wish to discuss this in the presence of the others, Brother," he said, "but my master occasionally breaks his vow of chastity. That night at the inn, I left the company and table of my fellow servants and found him a whore to serve his needs. He spent the night with her in the stable hay while I slept nearby, lest he require me for some other service." He smiled, a little too innocently. "I reveal this only to confirm that my master could not have harmed anyone. His attention was fully engaged in another activity."

With a sympathetic look he hoped would encourage even greater confidence and details from the man, Thomas indicated the fine cloth of the servant's robe. "At least your master rewards you well for the difficulties you must face in his service."

"My master has given me a warmer robe, but he has more pressing needs which demand precedence in his generosity." Didier's servant winked. "So I find no sin in seeking an extra coin or two here and there, Brother. Should you or someone in your priory wish any service…?"

"When you were so engaged outside the inn, did you see anything else untoward?"

"Only Abbots Tristram and Mordredus rushing for the jakes."

"Nothing of the man who helped you serve supper to the abbots?"

The man shook his head. "But I can confirm that those who claim to have sought the stables early were there as they said. They would never admit to this, but a few took awhile to fall asleep. It seems they found the antics of my master and his whore quite interesting, even inspirational."

At least the man had been honest, despite his arrogance and the sinful activity of Abbot Didier. The innkeeper's story had also been essentially confirmed, although Thomas' interest was aroused by the reference to this helpful inn servant. The innkeeper claimed no one of his had served the abbots, yet had mentioned someone Abbot Odo brought to the kitchen to serve the supper. It was a contradiction and a puzzling detail he must pursue with the crowner.

But that question to Ralf must wait, the monk thought. First, he had to go back to Signy's inn because of the young woman who was bleeding and the man with the rash on his hand. If he were fortunate, this mysterious servant would still be there and could answer any questions Thomas posed. Signy had had time to reflect and would be able to identify others who arrived around the same time as the abbots and their servants.

Thanking Didier's servant and then leaving the guest quarters, Thomas prayed that God would let him find this servant. If not that, at least someone who could reveal some detail to help him unravel the secret of how and why the dead abbots had been poisoned.

Chapter Eighteen

Gracia had always loved the warmth and bustle of Tyndal's kitchen. When Sister Anne first brought her here five years ago, Sister Matilda had cried out in horror at the sight of her emaciated body. From that moment, she had taken on the task of fattening her. At first, Gracia resisted but eventually surrendered and developed a deep affection for the often sharp-tongued but always loving nun.

It was for this reason that Prioress Eleanor had suggested that Gracia talk to Sister Matilda about the serving and cooking arrangements between the original kitchen and the new one. The nun might truly fear condemnation if her prioress visited with yet more questions. If Gracia asked them, the conversation might be less fraught.

Nonetheless, Sister Matilda was wary and eyed the young woman standing before her with caution. "You did not come to question me about the cost of seasonings, my girl. What new fault has our prioress discovered in my work since our last discussion?"

"None, Sister, but she confesses she suffered willful pride in the matter of this additional kitchen and failed to properly plan the overseeing of the work there. Prior Andrew has tried to do so but freely admits he is no better at it than Brother Beorn. With deep humility, Prioress Eleanor begs your advice on how to immediately improve the methods used to cook and serve, so our future guests must seek elsewhere should they wish to find cause for complaints."

Sister Matilda's look softened and she gestured her visitor to a seat on a bench against a wall. "I cannot stand as long as I once did, child. My joints protest too much."

"I am grateful," Gracia said to keep the nun from feeling ashamed of any perceived weakness. "I have been walking all day."

Looking around, she noted that the preparations had begun for the baking of tarts made of apples taken out of the winter store from the priory tree harvest. They were being sweetened with honey from Tyndal hives, and the aromatic scent made her hungry.

Her eyes bright, Sister Matilda went over to the nun forming the crust dough. She took an unused piece of it, rolled it in honey and spices, folded it, and hurried back with the treat to Gracia.

"You shall make me fat," the young woman said, taking the gift with a laugh. The comment had long been a standard jest between them.

"And it will take far more years for that to happen." Sister Matilda sat and leaned her chin on her hand. "What does Prioress Eleanor truly need to know? In this priory, she has never used spies to seek out faults. We honor her too much to lie, and she is always fair in her punishments. I shall answer her required questions frankly, even if the truth reflects badly on me."

"Her confession of pride and longing for your advice are sincere," Gracia said. "But she also needs your thoughts on what might have occurred earlier."

Sister Matilda relaxed.

"You have heard that one abbot died at dinner today. Another sickened but may live. Prioress Eleanor and Sister Anne are convinced the two men were poisoned."

Stiffening, Sister Matilda grew wary once more.

"No one doubts you are innocent of any wrongdoing. What Prioress Eleanor must know is where poison could have been added to the food. Only you understand all the faults this new kitchen must have. She relies on your experience and knowledge to enlighten her." She reached out and gave the nun's hand an affectionate squeeze. "Our prioress needs your help so much!"

Taking in a deep breath and closing her eyes, Sister Matilda thought for a moment. "I oversaw the preparation of the roasted vegetables and the mushroom tarts here in this kitchen. As I always do, I sample the food at various stages to make sure the taste is pleasing and the texture of each ingredient is perfect. The lay sisters who work here are experienced, known to us all, and are utterly reliable. At no time could any poison have been administered in this place." She jabbed her finger at the floor in emphasis, looked around, and scowled. "I shall personally check the spices…"

"That shouldn't be necessary," Gracia said. "The poison has been identified as the leaves of monkshood."

For a woman whose joints gave her pain, Sister Matilda jumped to her feet with impressive alacrity. "Sit while I check our supplies of seasonings," she said. "Now that I know what the poison was, I can quickly see if anything has been contaminated."

It did not take long before the nun returned with a look of relief and a cup in her hand. "All is well. No monkshood came from my kitchen." She held out a mazer of ale. "You look cold, child."

Gracia thanked her and sipped. "Were the foods cooked here and transported to the guest quarters?"

"Since the only oven is here, we baked the tarts as we always do but did not cook the vegetables except for boiling. Those were cut, seasoned, and tasted by me in my kitchen." She looked heavenward. "I prayed before sending them to be pan-roasted in the new kitchen, but we followed our usual custom in the delivery of the food. Lay sisters took the tarts and seasoned vegetables to the hole in the wall between the monks' and nuns' quarters and passed everything to lay brothers. Those men have been with us for many years, as have the lay sisters. This has been their duty since our prioress arrived twelve years ago. Nothing was left unattended."

"So only the vegetables were finally cooked in the new kitchen by the lay brothers assigned there?"

"That was the plan. They did heat the tarts with instructions sent by me. But it was decided that this first test of their skills

must be an easy one. Pan-roasted vegetables are not difficult…"
The nun tightly closed her eyes and sighed. "I begged God to
bless their attempts so they would not burn them."

Gracia stifled a laugh at the nun's use of the word *attempts*.
"Did Prior Andrew choose the lay brothers?"

"Brother Beorn eventually did. As our oldest lay brother, he
knows their skills best. But Prior Andrew decided they should
follow the Rule and let all the older lay brothers take their rotation there. Brother Beorn was opposed."

"And spoke with great passion against the idea?" Gracia grinned.

"We could hear them arguing through stone walls," the nun
replied, and a flash of humor finally sparkled in her eyes.

"No rotation had taken place before the arrival of the abbots?"
An idea was beginning to form in Gracia's mind.

Sister Matilda shook her head. "There was no reason to do
so. This kitchen had just been completed, and we did not have
guests before the abbots arrived. The kitchen brothers had not
yet performed any of the duties."

Gracia fell silent, thought for a moment, and decided to go
on to another issue. "When the mushroom tarts left here, were
they adorned with a sprinkling of herbs on the top or were any
decorative herbs sent with those tarts to be added before serving?"

"No! We do not decorate food in the priory like they do in
the king's court. As God's servant, committed to a simple life, I
believe that food should nourish both body and spirit, but adorn-
ment is affectation and pleases only the Devil's eye!" She snorted
in disgust. "Dyeing food with alkanet root to make something
look like dragon's blood?" Slapping her hand on her thigh, she
muttered, "And does it not take enough time to pluck a bird?
Why would I wish to put the feathers back on?"

"Let me make sure I am clear on what did happen so I can
explain to our prioress."

Sister Matilda nodded.

"According to common practice, and using the monastics who
have been doing these tasks for years, the food for the abbots'
midday dinner was prepared under your eye in all respects, except

for roasting the vegetables, and delivered to the lay brothers at the dividing wall. They carried it to the new kitchen where the lay brothers, chosen by Brother Beorn, finished the vegetables and reheated the tarts. Nothing was sprinkled on top of the tarts after cooking as seasoning or ornamentation."

"There are no supplies of seasonings in the new kitchen," the nun said. "It was the one battle I won. Until we can trust that the men can cook, all dishes would be started here where I can taste them."

Gracia was beginning to understand how complicated the running of two kitchens might be and why her prioress missed the help of a sub-prioress. It would be a long process to find a man who had Sister Matilda's fine sense of taste and quality. "A wise decision," she said.

"I cannot swear to the details of what happened in the new kitchen, but Brother Beorn would never choose lay brothers of questionable character for the task." She winced. "At least I have no quarrel with that," she murmured with her head bowed.

"Did these same lay brothers also serve the abbots?"

"That was the original intention. You should ask either Prior Andrew or Brother Beorn if it was followed. Since this was a new experience, it is possible that a change was made and other lay brothers served. But I repeat my conviction that Brother Beorn would not choose men who were new in the priory or of unproven character for such an important task. Consider the rank of the guests served!"

Gracia drained her cup of ale and thanked Sister Matilda for the help she had given to Prioress Eleanor, then hugged the woman she loved as if she were blood kin. "Prioress Eleanor gives you her word that your knowledge shall rule in reorganizing the way this new kitchen is run after the abbots have left."

Sister Matilda pressed some dried fruit into Gracia's hand and shooed the young woman on her way.

Hurrying back to Prioress Eleanor, Gracia grew more excited about her new idea on how to discover any problems in the second kitchen and perhaps even reveal the poisoner.

Since the prior wanted the kitchen staff rotated according to the Rule, Brother Thomas might be willing to volunteer himself as an act of humble service. For a reliable assistant to him, she would suggest the young lay brother, Brother Anthony. Whatever her errant feelings for him, he had impressed her as clever and observant. He asked good questions of Sister Anne or Sister Oliva, and she had never overheard him engage in gossip. That suggested he was discreet. Brother Beorn would know him best, however.

As Gracia climbed the stairs to the prioress' chambers, she began to add more details to her idea and was sure Prioress Eleanor would be delighted, both with her plan and with her discovery of this clever young lay brother.

Chapter Nineteen

The next morning, no one could be sure where the Earth stopped and the sky began. The spiritual and physical realms had united in shades of white. Falling snow looked like tiny petals made of ice. Sniffing the air, fishermen whispered to each other that a bad storm was nigh.

Inside the guest quarters, Brother Thomas and Crowner Ralf stood facing those three abbots still untouched by the anonymous liegeman of Death. A fire crackled joyfully in the dining hall, but there was no merriment in the assembled group.

The expressions on the faces of the abbots ranged from angry to fearful. Only Abbot Ancell exhibited the calm expected of a man whose dedication to God must mean he believed the life after death would be far superior to anything the mortal world had to offer.

Brother Thomas turned to him first. "When you were at the inn, there was another man besides your usual servants who spent time with you. What can you tell us of him?"

Ancell expressed surprise. "I recall no one like that. We specifically asked that only our men wait on us. The inn was teeming with whores. The very thought that our food would be touched by a woman was an affront to our vows. Just imagine how our meal might have been polluted! It makes me shudder even now."

Ralf opened his mouth to speak but restrained himself with great effort. Whores were plentiful at the inn, and reasonably avoided, but other women had cooked their food. The person in charge of their meals in Tyndal Priory was a nun. Clearly, these abbots were willing to compromise when it came to the dangers of women. No matter how austere some tried to be, none would go so far as to starve. Growling to himself, he felt contempt for all these abbots, not just his brother.

Thomas was more amused by Ancell's bad logic. As he imagined Sister Matilda's likely reaction to such denunciation of herself and the lay sisters in her kitchen, the monk struggled to hide his mirth as he continued with his question. "Nonetheless, a man who was not in your party did join those whom you brought with you."

Ancell shook his head and looked at Didier who did not respond.

"I recall the man." Abbot Mordredus said. "He was an inn employee who approached me when we arrived. He begged me to let him join us on the way to Norwich and offered to serve any of our needs until we left the next day. When he said he was troubled by the whores at the inn, and feared for his virtue if he remained any longer, I naturally agreed to his request. A godly man!"

Didier scowled. "I do not remember him at all."

Looking smug, Mordredus continued. "He said he would apportion the food from the pot to each of our servants. Since most of those are lay brothers, he was willing to protect them from the evil temptations of the daughters of Eve at the inn kitchen. He later ate his meal with the servants and did accompany our party in the morning, a group which grew in numbers and offered safety on the road near forests."

Ancell did not look pleased. "I wonder why he asked you and not another for permission to travel with us."

Mordredus beamed. "He confessed that he had prayed for guidance and believed he was led to me as the most virtuous of the seven abbots."

Didier laughed.

"You are not the one best able to question his opinion." Mordredus almost spat at his fellow abbot but quickly regained his composure before continuing to answer Thomas' question. "I also referred him to Abbot Odo for further instructions. Our dear brother is quite skilled in matters involving food and the service thereof."

Ancell walked away from the gathering and stood by the fire.

Thomas was puzzled by that reaction, wondering if he had some reason to avoid any more questioning. But the monk quickly grew charitable. As an old man, Ancell probably felt cold and needed a fire's warmth. It was Mordredus who seemed to have the most knowledge of the unidentified servant.

The monk looked back at the more helpful abbot and asked, "Did the man accompany you to Tyndal Priory when Abbot Ilbert fell ill?"

Mordredus thought for a moment. "No, he did not, but I didn't notice his absence until now when you asked. With the tragedies besetting us, I forgot about him. He may have helped us at the inn, but he walked with the other travelers and spent no more time with any of us, even to seek righteous guidance to virtue's path."

"You know well all the men who came here with you from your abbeys?" Ralf's tone was sharp with impatience. Had he been in charge of the interrogation, he would not have tolerated such willful forgetfulness about details, and it would not have taken this long to get clear answers. He understood why Brother Thomas had to treat men of such high religious rank with caution, but the crowner also wanted to get home to his family before dark or any storm arrived.

Ancell turned around but placed his hands behind him to keep them closer to the fire's heat. "Those men serve us and therefore God, Crowner. I resent your accusatory and insolent tone. You have no jurisdiction on God's land. Remember that and stay humble." He looked at Thomas. "I do not understand why this king's man was allowed to come here. Insulting us seems to be his only purpose."

"I asked him here because he must listen to all the statements given. If need be, Crowner Ralf can go where we cannot," Thomas replied. "His brother is also the stricken Abbot Odo.

Surely you understand how deeply troubled he is by that, as well as the other deaths."

Ralf snorted but quickly tried to hide his contempt with a cough. "I meant no disrespect," he said in a civil tone that was almost convincing. "As you noted, I am a worldly creature, a blunt man with few manners."

"The Abbot of Caldwell's brother? Although I had not noted it before, I now see the similarity to our brother in Christ." Mordredus' muttered remark was contemptuous but not quite low enough to remain unheard.

Thomas grasped Ralf's arm as a plea for caution before his friend could react.

Ancell returned to the circle of abbots. "Since this man at the inn has been further described, I do recall someone talking to Abbot Mordredus when we first arrived at that insidious place. I can confirm that a similar man joined our little party of pilgrims, including other faithful when we left the next morning." He looked with regret at Thomas. "But ask me nothing more about him. He was of no interest to me."

Thomas was intrigued by Ancell's description of themselves as pilgrims. Although he did not doubt that they would worship at the shrine of Saint William before starting on the journey back to their abbeys, he knew their true intent was a far worldlier one, seething with greed and ambition. Or did Ancell have a different purpose from the other abbots going to Norwich? Perhaps, for him, it was a pious journey.

"Can any of you describe him?" Ralf looked around as if hoping there was an ewer of wine to help him through this unpleasant interview with a group of religious men he deemed hypocrites.

Mordredus hesitated before saying, "An ordinary man. One of low status, from his speech and rough manners." His eyes narrowed, and he looked at Ralf. "A beard. Eyes narrowly spaced?" He waved his hand dismissively. "I did not notice much about him for it was nearly dark when we spoke together."

"Yes, he had a bushy beard. I noticed because our lay brothers are clean-shaven, and the two who are not serve Abbots Didier and Mordredus." Ancell's brief smile suggested the word *serve* had more than one meaning.

That smile sparked Thomas' interest, and he studied Ancell further. Not a man adverse to a little subtlety, he thought.

This abbot was much older than the others, his face deeply lined and his remaining sparse hair an icy white. His hands, folded prayerfully, included long fingers remarkably unswollen by the joint disease. For a man of his apparent age, his movement was easy, suggesting he might be stronger than one would expect of an aged man. And, as Thomas recalled, this abbot has shown more calm than the others in the face of appalling death. Was he a man of greater virtue than his fellows or was he simply less engaged in the world as he grew closer to death himself?

The abbots were engaged in a petty quarrel over whether the man had a well-trimmed beard or an untamed one, as well as when he was last seen.

Ralf gnawed his lower lip with impatience.

Of all the abbots on this journey, Thomas wondered why Ancell had come. His age suggested he had little reason to think a bishopric might be bestowed on him. Perhaps this was the one man who did come simply to honor Rome's special envoy, offer his services in preaching the crusade, and serve some secret penance by traveling in the winter season.

Yet all had been invited, had they not? Perhaps the envoy was solely interested in how to increase enthusiasm for the crusade and to accumulate gold to pay the cost of holy war. Maybe it was only Ancell who understood there was no hidden intent, and none of them would be examined as potential future bishops.

Didier began to mutter something to Mordredus. His expression suggested the conversation between them was not a friendly one.

Thomas abandoned his musing and turned a questioning eye on the two abbots.

Mordredus blinked first. "My brother in Christ has misinterpreted my comment that the man may have left our party when he discovered that we were not all as virtuous as he had assumed. I meant only that we, as mortal men, are all sinners. Not one of us is a saint." Mordredus glared at his fellow abbot.

"You now remember that he left?" Thomas looked hopeful. "When did he do so?"

"He must have," the abbot said. "I have not seen him here."

"I finally recalled that he did leave our party," Didier said. "When Abbot Ilbert began to vomit and Abbot Odo urged us to take the road to your priory hospital, the man went with the remaining pilgrims to the village. I assume there is an inn there?"

Ralf nodded.

"There were others besides that one man who traveled with you that day?" Thomas tried to keep the deep longing for useful information out of his voice. "What do you recall of them?"

"An elderly couple," Mordredus said, pressing a finger to his mouth as if fearing such worldly observations were somehow sinful and ought not to be uttered.

"And a young one," Didier said, but his eyes were shining. "The woman was pale but quite lovely." He squeezed his eyes shut. "Her pallor reminded me of a painting in my abbey church of St. Wilgyth watching her stepmother kill her two sisters."

"Surely others, but I did not concern myself with them other than bestowing a few blessings," Ancell said. "Our journey was so arduous that we missed many of the Offices because the threatening weather did not permit greater delay. I attempted to pray as much as possible as we rode to atone for those sins of omission."

Ralf leaned toward Thomas and whispered, "The man may still be at the inn, Brother, unless he chose to travel back to the place from which he had come. He couldn't go on to Norwich for the same reason these abbots had to stay here."

"I have spoken with Signy about those who arrived at her inn when the abbots came to us. I plan to go back there as soon as I can," the monk murmured back.

Ancell gasped. "Might this man, in whom you show so much interest, be the one who poisoned our beloved brothers, Gifre and Odo? And might he still be nearby?"

"You have nothing to fear, my lords," Thomas said. "Prioress Eleanor has a plan to keep you all safe."

The abbots murmured politely, but their expressions loudly proclaimed that they had absolutely no confidence in anything she would put in place.

Chapter Twenty

Nor did Brother Beorn have much faith in his prioress' plan either, and that was unusual.

He had served Prioress Eleanor with profound loyalty and sincere respect since her arrival at Tyndal many years ago. At first, he had assumed she would be nothing more than a witless girl from a family honored by the king, but he was soon convinced that she truly did represent the Virgin Mary on Earth, which was the expected responsibility of prioresses and the abbess in the Order of Fontevraud. As he glanced at the raw-boned youth beside him, whose robe flapped about his body like laundry drying in the wind, Brother Beorn, for the first time, doubted his prioress' wisdom in this one venture.

His heart burned with agony over that.

The lad, who might have seen fifteen or sixteen summers, looked up at this ill-tempered man and grinned. Unlike many youths of his age, his skin was still as pink and soft as a girl's, although there was a slightly coarser sprouting of hair on his cheeks. His teeth flashed white and straight.

Without question, Brother Beorn decided, Brother Anthony has immense charm, but that particular appeal was often more the Devil's gift than God's.

"I am humbled by your confidence that I can perform this work in the kitchen," the lad said, his eagerness already bubbling like a pot of stew.

Or else you assume the labor will be easier than clearing paths of snow to the hospital and church so pious villagers might walk them with greater ease, Brother Beorn muttered to himself. Aloud, he grunted. "Did I give you permission to speak?"

The youth's cheeks flushed a rosier shade. "Forgive me! In my eagerness to start my new task, I forgot your lessons in humility and have sinned."

"I fear that is not your only wickedness." The elder man stared meaningfully at the lad.

Brother Anthony paled as if his master had discovered something he had thought hidden.

The elder lay brother might be rough in manner but he possessed a kinder heart. He stopped and put a thin hand on the youth's shoulder. Had the boy feared he meant those sins born of dreams from which Beorn no longer suffered but which he did recall well enough? "Nay, lad, I do not mean a transgression all men suffer when a succubus attacks us in our sleep. That you must confess to a priest. I mean a more willful offense."

With a relieved sigh, the youth looked up at his lanky mentor with a confused expression. "I do not know what you mean," he said. "Teach me, for I am so ignorant of all the ways Satan drives us from God."

"Think on it a while longer," Brother Beorn said, and they walked in silence for a short distance. The older man prayed the younger one would realize by himself where his wickedness lay. Such awareness would be a good start on the path to greater virtue.

But the lad remained perplexed, and his face grew paler with increasing fear over what he did not understand.

Beorn chose mercy. "Where did you meet Gracia, Prioress Eleanor's maid?"

"At the apothecary hut!"

The young man's instant and enthusiastic reply sent a troubling message that upset Beorn. He stiffened, and his eyebrows clashed with a forbidding grimness. "Have I not warned you to forsake the company of women unless you are in the company of a much older brother? Have I not told you that you will struggle with the vow of chastity and should flee the presence of all women? Why have you disobeyed me? Meeting with any woman, and especially the Prioress' maid, is an odious thing! You have not only your vows to protect but her chastity."

"Brother, forgive me for I misspoke. I did not go to the hut to meet Mistress Gracia. I met her when I went to see Sister Oliva with another lay brother who suffered an earache." He looked at Beorn with horror. "Knowing we would be in the presence of a nun, we went together, as you advised. Our purpose lacked all sin."

"You met Mistress Gracia there," Beorn repeated slowly. "Was she alone?"

"She was in the company of Anchoress Juliana's maid, as she often is."

"*Often is*? How do you know that?"

The gruff tone was like gravel rubbed on a wound, and the youth winced. "We, I mean all of us, frequently see them together when we set off to work in the morning. It is common knowledge that they spend time together."

"You notice them? Why do you seek to look upon them and not direct your gaze from the temptation?"

Brother Anthony's cheeks flushed a brilliant red. "We cannot turn away unless we see them, can we?"

Beorn pondered the tone and found it oddly innocent of impudence.

"They are not always in the same place," the lad continued and looked hopeful that this reply was adequate.

"But you must have spoken to Mistress Gracia."

"I heard her accent and realized that we had come from the same place. She is from Walsingham, as am I. Is it wrong to feel a kinship, almost as if we were brother and sister? If so, teach me my error, Brother, and I shall gladly suffer penance."

Beorn stopped to glower at the youth. Had he heard a hint of disrespect in his voice? Was there defiance in his heart? "Satan, begone!" he shouted and waved his hand in the lad's face.

Falling to his knees, the youth raised his arms beseechingly.

"Forgive me! I confess I liked Mistress Gracia but only in a chaste way. I felt no lust for her."

After a moment, Brother Beorn ordered him to rise. Although he feared there was less innocence in this apparently chance meeting than the lad himself realized, or perhaps Mistress Gracia did herself, he chose to withhold a scolding until he looked into the problem further. Most certainly, he must also report this all to the prioress. "We will talk of the matter later," he said, "and I do promise that you shall undergo a hard penance."

With that, he pulled Brother Anthony to his feet and marched him to the kitchen.

◇◇◇

Brother Thomas was already there, talking to the other two lay brothers. When he saw Brother Anthony, he greeted him with courtesy and began to discuss what he expected him to do.

Before the elder lay brother went back to his other duties, Beorn stayed for a few moments and listened to the way the youth responded to his new tasks.

The lad was bright and eager to learn, as well as serve as directed. That almost brought a smile to the man's lips. It would not take much to push a motivated youth back onto a righteous path, the lay brother decided. After all, Brother Anthony had chosen to take vows and did not do so because his father, a Walsingham butcher, wished it.

Leaving the kitchen, Brother Beorn retraced the path he had come, his large feet shattering the crust of icy snow and his mind now firmly on God.

Suddenly, a tonsured man emerged from around a corner and deliberately blocked Beorn's way. Hands on hips, the man scowled. "I am Abbot Mordredus."

The imperious tone caused Beorn to bristle, but he remembered in time that this man was an abbot. He bowed his head with obligatory respect.

"I seek the kitchen that serves the guest quarters," Mordredus said. "Perhaps you have not heard the news. Some of my fellow abbots have fallen ill on the food cooked there. I must speak with those who prepare our meals to make sure nothing like this happens again."

Beorn was outraged at the insult to the priory, and an unChristian desire to strike back at this man's rudeness surged through him. He raised his head, realized the abbot was shorter than he, and found a sinful pleasure in looking down at Mordredus.

"My lord, I shall gladly take you to the kitchen, but you may rest assured that your concerns have been addressed. Prioress Eleanor has sent Brother Thomas to make certain you are all safe and will suffer no further distress. Indeed, he is speaking to those in charge of the meals while we stand here."

Abbot Mordredus tilted his head and stared at the lay brother in amazement. "A mere monk? Not Prior Andrew? What was she thinking to make such a choice?"

Beorn knew he must confess, as soon as possible, these sins of impertinence that he was in the act of committing, but his immediate duty was to defend his prioress and Tyndal Priory. He picked his words carefully in reply to this man who dared to question Prioress Eleanor's decision.

"Brother Thomas often acts for Prior Andrew in matters that require special attention, my lord. The good monk is well regarded by us all at Tyndal for his skills and especially his virtue."

Mordredus blinked, silently spun on his heel, and crunched his way back toward the guest quarters.

With a victorious joy he knew was wicked, Beorn watched him leave and then changed his own route to go to the church.

There was one transgression that he must confess immediately, a sin that was more grievous than all his others. He would beg a severe penance for daring to question any decision his beloved prioress ever made.

Chapter Twenty-one

Thomas was well-pleased with the lay brother recommended by Gracia to work with him in the new kitchen. Brother Anthony seemed a clever lad with a boy's enthusiasm for adventure and a man's desire to take responsibility for doing the task properly.

Although Prior Andrew had concluded that only two men were needed to perform kitchen duties during the abbots' stay, Thomas persuaded him to keep the two lay brothers originally assigned there while adding Brother Anthony and himself.

The first two men were both grieved and frightened that the food they served the guests had killed one abbot and perilously sickened another, but the monk assured them that they were guilty of nothing. After questioning them, he learned that no one had stopped them on their way to deliver the noon meal, nor had any unknown person come into the kitchen. Thomas swore to them that he would take responsibility for overseeing all future meals until the abbots left or the poisoner was caught.

The addition of Brother Anthony, he explained, would allow them to prepare the meals without worrying that something might happen when they were too busy to notice. The youth could even be taught some basic cooking skills to ease the burdens of the two men. Brother Anthony was not only eager but obviously had too many wits to spend his earthly days cleaning moss from chapel windows or feeding the large priory chicken flock.

Deep in thought after he left the kitchen, Thomas did not hear the bell tolling the next Office so was surprised to find the guest quarters empty, silent, and the chamber doors shut when he arrived to tell the abbots they could be confident that no more poisonings would occur.

Standing in the dining area around which the guest rooms were built, he felt the stillness fall on him with a heavy weight. The ensuing melancholy allowed the pain of his recent and very private sorrow to attack with an agonizing blow to the deepest part of his heart.

Durant of Norwich, wine merchant and spy for the king, had sent him a message with his trustworthy servant who delivered wine to Tyndal Priory. Some years ago in Walsingham, when they worked together to catch an assassin, Durant and Thomas had formed a deep bond and swore a vow of brotherhood. But the love between them had become an attachment more passionate than the one between brothers, and their meetings since had grown strained.

The last time they had met, the two had clung together with a fervor that made both dizzy with lust, but each stepped back before a greater violation of vows and law had been committed. Without a word, Durant fled. With a numbing silence, Thomas watched him leave. His longing to lie with the wine merchant until their bodies were both sated was unbearable, but he had not called to Durant, begging him to come back. In that moment, he found he had lost all power of speech.

A month ago, this man Thomas allowed himself to love had written that they must no longer meet. Although he sinned often enough, Durant had said, he could not commit the ultimate blasphemy of seducing a man vowed to God into breaking his sacred oaths.

Thomas groaned in memory, clenching his fist in his ongoing protest to God.

"Are you in pain, Brother?"

The monk opened his eyes and saw Abbot Didier standing before him. The same question from Sister Anne would have meant concern for his health. The abbot's expression revealed a man who feared most for his own safety in the face of any errant plague.

Forcing a smile, Thomas assured the abbot that all was well and he had only suffered an inconsequential pain in his gut.

Didier still looked uneasy. "An attack of the wind? Abbot Ilbert suffered that."

Thomas denied the cause. "A minor twinge," he said dismissively. "I ran up the stairs too fast."

The abbot sighed with relief and motioned to the now open door of his chamber. "We are well met then. I wish to speak privately with you. This is a matter so troubling that I was unable to accompany the others to prayer because I could not concentrate on God. That was impious of me. I must end this wickedness by revealing my concerns to a man of God."

Thomas followed him into the chamber and looked around. There was a ewer sitting on a chest. He glanced at the abbot and pointed to the object.

"Fear not, Brother." My servant has brought this wine to me, and it is from my own store. I have already drunk of it and, as you see, I remain upright."

Thomas chose not to remind Didier that Abbot Tristram had felt ill, recovered, and later died. Instead he said, "It might still be wise if you ate and drank nothing but what we serve you here."

"And die like Abbot Gifre?"

"That problem will not occur again."

"Your prioress may be without equal among her peers, Brother, but in matters of mortal evil, she still suffers the deficiencies of all women."

Such was the ignorance of those who did not know his prioress, Thomas thought, but he was accustomed to this, as was Prioress Eleanor. "You have my oath that Death will be barred from your company henceforth, my lord. I am responsible for all arrangements to keep you safe at meals." He bowed his head.

"Ah, so I may truly hope that the plan will be good."

"But I must beg forgiveness for the delay in letting you speak of this matter which so unsettles you."

Didier looked over his shoulder before choosing to shut his chamber door. "As deeply as this grieves me," he said, walking back to the monk, "I must tell you that I believe one of us is guilty of these heinous acts of murder."

Thomas tried not to show his surprise. "Please explain, my lord."

Didier poured himself a mazer of the wine.

Thomas winced but said nothing. When the abbot failed to offer him any, he was grateful.

"You know that we were all traveling to Norwich to meet the special papal envoy. The stated intent was to discuss how best to preach the crusade as well as to confess the problems in our respective abbeys and the plans to correct them. The underlying purpose was the longing in each of us to impress Rome with our competence and worthiness to receive a bishopric when next an opening occurred."

At least the abbot is being forthright, Thomas thought, and encouraged Didier to say more.

"I fear that one of us may have succumbed to worldly ambition and chosen to remove some of the competition."

"I understand your point. Please elaborate on your specific concerns."

"I have learned that Abbot Mordredus wrote to Rome in the summer of last year and condemned each of us for some terrible sin. He himself is guilty of ambition beyond a righteous desire to serve God in a more responsible role. His envy is a gangrene rotting his soul. Satan himself could not be more wicked. Of course, he failed to mention any of that!"

"If you will, what were the sins of which each abbot was accused? I ask only to clarify the magnitude of his deed."

Didier sipped at his wine. The deepening flush on his cheeks suggested he had been drinking for some time.

Unless, Thomas thought unkindly, it indicated his great eagerness to expose his fellow abbots.

"First, there is Abbot Ilbert," Didier said. "He was a man infamous for cruelty and wrath. He almost beat my nephew to death in a fit of temper over a minor infraction."

Thomas voiced the expected astonishment.

"Abbot Tristram was notorious for taking credit for every success in his position, although we all knew others did the work. There was no man more slothful."

Thomas shook his head with proper dismay.

"Abbot Gifre was infamous for channeling funds into his own pocket rather than to the poor. His collection of plate is wondrous, while even his clerics are ill-clad and poorly fed. He exemplified greed."

Didier poured more wine, drank with evident pleasure, and looked at the monk for encouragement.

Thomas willingly gave it.

"Abbot Odo, of course, is known for his gluttony. Abbot Ancell was born into a family of high rank and never lets anyone forget it. Of those of us still alive, neither Odo nor Ancell deserves a bishopric, a position where a man should exercise denial and humility. Abbot Mordredus is, of course, the Devil's twin and should not even be in the position he has. Surely you agree?"

"Humbleness is a great virtue, my lord, and the suppression of the body's desires is part of our vows." Although he had tried to be supportive while remaining vague, Thomas was almost overcome by a surge of embarrassment. Just how hypocritical was he, considering his most recent encounter with Durant? He forced his mind back to the question of murder. "But you have not said of what sin you were accused."

Didier snorted. "A lie, of course. He especially vilified me because I was the only one he could not slander honestly." The abbot raised his chin in defiance. "He accused me of lust!"

"Indeed!"

"There is a woman who lives near my abbey. A whore. She has several children, all by different men, or so I have been told. They are not mine, as Mordredus claims. On several occasions, I have visited her with a virtuous longing to direct her into a godly path and thus save her soul. Each time, my servant has accompanied me. There is no reason, other than a craving to belittle, for accusing me of breaking my vows."

And, Thomas thought, the servant probably waits outside the woman's hut while the abbot preaches the doctrine of love to her in his own special way.

He flashed an expression that suggested sympathy. "Since three of the abbots accused of vices have died, and one has fallen seriously ill, we can eliminate them from suspicion of murder," the monk said. "Which man of the remaining abbots do you think most likely to be guilty?"

Didier looked horrified. "Surely you do not expect me to point a finger at one!"

"I beg for your well-considered opinion, my lord. If you are wrong, no one will know. If you are correct, I shall praise you for leading us to the solution."

"Of course, I am innocent. As for Odo, I could disregard him. He does not have a polished wit. If he did, he might have made himself sick, but not fatally, to direct suspicion to others."

Thomas had not thought of that. Unlike Didier, he did not disparage Odo's intelligence, nor did Ralf, despite his scorn for his brother. Nevertheless, the idea of Odo killing all these men troubled the monk. He hated contemplating the possibility that his friend's brother might be a murderer, but he knew that he could not ignore it just because of his friendship and loyalty to Ralf. It would still be a cruel blow to the crowner's family honor if true.

Didier's expression was somber with reflection. "Thinking more on this, I truly cannot ignore the Abbot of Caldwell. He may not have a refined and well-educated mind, but he is quite clever in a rough sort of way. Yet I have my doubts about his guilt. I never thought he was a man willing to endure suffering of any kind for any reason." He glanced into his ewer and found it empty. Raising his cup, he savored the last drops of wine.

Thomas waited for him to finish drinking.

After a sigh of pleasure, Didier continued. "Nor do I see good cause to accuse Ancell. He is far too arrogant to think another would be chosen over him, even if we had all remained alive. He is also aged. These murders require a younger man's energy and the passion of hate."

For a moment, silence fell as Didier formed his closing argument in favor of his chosen poisoner.

Thomas heard voices outside and realized the other abbots and the servants were coming back from prayer.

"I think the killer may well be Mordredus," Didier said in a hushed voice. "He was the one to write to Rome. He is the one who yearns for the bishopric the most. Indeed, his greatest sin is envy. He is jealous of us all."

"I shall take these ideas to heart, my lord, and will use them to investigate further. My gratitude for your information and flawless logic is boundless."

With that Thomas bowed and left, just as the others were filling the dining hall. They fell silent when they saw him. His gaze meekly lowered, he passed by without speaking. Walking down the stairs to the outside, his mind again fled from the issue of murder and stubbornly returned to his angry quarrel with God.

Enlighten me, he muttered in silence to the Deity he served. Why may the sin of lust be forgiven so easily in one man but not in another? Didier keeps a mistress who is only a convenient vessel in which to spill his seed. Other women equally serve his desires. For these transgressions, the abbot is condemned but also excused, as long as he confesses and does penance for sins he commits repeatedly. But what of men like Durant and me? What if we had lain together that one night and then sincerely asked for penance and never repeated the act?

Thomas knew that many in England wanted to burn those who committed sodomy with another man. According to some tales, the half-brother of England's queen, King Alfonso of Castile, had ordered his brother strangled and the man's alleged lover burned at the stake. There was no trial and no offer of penance. How was this just?

How could God, who spoke of compassion and forgiveness, countenance such a harsh penalty? Why were he and Durant condemned as more wicked than Didier, a man who never denied himself a woman's body, eagerly broke his vows, and offered only hollow repentance?

Thomas slammed his fist on the rough stone wall and did not even feel the pain.

Chapter Twenty-two

Odo picked at his blanket. "Although you may wish it otherwise, Ralf, I am no killer."

Ralf shot him an unconvinced look.

"If I were, I would have murdered you many years ago. My forbearance then argues for my innocence now."

"Not that you would hang anyway," the crowner replied.

"Spare me a recitation of your impious opinion that putting a man to death is superior to godly penance that cleanses the soul from the taint of sin." The abbot grunted. "Or that penance is easier to bear than execution. Death, no matter how agonizing, is of brief duration. I find hanging preferable to being locked into a penitential cell for the remainder of my life without the small comforts and sustaining meals I enjoy in my chambers at Caldwell Abbey."

Ralf chuckled. "You have finally convinced me, Odo. The meals, not the penitential cell. If you were locked away with no sunlight but given fine haunches of venison along with a good red wine, you would be content enough."

The abbot looked around with impatience. "Where is that servant? I need something besides tasteless water to drink."

"You have been forbidden anything else by Sister Anne until your humors recover from your near-death."

"What does she know? She's a woman."

"Have you forgotten the time, before our father died, when she saved your hand after it grew foul from the knife-cut?"

Odo looked at the jagged scar still visible on his palm. "That is the same woman? She became a nun? I thought she was your whore."

Ralf leapt to his feet and wrapped his hand around his brother's throat. "Apologize, you cur, or you'll not live to eat again!"

"Sit! I remember now that she married the apothecary in the village, and you went off to sell yourself to the highest bidder who needed a sword. I was confusing her with another." His words sounded brave enough, but his bulging eyes betrayed his terror. The green pallor of his face briefly turned into a reddish shade.

Ralf sat, but his teeth remained bared with rage.

For a long moment, the brothers stared at each other with mutual and palpable hate.

"I want my servant. Where is the man?"

"He has been sent off to the far side of the priory on an errand for me." The crowner did not mention that it was an easy one made more pleasant with the suggestion that the man take his time sampling the famous priory ale on behalf of his master. For an older man, he had sped with alacrity to the task.

"What do you want from me? This fraternal visit is a pretense. We both know that. Get on with your purpose. The sooner done, the sooner I can be left in peace."

Sitting back, Ralf folded his arms and began. "When you arrived at the inn the day before you came here, you were greeted by the innkeeper. Was there another man who chose to approach you? If so, describe him."

"Anyone who said the man chose to approach me lied, but I did see the one you mean. You want a description? He was unremarkable. Of average height and appearance. Light brown hair, I think. A scruffy beard of a darker shade. Grey eyes? Light ones, certainly. No visible scars."

"You recall him quite well despite his unexceptional appearance."

"Even you would have, most beloved and witless brother. I saw him loitering by the inn door and didn't like his look. While the rude innkeeper was arguing over our simple accommodation requirements, I continued to wonder if the man was lawless, assessing what might be stolen from all those who stopped by the inn. It wouldn't have surprised me if that innkeeper allowed him to do so for a cut of whatever the man's wicked fellows acquired down the road."

"Do you think he was in the hire of the innkeeper?"

Odo thought for a moment. "In truth, I do not know. He did not speak to the innkeeper and waited for him to leave before he approached our party. Either he and the innkeeper were clever enough to hide their felonious alliance or there was none."

"If not you, to whom did he first speak?"

"Abbot Mordredus."

"What did he want?"

"I did not hear the entire conversation, but I noticed that he groveled on his knees to the abbot as he spoke. Then Mordredus summoned me and said that he had resolved the problem of pollution from whorish women. This man could be the barrier protecting our virtue." Odo snorted and rubbed at his nose. "Mordredus is a fool, yet has always thought himself above the rest of us. I thought it quite likely he had just engaged the services of a man who would later attack us on the road."

Ralf might hate his brother, but he knew him to be no such fool. The crowner had bought him a position in the abbey at Caldwell, but Odo had advanced to lead it on his merit alone. A curse on him, Ralf thought, but I can trust most of his observations, other than his opinions of me.

"Did he help your men wait on you at the meal?"

"I took him to the kitchen and explained both to him and the scabby wenches there what his duties were. The cook was ordered to provide for our needs first, and I took special care to make sure he knew each abbot's preferences on portion size and a few other details, or at least those that could be met under such rough conditions."

Ralf tried not to grin. He was surprised there was anything left of the aged ox after his brother got his supper that night.

"Our own servants first poured the ale and brought that to us while the man ladled the stew into the bowls and carved more from the roast for us. For a simple man, he learned remarkably well from my instructions. Ancell's portion had smaller bits for easier chewing, for instance. The abbot suffers from sore gums and loose teeth."

"So you concluded the alleged servant possessed a few wits?"

Odo coughed and began to look like he was rapidly tiring. "Or Mordredus had told him already. Or he knew more about us than he ought for other reasons." Odo pulled his blanket up to his chin and sighed. "God endowed us with the ability to be suspicious for good reason."

No, his brother was not easily duped, the crowner reminded himself. If the mysterious man did know more about the abbots than he should, who was the source and what was the purpose? He doubted it had anything to do with anonymous thieves living in the woods.

"Why do you think he went to Abbot Mordredus when you were the one discussing the terms of your stay with the innkeeper and appeared to be in charge of the traveling party?"

"I cannot answer that question. As I said, Mordredus lacks a few wits, but that is a fact not necessarily or quickly observable by a stranger. Perhaps he found me too intimidating."

That was possible. Ralf had long concluded that his brother's size alone would frighten even a sea monster.

"Yet I was troubled the next morning when Mordredus told me that the man had asked to accompany us to Norwich. Was this a sign to outlaws in the forest that we were suitable prey? Or did the man have another questionable reason to escape the inn under the cover of pious companions? He gave Mordredus no reason for his journey, or at least none that the abbot wished to tell me."

"You said nothing about your worries to Abbot Mordredus?"

"No. Although I did not like the creature, I had no proof that he was anything except what he claimed to be. When I took him to the kitchen, I carefully mentioned we had sufficient servants.

That may be why he sought permission from Mordredus, rather than me, to travel with us to Norwich. With a bit of flattery, my fellow brother in Christ would have given the Devil's most favored imp permission to travel by our sides. He does so love the power that authority brings."

"Did you learn the man's name?"

"In that I was the fool. He neither gave one nor did I ask. Perhaps the Abbot of Envy knows."

Ralf was amused by the name his brother gave Mordredus and wondered what that abbot called Odo. "Might this man have had cause to poison members of your party?"

The corners of Odo's lips twitched upward. "That is for you to discover, Ralf. I thought he had hopes of cutting all our throats, yet he didn't. When we escaped the forest with no harm, I assumed I had been wrong about him. Instead, I was more annoyed by the delays caused by Abbot Ilbert and his constant need to pee."

"Do you remember when the man left your company?"

"When Ilbert began to foam at the mouth, and I insisted we ride swiftly to the hospital here. The others, including this man, went to the village and, I assume, the inn there." He watched his brother for a moment before adding, "And if you want to know, I remained aware of him until then because I never fully trusted him."

"You are sure he did not go back the way you had come, perhaps to the inn where you had stayed the night before?"

"I cannot swear to what he might have done after we went down the road to the priory. It would have been foolish of any man to travel after dark, so I must assume he probably went into Tyndal village with the others." Odo exhaled with impatience. "As for everything up to the moment we parted from the other travelers, I have told you what I saw. I can assure you my report is accurate. As even you know, I have never been inclined to dreaming while awake."

"I only asked because you might have been distracted with the illness of Abbot Ilbert."

"Ilbert?" Odo's laugh cracked into a painful cough. "The man was a brute. Since God is just, the man's soul is surely being whipped with the ferocity he inflicted on many. No, other than the mercy we owe all mortals by getting him to the hospital, I was not worried if he lived or died. I also wanted to make sure we were in the priory where we would not have to listen to men singing ribald songs and watch whores ply their trade. I was weary of such pathetic and worldly pursuits."

Ralf paused and studied his brother. "You never liked women?"

"They are the daughters of Eve who forced us from the Garden. If she had not sinned, we would have food in abundance and suffer no pain. Of what use is Woman? She is like a cow with flesh hanging from her chest that would never be needed without the breeding of children in beds of lust. She foully bleeds on a regular basis. She keeps men from a virtuous life with her wiles and, unless God grants her the gift of a man's intellect, she is infernally boring and stupid. The better question, Ralf, is why so many men find them tempting."

The crowner shook his head. There were many reasons he and Odo never got along. This was one. His wife, Gytha, was neither boring nor stupid, and they had much joy in the marriage bed. Perhaps Odo had never forgiven that cow that once kicked him as a boy and thereafter blamed all females for the sins of one bovine? He swallowed his laughter.

"Are you finished? I am exhausted."

"One last question. Which abbot spent the night in the hayloft with a whore from the inn?"

"Didier. He is the second son and never wanted to take vows, but his father marched him to the abbey as a boy. As I heard the tale, Didier kicked and screamed the entire time and was locked away in a solitary cell until he saw reason. He has since found himself a whore and spawned many bantlings in her. On journeys, he always finds consolation." Odo closed his eyes and faced the wall. "Please leave me, Ralf. I am weary unto death."

Ralf realized that his brother was not complaining without reason. Odo looked terribly ill as, in fact, he was. For just an instant, he felt pity but swiftly exiled the emotion. "I shall recall your servant and send another lay brother to attend you until he arrives," he said.

Odo did not respond.

Ralf began to walk to the door, then turned around and looked at his pale brother. "You have helped more in this problem of murder than any of the others. For that I thank you." His tone was civil, even gentle.

Odo sighed.

With no further comment, Ralf hurried from the room. Had he looked back again, he might have seen his brother wipe a rebellious tear from his cheek.

Chapter Twenty-three

"Crowner!"

Ralf had barely shut the door to his brother's chambers when he saw Abbot Ancell waving to him.

He winced. The crowner had had enough of men vowed to God after enduring the conversation with Odo. Despite Gytha's influence and his friends within Tyndal Priory dulling his contempt, he still preferred straightforward thieves to men who enjoyed mortal foibles but pretended to be holier than more honest sinners. Grumbling to himself, Ralf steeled himself to face this unwelcome encounter.

"May we talk together?" The abbot gestured to the dining table in the middle of the room and, assuming the crowner would follow, walked to a bench and sat down.

Suppressing a groan, Ralf joined him.

"Sit closer," the abbot said, gesturing to a spot nearer to him. "I wish to speak in a low voice so others do not hear." With a significant look, he indicated the doors to the surrounding chambers of his fellow abbots.

Reluctantly, Ralf inched closer.

"You surely know by now that Abbot Gifre's murderer is one of my fellow abbots." Ancell leaned nearer.

The crowner nodded. For an elderly man, he thought, this one still has a bright eye and lacks that musty smell so many men of his age possess. His breath stank, but even the young suffered from rotting teeth and pustulous gums.

"Good!" Ancell put his hands together and grinned like a teacher faced with a student who has just unexpectedly answered a question properly. "Do you not think it odd that Abbot Gifre died but Abbot Odo did not?"

The crowner sat straighter with amazement. "You wish to denounce my brother?"

"I condemn no one. I wish only to pose questions for your further consideration." He sat back and studied the king's man sharing his bench. "I did not think you would find my suggestion of your brother amiss. There has never been great love between you, and I have heard you are an honest man."

Swallowing a brusque retort, Ralf urged him to continue with his remarks. In the back of his mind, a tiny voice, which sounded a bit like Odo's, whispered: *How does this man know that my brother and I do not get along?*

"A guilty man may injure himself to appear innocent. Have you never seen such a trick?"

The crowner confessed that he had.

"So Odo might be the guilty one. His illness does not make him innocent, and our dear Abbot of Caldwell is a most ambitious man. Or the poisoner could be Abbot Didier, who needs a higher position with more rents so he can pay for his mistress and their growing family of bastards. Despite being a wicked man, Didier is fond of his children and wants them fed and clothed, although his fidelity to their mother is questionable. I am sure you have heard that he pokes any woman whenever he can and did so with much merriment at the inn."

"You believe ambition to rise to a bishopric led one of the abbots to murder? Isn't that a particularly vile sin committed for an ignoble purpose?" Ralf deliberately blinked with an expression that he hoped suggested an innocence he did not possess.

"Men of God are still men, Crowner. Surely that does not surprise you. Few of us deserve the positions to which we rise. It grieves me as much as it does any other man of profound faith that virtue is not always the primary quality needed to gain honor in the Church."

Ralf was a bit taken aback by Ancell's frank remark but decided that the man's observations might be more useful than he had thought. Oddly enough, he was growing fonder of this abbot whose refreshing honesty was needed after breathing the fetid duplicity that always surrounded Odo like a second cloak.

"Abbot Didier has been exposed for his lust by Abbot Mordredus in a letter he wrote to Rome. He included no proof of Didier's transgressions but stated that such could be obtained easily. For this act, I fear for Mordredus' life."

"But he remains alive and others have died."

"As I am sure you and others must suspect, Abbot Ilbert may not have suffered a natural death, nor did Abbot Tristram. Abbot Gifre was certainly murdered. If you were an ambitious man with a terrible sin you wished to hide and you wanted to eliminate rivals, might you not be tempted to kill those who could gain what you so desperately desired?"

"Yet to leave one man alive would be ill-advised. He would surely be the killer."

"That is why I mentioned that Odo did not die but suffered nonetheless."

"Might your life be in danger as well?"

"Although I am the least of the threats to the killer's advancement, I may die. That is true. If the poisoner is Mordredus, Didier will die. If Didier, Mordredus will succumb to some fatal act. Either Odo is the killer or he will soon be dead." His expression saddened. "It is also possible that the killer will let me live so I become the suspect. Wouldn't that be clever?"

"With two of you alive, one is surely the murderer."

"Then I return to Abbot Odo. If he has suffered so much, why suspect he would be the culprit? If I am alive and unharmed, does that not suggest I am the more likely killer? Or you might begin to fear the poisoner is not among the abbots. Maybe he has escaped, and you have failed to identify him in time."

Ralf grew uncomfortable. Ancell had made a good point.

"Of course, I have a motive, as does each of my fellow abbots. Like all men, I have my fallibilities, and Mordredus surely mentioned them to Rome. But they are minor compared to the others." He rubbed his hand over his eyes. "I am an old man, Crowner, and have little left to hide. Yet my age may make me the most dangerous to the killer. A bishopric bestowed on me would not remain filled for many years but perhaps long enough that others might rise to the attention of Rome and the chance lost again for the murderer." He fell silent as if wanting to let that statement sink in. "That is all I have to say, but I had to offer you my questions born of sorrow in this heinous matter of untimely deaths."

Ralf was pleased the abbot was rising from the bench. Perhaps he could finally escape this cauldron of religious ambition and escape to the arms of his beloved wife and children. "I am most grateful for your opinions, my lord. But be assured that you are safe if the killer chooses poison. Prioress Eleanor has a plan to keep your food safe from deadly contamination."

Abbot Ancell smiled and bowed his head in a practiced display of gratitude.

Ralf was not fooled. As he watched the abbot disappear into his chamber, he suspected that Ancell did not believe, any more than any of the others, that a prioress was capable of protecting anyone.

As the crowner left the dining hall and the priory itself, he was surprised to realize that he was convinced Odo could not be a suspect. His brother was a clever manipulator, and he might eventually stuff himself so full of food that he killed himself, but he would never kill another man.

"My brother has never even liked to hunt," Ralf muttered.

Chapter Twenty-four

Abbot Ancell retreated into his chamber for prayer and reflection, grateful he had done what he should. Now he could leave the secular world and the king's man behind.

Although he was an old man, he suffered less than others from the troubles of decaying flesh. Of course Death might come for him soon, but he was confident the pale rider would not arrive quite yet. Had he believed otherwise, he would not have come on this journey to Norwich to meet the papal envoy and hope for a bishopric. Despite appropriate denials to the contrary, he knew that his birth, his proven administrative skills, and his virtue qualified him for one. Advancement in the Church was a holy ambition if desired by an unsullied heart, and his was as pure as any mortal's could be.

The orisons he now offered God were short, but he concentrated on uttering each word with passion as if it were the last one he would ever voice. It mattered less to him what the words meant. They were sacred utterances. That was sufficient.

Rising to his feet, he was pleased. He might have minor aches in his back, but his knees were unaffected by the joint disease. God obviously was pleased with him if He allowed him the mercy of praying without discomfort. As for his tender gums, they troubled him very little. He had never cared much about food and, for many years, had abstained from meat unless it was softened in stews.

His servant had found him a chair and pillows for his chamber so he might read in comfort. Walking over to it, he sat with pleasurable anticipation. The book he wished to study was lying on the table next to a ewer of ale from the Tyndal's own brewery. Although he preferred wine, he demanded that his soul be grateful for the simple gift which this remote priory had offered. Indeed, he found the drink palatable enough and poured some into a mazer to sip.

Preparing himself to be worthy to read Matthew Paris' *Life of Saint Edmund, Archbishop of Canterbury*, he closed his eyes and chased away all earthly thoughts, although ones involving his fellow abbots were harder to dismiss.

It was unfortunate that three had died, although God must have wanted the deaths or they would not have happened. He had prayed hard for their survival, but God had chosen another path. "Thy will be done," he whispered and acknowledged to Him that he accepted the deaths and would set aside any lingering sadness.

After a moment of silence and a wordless prayer, Ancell slipped his hand under the volume and pulled it toward him.

He felt a sharp pain in his hand and yanked it back.

There was a brown spider on his hand, less than an inch in width with a marble-like pattern on the back. The bite was already turning an angry red.

Ancell screamed and killed the creature with the slap of his other hand.

Then he lost consciousness.

Chapter Twenty-five

When the monk told his prioress and Sister Anne that he was going to the inn to treat the young wife who had not yet healed, the sub-infirmarian suggested he take another woman with him. It was an unusual idea, but the logic was sound. He was forbidden to touch the wife, but, if needed, a woman could with his direction.

To the surprise of all, Gracia volunteered, if no qualified lay sister was able to go. Although Prioress Eleanor hesitated, she gave the requisite permission. Sister Anne expressed gratitude for the girl's offer. With the latest storm, many sick had come to the hospital, including children unable to breathe, and the sub-infirmarian decided the latter had more immediate need of her attendance than the young wife.

Now Brother Thomas and Gracia were walking along the roadside to the inn, traveling in easy silence and carefully avoiding the dangerous frozen ruts disguised by snow.

Thomas glanced at the young woman and wondered if he should take advantage of this time alone with the girl to encourage a confidence. He knew Gracia was distressed over the decision she must make about her future and considered what he should do or say. His anger with God having abated, he felt more able to offer counsel—if, indeed, Gracia even needed his advice.

He chose to circle the problem.

"This matter of the young wife may be troubling," he said. "Are you sure you are comfortable helping?" As he looked down at Gracia, he tried to read her expression. Thomas prided himself on hiding his feelings, but he decided that the prioress' maid might just be his superior in the craft.

"I am, Brother. You explained she had lost her child. All I wish is to help ease her suffering. If I can also bring her a little solace, I shall be content."

"Then you most certainly shall succeed. At the priory, you have had ample opportunity to learn the many ways a soul can find consolation." He kept his tone light to mute the implications of those words.

Her expression was polite, but the look in her eyes suggested that he had not fooled her in the slightest. "I am grateful beyond measure for those lessons, Brother, but often wonder if I am worthy to be there. You know my past. I am not without grave sin."

"None of us is. God does not expect perfection, my child. He asks only that we strive to understand His intent within the words of His laws. For ourselves and others, we must practice compassion, forgiveness, and charity. The embrace of love is God's way. Hate and anger are Satan's." Thomas realized he should probably take his own advice more than he did.

Gracia slowed, face flushed, and stared at the white road ahead, framed by black trees with skeletal branches.

"I know the sin you mean, child," he whispered. "It was not your sin, for you did nothing willingly. The evil was committed against you."

"If so, Brother, I should long to avoid the company of men. Yet I do not fear all of Adam's sons. Indeed some are most pleasing to me. Is that not a sign that I must have consented to the acts, even if I have denied it to you and in my heart?" Her words were barely audible.

Thomas took a moment to consider his answer. Perhaps he had succeeded in healing some of the deep wound she had suffered from the rape, and for that he thanked God, but scars remained. Not all would agree with his complete exoneration of her, but his soul rebelled at the idea that a child should be blamed for an act of sexual violence just because she was Eve's daughter.

"The answer to your question is simple. You consented to nothing. A child is unformed and thus incapable of either an adult's sins or responsibilities," he said. "God wept over your pain. As for the nature of mortals, we are all sinners. Yet some strive more than others to virtue. If you do not hate the innocent along with the guilty, you have begun that long journey to righteous wisdom. Not all men are like the one who sinned against you."

"Have you ever hated mankind, Brother? Men or women?"

Her words brought both searing memory to his heart and bile into his throat. Thomas forced himself to dig far beneath his anger at God and the agony of his own rape in prison. Gracia had asked an important question. It was one that demanded a fair response.

"I did hate. As mortals, we all suffer that weakness. It is part of our frail nature that we are inclined to sin in that way. But God believes his creatures have hearts capable of learning a better way. He only condemns those who willfully reject the harder road to love and choose instead the easier path of hate."

Gracia grew pensive, and the pair walked on in silence.

Suddenly, she stopped. "How can there be love between a man and a woman without offending God? Lechery is a sin, is it not?"

Thomas was at a loss for words as he gazed down at the young woman, her brow furrowed and eyes narrowed with bewilderment. How could he respond when he was still struggling with an answer for himself?

Love between adults was a complicated thing, sometimes combined with lust, other times not. Didn't he love Sister Anne and his prioress? Yet he had no wish to lie with either. He loved Ralf, but had no yearning to couple with him. From time to time, he had lusted for the bodies of other men, and the pain of denial had been a sharp but brief agony. His couplings with women had brought relief but never joy. Only twice in his life had he felt love and desire entwine. The first had almost killed him. The second?

He clenched his fist and swore an oath that his love for Durant would not be destroyed like his love for Giles had been. All he wanted was that peace he found in the wine merchant's arms before their mutual passion drove them apart. Surely there was a way....

Gracia was looking at him, her eyes begging for an answer now.

"Lechery is a thing that sparkles, delights, and quickly loses its glow, child. Love is a gift from God, enduring, a source of strength and of joy." Was that enough? He feared it wasn't for her any more than it was for him.

"Then a man and a woman, who yearn to lie together, cannot also love because the body's passion is a sin."

"The two emotions can be felt together, although not always. But God allows desire to be satisfied in the marriage bed, and marriage is no sin."

"But to love without marriage?" She shook her head. "I am not sure what I mean, Brother. I do not mean those who couple together without God's blessing. But surely lust kept solely in the heart is... I cannot explain myself at all. I am so confused."

"You are not alone. It may require a lifetime to understand the nature of love," he said. "I pray daily for the patience to improve my understanding. All I do know is that God does not condemn those who struggle, doubt, and question..." He stopped, unable to find the right words. Indeed, he had never had them.

Suddenly, Gracia looked down the road and pointed.

Nute was running toward them. "Brother Thomas!" he shouted.

The monk and Gracia hurried to meet him.

"You must come quickly," the lad gasped.

"What has happened?" Thomas felt an unearthly fear. Had they all been wrong about the abbots' illnesses? Was there a new plague in the land?

"Just follow me, please. My mother begs you not to delay."

The trio rushed to the village inn.

Signy was waiting for them at the door, her face pale with fear. "I'm grateful you were so close, Brother."

"This is the salve for the man with the rash. I do not know his name." As he gave her the jar, his soul trembled.

"He calls himself Ned." Her voice shook. "I'll pass it on to him, but I sent Nute because I fear for the young couple. The wife has collapsed. She is gravely ill!"

Sensing that this condition might not be good for Gracia to see, Thomas told her to wait, then hurried to a room that Signy had created by surrounding an area with cloth for a rare privacy at an inn. Entering, he saw the husband kneeling by his wife's straw pallet bed. The man wept bitterly as he held her hand.

It took Thomas one look to know that the young woman was dying.

Chapter Twenty-six

"My lord, my work would be finished sooner if you held your hand still." The young hospital brother clenched his teeth to keep from uttering oaths he had vowed never to speak again and especially not in the presence of an abbot.

Abbot Ancell glared at him in response. "Was the bite poisonous?"

Sister Anne had been watching the treatment from a suitable distance. Noting the abbot's pallor, she felt a brief twinge of sympathy. "It is," she said, "but it will not be a mortal one. The common biting spider causes a red and painful swelling. This remedy will dull the soreness…."

"It is not sore! It burns!" He pressed a hand to his chest. "And I have a pain here!"

"That is a common symptom with this kind of spider bite, my lord." Sister Anne struggled to ignore the undisguised delight on the lay brother's face over the abbot's mortal fear. "It shall pass soon." But she caught herself hoping it would not pass too soon.

Tying a piece of clean linen around the hand, the lay brother dropped the abbot's hand. "I have finished," he announced and swiftly fled from the apothecary.

"But I have questions for him," Ancell muttered as he pointed at the rapidly vanishing man.

"Questions I may be able to answer with the help of God." Anne modestly folded her hands and humbly bowed her head.

"I would rather speak with Prior Andrew or even Brother Thomas." The abbot stood up from the stool on which he had been sitting and walked to a spot as far from the nun as he could.

"Brother Thomas is in the village, taking medicine to the sick. Prior Andrew is directing an urgently required repair of a leak in the monks' dormitory roof."

"Then Prioress Eleanor must be summoned. You," he pointed to her lest she be in any doubt over whom he meant, "must leave my presence. She must bring a proper attendant to protect our sacred vows. I shall be praying in the chapel."

Sister Anne left to send a messenger to the leader of Tyndal Priory. Having been married in the secular world, she was experienced in the many joys of the marriage bed. The idea of any woman being tempted to sin with Abbot Ancell required more imagination than even her wicked soul possessed.

◇◇◇

Prioress Eleanor was used to dealing with the difficult and told the young messenger that she would attend to the abbot immediately. No matter what opinion she held of Abbot Ancell, or any of the other abbots for that matter, she honored courtesy and always considered diplomacy to be the most successful approach in the majority of situations. Thus she lowered her veil over her face and arrived in the chapel with a nun and one of the hospital lay brothers in tow.

The abbot was kneeling in prayer while tenderly cradling his bitten hand.

Eleanor waited until the man decided he would notice the sound of her arrival and finish his orisons. The delay, as she knew, was a calculated display of the abbot's power and status.

"We have been lied to," he said, rising to his feet and glancing with satisfaction at the man standing near the door and the nun by her side.

"Please explain what you mean, my lord." The prioress was impressive in her calm.

"Brother Thomas, the crowner, and even a lay brother have assured us that you had taken adequate measures to protect us. Yet this has just happened!" He carefully waved his bandaged hand.

"A spider bite," she replied.

"A plot," he retorted.

"That was done by a common spider. We have seen others inside during winter."

"It was deliberately hidden in my book," Ancell said, emphasizing each word. "Three noble abbots have died, and one is fighting to keep his soul out of Death's hand. Now I have been attacked. What other conclusion could anyone endowed with reason make?"

Opting not to explain the difficulty of hiding a spider under a book with the assumption that it would wait until a particular time and the targeted hand was nigh, Eleanor bowed her head. "I have sworn to keep you all safe," she said. "Have you some suggestions for improving the protection since you have suffered this bite?"

He glared at her, although her tone had not suggested any sarcasm. "Godly men must be assigned to protect our quarters. Our food and drink must be tasted by your lay brothers before it is served to us."

The kitchen brothers had already been ordered to test the food with a cage of mice, but she wondered why any abbot, of more mature years and surely longing for Heaven, would demand a young man sacrifice his own life so the elder might remain even longer in the sinful world. As for godly men, she was curious if he had a special definition, since all in the priory were as vowed to God's service as were the abbots.

"You have no response? Has God silenced your woman's tongue?"

"Our priory is small, especially compared to your abbey," she said, "and lacks the number of men needed to guard your chambers. Perhaps your servants could do this." She saw that he was about to protest and quickly added, "Our lay brothers could not possibly be as devoted to you as the men you trusted enough to bring on this journey." She carefully omitted any specific mention of having tasters for the meals.

He shut his mouth, and his expression suggested he was willing to consider this option. "Very well," he said at last. "Our servants shall do this, but their other duties cannot be left undone. Your religious will have to perform some of their tasks."

Eleanor agreed that linens would be changed and washed by her people as well as any cleaning of the rooms. All, she said, would be done under the watchful eye of the abbots' servants so no more errant spiders could be hidden.

Having established that the abbot had no further demands, Eleanor departed with courtesy and walked back to her chambers, taking the long way around through the snow-softened cemetery. The sharp air and numbing cold beneath her feet distracted her from her anger.

Glancing at a rounded grave with no markings that lay just outside the sanctified ground, she brought to mind the story of the man whose corpse lay there.

Murder was a grave sin for any mortal but especially for this man who had sworn himself to God's service. So which one, of those remaining alive in this party of brother abbots, was also committing the heinous sin that had caused God to brand Cain?

Chapter Twenty-seven

Prioress Eleanor noticed that Gracia had been especially quiet since her return from the village with Brother Thomas, but the young woman claimed the events there had not troubled her beyond a very human grief. After a short while, she asked permission to visit Eda in the anchorage later in the day, a request Eleanor most readily granted.

If her maid wished to seek counsel from the anchoress or her friend, the prioress willed herself to be content. She would have preferred that Gracia seek her advice, but, depending on what the young woman wanted to discuss, she knew that she might not be the wisest one to give it.

As Thomas led Crowner Ralf and Sister Anne into her audience chamber, Eleanor glanced at Gracia who was already heating the wine with a poker from the fire. Even if the young woman was troubled, she still thought first of the comfort of others without being asked. Once again, the prioress prayed that the girl would stay at Tyndal while acknowledging that her desire was selfish as well as pure. At least God was used to the flawed mix of emotions from her, and she silently expressed gratitude for His patience.

"The abbots are restive," Ralf said after taking a cup of mulled wine. His nose was red from the bite of the outside air.

"Abbot Ancell is convinced the spider that bit him was planted under his book to poison him." Sister Anne briefly smiled.

"And you, Brother? What cheerful news have you to bring us?" Eleanor meant to lighten the mood but then remembered what he and Gracia had found at the inn. Begging God for forgiveness, she deeply repented her frivolous tone.

"I fear none. The young wife died at the inn, my lady. She was almost dead when I arrived. Even if I had gotten her to our hospital, she would not have survived."

Grateful for his tactful reply, Eleanor apologized for her unintended lack of compassion and promised to pray for the woman's soul. When she stole a look at Gracia, however, she saw her maid turn away as if wishing to hide her face. Sorrow stabbed at her, and the prioress regretted letting the girl go to the inn with the monk.

Yet that is a foolish lament, the prioress thought. Death stands next to us with a stubborn fidelity from the moment of our birth. Did the Reaper not take Gracia's family when she was a child as he did my own mother?

"Was she the one who was bleeding when you first met her?" The sub-infirmarian had not yet heard this news.

Thomas nodded. "Her husband said she had bled on the way to Tyndal, but the flow diminished significantly by the time they reached the inn. Yet it never stopped and was clearly not her normal courses."

Perplexed, Eleanor asked, "I was never sure whether she had given birth to a dead child or lost the baby before its time?"

"I fear she tried to abort the babe and was struck with the fatal rush of blood for her wrongdoing." The monk had never mentioned his suspicion before and sadly wondered if he had erred in not doing so. She would have died anyway from the sudden hemorrhage, he thought, but that did little to dispel his sorrow.

Anne gasped. "Was she able to confess the deed before she died?" She bowed her head with embarrassment. "That was not a question I had the right to ask," she said. "I apologize, Brother."

Thomas shook his head. "She was unable to speak by the time I arrived, but, from her repentant gaze and sighs on my previous visit, I believe she sincerely lamented her deed. I asked God to allow that as her confession, accept her painful death as her penance, and forgive her transgression."

"Why did they succumb to the Devil and commit this evil?" The look in Sister Anne's eyes was unforgiving.

"Are you certain she sinned?" The prioress was watching Gracia.

The young woman wiped tears from her cheeks.

"She never told her husband she had, although he suspected what she had done. He had no work, and they were traveling to Norwich in hopes of finding some. When his wife discovered she was pregnant, they both feared that the babe would die of starvation or illness. Indeed, the couple had little enough to eat themselves, and she worried she would be unable to nurse. The only reason they could stay at the inn was that the husband managed to steal some coin from a pilgrim." Thomas glanced at Ralf.

The crowner shrugged. "Or so he says. Perhaps he did not want to admit to a charity. I have heard no complaints. Have you?"

Thomas confirmed that he had not.

"There, you see? I have no cause to look into this matter."

Hiding her relief, the prioress was grateful. Many condemned Ralf for his rude ways and roughness with felons, but he also had deep compassion which he kept carefully hidden from most.

"The husband says she might not have been able to bear the thought of a child dying with cruel slowness and decided to murder it quickly. Although he did not know where she had gotten them, he saw juniper berries in her pouch and asked her the intended purpose. All she said was that she had been given them to infuse their ale with flavor one day, and he inquired no further."

"Juniper berries cause abortions," Sister Anne murmured.

"As he feared but was not certain," Thomas replied. "He did not want to condemn her for a sin she might not have committed."

"He knew and did not stop her." The nun looked at her hands and clenched them.

Thomas looked at the prioress.

"We shall pray that God have mercy on both their souls," Eleanor said and briefly touched the sub-infirmarian's arm to comfort. Abortion was an acknowledged sin, but it was also committed often enough. Many sympathized with the parents and supported their claim that the loss had been a natural thing. Sister Anne, having seen her only child die and never ceasing to grieve, was not one of them.

"There is one more thing you should know about this tragedy," Thomas said. "The young husband was distraught over what might have happened and knew he shared guilt if his wife had taken the berries he had seen in her possession. Yet he still doubted she had done such a thing and wondered if the loss of the child had been God's kindness to them. He visited our anchoress one night for advice but fled because he found himself unable to give full voice to his doubts. He was both grateful his wife had lost the babe and terrified of sin."

"So the strange visitor to Anchoress Juliana was not the one who struggled with his conscience over the deaths of the abbots." Prioress Eleanor sighed with regret but was careful not to ask if the suspect juniper berries were still in her pouch after the woman's death. That Brother Thomas had shrived her was sufficient.

"Nonetheless, I do believe that this elusive servant must still be at the inn," Thomas continued. "Only a few have turned back to their homes, and no one has gone in the direction of Norwich."

"Did the salve I sent help the man with the reddened hands?" Sister Anne had finally calmed and sipped her drink. "I pray that we have done some good."

"I gave it to Signy. He may not have been in the inn when I rushed to the dying woman's bedside, nor did I see him seated with others when I left to return here. I shall go back to examine him."

"Meanwhile, your priory guests accuse each other of plotting to kill their fellows," Ralf said. "One claims my brother is the most likely." He muttered a probable curse under his breath.

"Abbot Didier has pointed to Abbot Mordredus because he wrote a letter to Rome before the arrival of the special envoy sent by Pope Martin IV. In it, he detailed the sins of each of the other abbots in the party that traveled together to Norwich to meet with this man," Thomas said.

"It was Abbot Ancell who first suggested my brother might be guilty and have taken just enough of the poisoned food to make himself sick, thereby removing himself from suspicion. Next, he argued for Abbot Didier as the culprit."

"Abbot Ancell was bitten shortly thereafter by a spider and blames the murderer for the deed." This time Sister Anne did not smile.

"And thus becomes a victim himself, or so he believes. Since my brother has been too weak to leave his bed, the guilty one must be Abbot Didier or Mordredus." Ralf's face reddened. "As I have often said, my brother is an odious man and I bear no love for him. Ambitious, he most certainly is. To win a bishopric, Odo would lie and scheme to place any other contender in a terrible light so he might best him. All that acknowledged, I do not think he would stoop to murder." The crowner drained his cup. "But I am his kin, and my word cannot be given credence. He must rank as high a suspect as any other."

"In theory, Ralf. Only in theory," Thomas said.

"Obviously, I do not think the spider was planted," Anne said to Eleanor. "That seems to be a genuine accident. Spiders live indoors in the cold weather. This one had simply found a sheltered place that happened to be the abbot's book. It was a fatal choice for the spider."

"I agree that the spider is an improbable murder weapon even if Abbot Ancell believes otherwise," Eleanor said. "I take it he has no chance of dying?"

"All wounds can fester, but this is a minor bite. He will suffer for a few hours and heal quickly thereafter, unless there is something else malignant in his body." She looked disgusted.

"For that small mercy, we must be grateful," Eleanor replied and tried not to dwell on their equal certainty that the now-dead Abbot Tristram would live.

"If only we knew more about the health of the dead abbots before they fell ill," Sister Anne said.

Eleanor agreed. "We have been told that no one was taking any new remedy to which he was unaccustomed. Yet these men were not traveling with a physician, and it is winter. They are older men and most prone to sudden ailments." She looked at the monk and crowner, both of whom agreed.

The sub-infirmarian did as well. "Some slight complaint or pain might have struck either of the two abbots, one that no one thought significant enough to mention. Perhaps someone along the way suggested a temporary relief until the abbot could reach Norwich and consult a physician. We often take more of an herb or draught on the assumption that more is better if knowledgeable guidance is not given."

"I do recall one minor thing," Thomas said. "Abbot Didier mentioned that Abbot Ilbert had complained of flatulence on the journey. Then he remarked that Ralf's brother commonly suffered those symptoms and may have shared information on his remedy. Abbot Odo was outraged over the suggestion, denied Ilbert had ever approached him, and accused Mordredus of insulting him."

"Odo lied. He suffers from it," Ralf snorted and thanked Gracia for refilling his cup.

"It would not surprise me if Abbot Ilbert had begun to experience this. His humors were unbalanced, or he would never have suffered from such great wrath. On the journey, he was eating food to which he was unaccustomed. I wonder if Abbot Odo did suggest anything?" Sister Anne looked at the crowner. "It was surely meant as a kindness if he did."

"Kindness? My brother?" Ralf feigned a shocked look. "Yet it has been reported that he denied doing so, and he did not mention it when I spoke to him. Shall I go back and ask him?" The very thought made him growl with such ferocity that a wild dog would cringe.

"Let me think on this a while longer." Anne fell silent.

"The illnesses of Abbots Ilbert and Tristram aside, I do not understand how the poisoning with monkshood occurred," Thomas said. "If one of the abbots is at fault, why have the others not remembered something that one of them did that he shouldn't have? Even now, as each of the remaining claims one of the others is the perpetrator, no one has pointed to any proof."

Eleanor set her untouched wine aside. "The mysterious servant could have done something at the inn, either on his own or under the direction of someone else. But he is not at Tyndal Priory so could not have poisoned that tart."

Ralf suddenly brightened at the thought of food and looked around with the hopeful expression of a hungry puppy.

Catching his eye, Gracia sadly shook her head.

"We are quite certain he is not in residence here," Thomas said, "but we do not know if he has found a way to lurk nearby."

"At least we only have three likely suspects left among the abbots," Eleanor said.

"Four, as we must include my brother," Ralf added.

"As you will." Eleanor agreed but her expression suggested she did not think Odo was guilty. "Have we all shared everything we know from speaking with the innkeeper, abbots, and servants?"

Both Thomas and Ralf quickly summarized what each had gleaned in case either had forgotten to mention a detail.

"Has anyone a question they have not yet thought to ask?" Eleanor reached out and touched her distracted sub-infirmarian's arm.

Sister Anne blinked but quickly shook her head. "I have found nothing in my herbals," she said and quickly went back to her thoughts.

The prioress turned to her monk. "I think you should visit the inn again and talk to anyone who was with the traveling abbots. Signy has probably remembered others. You must identify which one is the missing servant."

"I shall leave immediately, my lady," Thomas said as he stood. Given permission to leave, he still took a moment to pet the great orange cat that had just risen from his place by the fire and awaited the show of respect to which he was due from those he favored.

Eleanor laughed at the sight of King Arthur's namesake purring and rubbing against the legs of his beloved monk. It was a moment of innocence she needed to keep her from being overwhelmed with the evil of these murders.

"And I shall seek the help of Sister Oliva in consulting my herbals again. I must find a clue there." Sister Anne followed the monk out the door.

Ralf looked at the prioress with a questioning expression.

"Go home to Gytha and your babes," Eleanor said to him. "Let us see what Sister Anne and Brother Thomas can discover. We can always send word to you when you are needed. As for your brother, I do not think him a murderer any more than you do."

The crowner bowed. "You are ever kind, my lady." He hesitated a moment as if wishing to say more, then nodded and left.

Perhaps, she thought, he cares for his brother more than he wants to admit.

As Eleanor walked back to the fire, she noted that her cat had resettled into his place a safe distance from the heat. With little fuss, Gracia was removing the cups and wine. For just a moment, the prioress bitterly longed for the kind of peace this moment suggested before reminding herself that she had vowed to serve God at His will.

The resentment was brief, and she disappeared into her private chambers to pray for both strength and forgiveness.

Chapter Twenty-eight

Prayer had given comfort, yet Eleanor remained unsatisfied. She asked God why He had sent these crimes and destroyed the peace of her priory. He chose not to answer, and she feared she had offended by failing to show gratitude for the many gifts He had given her.

Since her last encounter with violent death, she had enjoyed almost three years of comparative tranquility. During that time, she had taken pleasure in the joys of family and friends. Ralf's wife had easily borne two children to give more siblings to his child from a prior marriage, and the entire family enjoyed good health. Eleanor's nephew, Richard, was absorbed by his studies and seemed content in Oxford. Her brother, Baron Hugh, was always a worry, but he was safe at Wynethorpe Castle as long as the Welsh remained quiescent. Their other brother, Robert, was married to a good woman, and she had just given him a vigorous son.

Even her sinful passion for Brother Thomas had mellowed into a quieter and deeper love, although she could hardly call it one common between brother and sister. Even if it had become a rare occurrence, the incubus who took on his form still invaded her dreams and reminded her of the power of overwhelming lust. But no other man had tempted her since that horrible time at the castle named Doux et Dur. Perhaps God had meant her to learn a lesson from that, and thus she had made peace with her mortal flesh and opened her heart to the wisdom He had intended to bestow on her.

As she hurried down the stairs from her chambers, she thought more about how deeply upset she was over this new trial God had sent her with the deaths of the abbots. Setting aside all selfishness, she realized that the feeling was less resentment, or even anger, than doubt. In the past, she had sometimes welcomed the adventure of matching wits with Satan. This time, she was strangely uncertain of victory, and that made her apprehensive.

Stopping outside the door to the cloister, Eleanor looked around. The garth was protected from the sharp wind but still bore the marks of cruel winter. Everything was covered with snow, and what plants there were had been hidden. Few walked here because of the bleakness. That might give Eleanor the privacy she wished, but it also made her sad.

Before her father's death, and soon after the death of the beloved aunt who had raised her in Amesbury, she had found this season oddly satisfying. It was a reminder of death but one that had always led her thoughts to Heaven. Since those two deaths, winter made her feel abandoned.

Heaven remained the goal of the faithful, and she knew her loved ones would be there to greet her after she had burned off her sins in Purgatory, but she suffered a very human feeling of loss with the deaths of those who had always been in her life. Her brother, Hugh, seemed to have leapt successfully into the baronetcy their father had bequeathed him. Eleanor still resented the changes her father's death had brought her, as well as the loss of Sister Beatrice's calm wisdom and broad experience.

Stopping at a bench, she brushed away the snow, then looked at the icy stone and decided not to sit and ponder. She would pace around instead and try to stay warm enough to think.

If she did not feel comfortable with these deaths in her priory, the best solution would be to set aside this insidious doubt and quickly solve them. With Brother Thomas going to the inn to discover the mysterious servant and Sister Anne researching poisons, it was her duty to discover the motive behind the murders.

With three of the seven abbots dead, she thought grimly, those likely suspects were at least reduced in number. She must regain her confidence. There was no reason why she should not be able to solve this crime as she had so many others.

"Let me start with the obvious," she whispered into the icy air, "and logically peel away the layers that conceal the core of the scheme."

Someone must have had a grievance against the abbots and chosen the trip to Norwich as the ideal time to wreak vengeance since all were gathered together. In truth, the murderer might be one of the abbots, one of the servants, the man who suddenly joined the party at the inn before they came to Tyndal, or someone else as yet undetected.

She was certain it was no one in her priory. The first two abbots fell ill before they arrived here. As for other members of the traveling party, Brother Thomas would find out at Signy's inn who was part of it and when they joined, whether from the beginning of the journey, during it, or later at the inn where Ilbert and Tristram fell ill. The monk had already questioned the servants and none seemed a likely perpetrator, although further questions might be required. At this point, she could dismiss only the dead from suspicion.

The remaining abbots were all frightened, other than Odo who was angry that he had almost died from a food he likely deemed unbearably plain. She did not find his anger suspicious and understood it was a way of disguising his terror at his near-death. She might not like Abbot Odo, but she was able to look at him with greater objectivity than did his youngest brother. Odo was no fool, but he was a pompous ass. Although kinship might make Ralf believe Odo was not guilty of murder, Eleanor had concluded that pompous asses rarely made clever killers. He would remain a suspect, but she placed him at the bottom of her list.

The mysterious servant troubled her. If he had a grudge against these seven men, he would have had a hard time planning the most advantageous time for the killings to take place. He had not been with the party before the night they arrived at the inn where Tristram and Ilbert were probably poisoned, but how could he have known that a delay would force them to stay there? Had the weather broken or the route proved easier to travel, the abbots might have reached Tyndal instead and he would not have had the easy access to them in the guest quarters that he did at the inn. Again, with good weather, the party would have traveled from here to Norwich the next day and settled into even more secure chambers.

Yet he had specifically waited for them at the ill-fated inn and taken on the duty of go-between between the abbots' servants and the tempting flesh of those more aged daughters of Eve who cooked at the inn kitchen. It was he who ladled out the portion for each abbot. How easy it must have been to slip something into the bowl intended for Abbot Ilbert, Abbot Tristram, or both.

Then he had begged permission to continue with the party, presumably to Norwich. Was his master there? Or was his master hidden among the abbots themselves or even their servants? Until this man was found and questioned, that solution to the crime might remain hidden forever.

Eleanor kicked at a mound of snow and watched it scatter in a cloud of icy fragments. If only she could find just the right clue. She looked around and listened to the empty whisper of the feeble breeze.

No gift of revelation arrived.

Shivering, she continued her circle of the cloister garth.

Once the abbots did arrive at Tyndal, the mysterious servant had chosen to leave the party of abbots and go with the others to Signy's inn. To the best of anyone's knowledge, no stranger had been seen lurking near the guest quarters. And from all she had learned from Sister Matilda and Brother Thomas' queries, no one could have had access to the mushroom tart that killed Abbot Gifre and sickened Odo.

What did this mean?

Eleanor banned all active thought and paced once more around the garth as she waited for some inspiration, a voice, even a vague but logical suggestion to slip into her mind. The grow-ing silence she encountered was as hard to bear as the chilly day.

Possessed of a woman's mind, the prioress often found solu-tions to problems in intuition, not from more masculine reason. Contrary to the beliefs of wise men, she had also learned to trust those instinctive opinions.

Perhaps there is also other merit in being a lesser creature compared to Adam's sons, she said to herself with mild humor. Such imperfection meant she was closer in nature to the major-ity of sinners and might therefore understand them best. Sister Beatrice would have laughed with great merriment at this con-clusion, the prioress thought, and missed her aunt all the more.

So what do I think? She shook her head and banished that idea. Nay, what do I feel to be the case?

"Were I to guess," she whispered, her breath turning the air as white as the snow, "I would say that the servant at the inn was used by one of the abbots or one of their servants to start the process of mortal accidents. Once they arrived at Tyndal, by accident or intent, the mysterious man was allowed to go on his way. Perhaps he was paid then and allowed to escape? Perhaps he was dismissed so he might never know his actions had resulted in death, and thus he would never point an accusing finger at the man who planned these crimes?"

Eleanor felt relief. This made sense to her. She might not have lost her ability to solve murders after all.

"Once at my priory," she continued to murmur as she passed by dark stone walls and emaciated limbs of naked shrubs, "the master of the crimes took over and somehow managed to kill one more abbot. Maybe he hoped Odo would die as well? Maybe he still has plans to kill him as well as the others."

But she realized that the killer, especially if he were an abbot himself, could not slay all his fellows. The last man left alive was most likely the murderer, and, if he wanted to escape, he would not be so dim-witted. This man, who had so cunningly planned these deaths, was certainly not stupid. This was another reason she was inclined to discount one of the servants as the perpetrator. From what Brother Thomas had told her, none seemed especially gifted with the cleverness required.

Abbot Ancell had made an excellent observation. A man might make himself ill, although not fatally so, to hide his guilt. That would suggest that Odo was a strong suspect. Thinking on this a while longer, she decided she still did not think he had killed anyone.

"So let me consider the other three," she muttered with determination.

Didier might long for a bishopric, but, despite his denials, he likely had a mistress and had fathered several children. For all his own faults, Pope Martin would not have welcomed such a man into a higher position in the Church. Had the abbot's sins not been enumerated by Abbot Mordredus, Didier would have had a good chance at advancement, being known as a capable administrator, but he certainly had little enough now. Did the abbot know this? Had he cause to murder his brothers in Christ so only he might be in line for advancement, despite his sins? A clever man could still hide his mistress or else lie convincingly. Mordredus had spoken in his missive only of the tales told to him, and all stories can be retold to suggest different conclusions.

There was also Ancell. He was elderly, although he seemed spry enough. He had readily admitted that his sins had been exposed in the same infamous letter to Rome, but he was little troubled by that. Perhaps he knew that his age might prohibit any hopes for promotion or he was simply confident that he had the best opportunity in this company of sinners. So what reason did he have to kill anyone if he did not care or he was confident enough in his selection? He seemed the weaker prospect for the killer.

Finally, there was Abbot Mordredus, a man who was as rabidly ambitious as Odo, but, unlike Ralf's brother, he had written to Rome, condemning his six fellows for their evil ways. Did he fear that the letter was insufficient for the papal envoy to dismiss all except him?

Certainly, the crimes of the others who had been killed were transgressions, but they ranged in gravity. Ilbert suffered rages and beat his clerics, one of whom was Didier's nephew. Tristram, on the other hand, was simply lazy and demanded others do his work for him while he garnered all praise. Odo's faults lay in gluttony as well as in an ambition matching that of any courtier seeking a king's favor. Gifre was rumored to gather plate like others do May flowers in the morning, and he made it a habit to mock any whose birth was lower than his.

Eleanor began to feel numb with the cold and realized she must seek the warm fire of her chambers. Shivering, she hurried back to the stairway.

If she had to point an accusing finger at the one abbot who seemed most likely to be behind the murders, she would pick Abbot Mordredus. After all, he had taken it on himself to write Rome and destroy the reputations of all who might be in competition with him. Such overweening ambition often did lead to murder.

Chapter Twenty-nine

Signy glowed with joy. "Brother, I am grateful to you. My foster daughter is well enough to seek the kitchen and ask to help the cook."

"Her healing is all due to God's grace," he replied, delighted by the news. "And does her poppet enjoy a similar return to health?"

"She left her in the bed this morning but did wrap her up well and cautioned her to rest quietly like a good girl." The innkeeper laughed and beckoned for ale. "Would you have some of our root vegetable stew?" She grinned. "I promise the broth comes from chicken, and today there is no other meat in it that Prioress Eleanor would find objectionable."

Thomas gratefully refused. "I come to ask a favor."

"A request I shall always grant if it is within my power to do so."

"When last we spoke, I asked which of the people here came with the party of abbots. You pointed out the tragic young couple and Ned with the rash. After reflection, can you show me any others?"

Signy looked around at the few customers. Some were eating while others stared into space as if bored. A few children raced around the benches, causing either laughter or ire among the adults who watched over the boisterous antics.

"There, I think." She discreetly pointed. "The elderly couple. They are on pilgrimage to the shrine of Saint William. As for the young couple, the widower no longer stays here. But you have spoken with him, have you not? I grieve for him."

"He has sought refuge in our priory to ease his anguish until his wife is buried in our cemetery. He has no other place to take her corpse."

Signy looked at him with some confusion but chose not to ask the question she was pondering.

But Brother Thomas suspected that she wondered if the loss of the child had been deliberate, a mortal sin that would ban her corpse from holy ground had she died before repentance was possible.

"God is so merciful. Her obvious sorrow over any earthly transgression spoke as loudly as words," he said, carefully avoiding the name of a specific sin. "Be comforted. She died as good a death as possible."

"You are a kind and good man, Brother, filled with compassion."

He bent his head so she would not see his expression. I most certainly am not a good man, he thought, and begged God to forgive him if he had, in any way, presented himself as more upright than he was.

With a serious expression, she continued to look around. "There is Ned. He sits by the fire, drinking ale. I gave him the salve yesterday."

"Surely there were others?" Thomas grew fearful. Perhaps the servant had left and they would never get the answers to their questions.

"A very few decided to travel back to their homes. Of those, I remember some pilgrims and one family with small children."

"Can you recall any details about them?" He hoped the servant he was seeking had not disguised himself as a pilgrim. It was unlikely that the couple included the man he sought. Nothing Thomas had been told suggested the servant had been familiar with any in the party of travelers nor had he newly befriended anyone in particular.

"The husband of the couple was a carpenter from a small village nearby. Our local carpenter told him that he might just as easily find work in Cambridge, and they seemed glad enough to try."

"The children were small?"

"One was nursing. The other was still unsteady on her feet."

The monk nodded, satisfied that this couple was of no interest to him. "And the pilgrims?"

"There were four of them. One lacked a leg. I fear the stump was rotting, for he stank terribly. Another was an ancient woman, her back bent so painfully she could only stare at the ground. She had come with a young lad who must have been kin, for he helped her in all ways and even served the other pilgrims."

Thomas asked for the youth's description.

"Tall. Thin as a tree branch. Beardless as a girl, and his voice was still breaking. Skin pitted from the pox. So blond you could see his scalp. About Nute's age, I think."

He shook his head, relieved that this boy did not fit even the vague description of the man he sought.

"The last in the party was a widow. I know nothing about her. She said little and her expression was always grim. I felt she had come to beg remission of some terrible sin." She thought again for a moment. "Ah, yes. A couple of men may have come at the same time but have since left."

This news did not please the monk. "Do you remember anything about them or the road they took?"

Signy shook her head. "The only passable road of which I have knowledge is the one to Cambridge. As for the men themselves, they stayed apart from the others. I paid no attention to them as they stayed only one night."

Thomas waited for more information and then said, "Those adults you mentioned were the only ones who came here at the same time as the abbots?"

"Aye, Brother. As you can see, the inn is not filled, although the strangers who usually come here at this time of the year are far fewer than this in number."

The four pilgrims, described by the innkeeper, were of no interest. But Thomas was uneasy. The two men who had left might have been involved in the murders. After all, the road to Cambridge went past the inn where the abbots had stayed.

Thanking Signy, the monk picked up his ale. "I shall question those who remain," he said and sought out the old couple first.

The wife brightened at the approach of the handsome monk. Her husband scowled, began to mash something in his bowl with a spoon, and bent to noisily suck up his broth.

"He cannot hear," she said. For a woman of her many years, she still had most of her teeth, although her white hair was so wispy it barely covered her head.

After a little companionable talk, Thomas mentioned that he was seeking someone who had come with the party of abbots.

"Describe the man you wish to find, Brother. I might answer you better if I knew what he looked like." Her eyes were bright with good humor.

Her husband had finished his meal, continued to ignore both monk and wife, and laid his head on his arms. He quickly began to snore.

Thomas gave a general description and added, "He joined the party at the inn the night before you all came here. He was traveling alone." He hesitated. "Perhaps with another man."

She rested her chin in her hand and pressed her fingers against her lips several times before answering. "The three couples, my husband and I included, all came together to the inn along with the abbots, although each couple joined the holy men at different villages. There were three other men who were already there waiting when we arrived, and they asked to join us. A far larger party was safer. Lawless men may not like to rob in the piercing cold any more than we enjoyed the journey, but their bellies rumble just like those of honest men."

"Are the three men still here? Do you know if any left the inn?" He looked around with pointed interest, straining to see around some of those walking about. "I do not see the one I seek."

Squinting hard, the old woman was doing the same.

Thomas' heart sank. If her eyesight was that poor, she would be of no help to him.

Finally, she sat back. "There were two men who have gone back toward Cambridge. They might have matched your description, but so does the young man whose wife just died, as well as that man over there." Pointing her finger, her hand trembled with a mild palsy at Ned sitting by the fire.

"Can you remember anything specific about the men who left?"

Her expression turned blank.

"Do you recall…?" Thomas had raised his voice.

"I heard you well enough, young Brother," she replied. "I was trying to picture the men."

With embarrassment, the monk apologized.

She dismissed that with a polite wave of her gnarled hand. "One had a severe limp when he first rose to walk, although that soon disappeared as he moved on. He was an older man with hair the color of iron. His companion was younger. I thought at first he was the elder's son, but they did not resemble each other." She mused for a moment longer, then shook her head. "The younger man was not memorable. A surly look, I thought, but that was all."

Thomas was pleasantly surprised. "I am most grateful to you for your information."

She tilted her head as she grinned at him.

For an instant, he could see the beauty she must have possessed as a young woman. "You are very observant."

"There is much in the world to enjoy, Brother. I have never lost my appreciation for a handsome face either, although I have always been a good and faithful wife."

He looked at the husband who lay on his arms, snoring and drooling. Suddenly, his heart filled with sorrow for the woman.

She read his expression well and bent her head toward her aged spouse. "You might not think it now, but he was a handsome lad!" Her words were soft with affection. "We had our joy of each other and healthy babes as well. Although our passions have faded, he still takes my hand and kisses it before we sleep. I pray to God every night that neither of us shall wait long for the other after death."

Thomas spoke for a while longer with the old woman. She had nothing more to impart, but she had eased his mind a bit about one of the two men who had left the inn. Of course, he would ask the abbots if the mysterious servant had limped at all, but he suspected that man was not the one he sought. The second of the pair might be. That possibility continued to trouble him.

Rising at last and taking his leave, Thomas gave the couple a blessing, even though the husband slept on.

"We are both grateful, Brother," the woman said. "Although my husband seems unaware of your blessing, his soul will know of it and be content. Is that not all that matters?"

He agreed and left, next seeking the man called Ned with the rash. As he did, Thomas prayed for the elderly couple, that they each might end their days with good and easy deaths and that one would not long survive the other.

◇◇◇

Ned was not as pleased to see him as the old woman had been.

"Any news on when the road to Norwich will be clear of snow?" The man's tone was peevish.

Thomas noticed that his hands were still red, although the color had faded a little. Yet he was annoyed by his blunt lack of courtesy, and he chose to ignore the question he had been asked. "How has the salve worked?" Thomas queried in response.

Ned looked at his hands as if surprised by the question. "Well enough," he growled. "They will improve when I get to my journey's end."

"The air feels as if another storm may come soon," Thomas replied and knew his pleasure at bringing unwelcome news was probably a wicked thing.

The man glared into his jack of ale as if it had offended him.

"I would like to ask some questions," Thomas said and sipped at his own ale.

"Why?"

"I am looking for a man who traveled with the party of abbots."

"I was with them myself. For what reason are you looking for this man?"

"One of the abbots was worried about him because he disappeared." That is a lie, Thomas thought, but Abbot Mordredus might have expressed such a concern if he had thought to do so.

Ned returned to staring at his drink.

Thomas vaguely described the person he sought. It was so general that almost any man in England might fit it, including, as the old woman noted, the one in front of him.

Swallowing the last of his ale, Ned awkwardly poured another drink from the jug. When he clutched the pitcher, it was obvious that his hands pained him. After a hesitation, he shoved the jug toward the monk.

Refusing the offer, Thomas added, "Have you seen the one I seek?"

"Maybe he has left. A few have given up their journey and gone back to their villages." He pursed his lips in thought. "A couple of men certainly did. They generally match your description. Rude, they were. Never bought a drink for anyone."

"When did they join your party? Was it the same time and place as you did?"

The man closed one eye and, with the other, stared at the monk with a look that suggested he might refuse to respond if questioned much longer. "Why would I care enough to notice?" he said and gestured at the elderly couple. "Ask the old busybodies. They notice everything and chatter endlessly between themselves about each of us. He can't hear. She is nigh witless." He mimicked speaking with his fingers. "I think they must talk even in their sleep."

Thomas watched as Ned clenched his mouth shut, curled his arms around his jack, tilted it, and lowered his head so he could drink without using his hands. His forehead was creased with dark displeasure or, the monk suspected, with pain.

I shall get nothing further from him now, Thomas decided. I am not the crowner and have no authority to pressure a man for answers. He rose from the bench with thanks.

The man grunted in reply, but the sound suggested less malice than rudeness.

Before Thomas left, he found Signy and told her he would be back. As usual, she refused to let him pay for his ale and sent him back to the priory with a coin for the poor at the hospital.

As Thomas stepped outside the inn, he looked up at the grey sky, felt the dampness in the air prick his skin, and sighed. Would this dark season never end?

Chapter Thirty

Prioress Eleanor and Sister Anne stood near the fire in the prioress' chambers and warmed their reddened hands while the dark orange cat rubbed his wet fur against their legs. Arthur had followed them out of the wind, eagerly bounding up the stairs in anticipation of a warm nap after ridding the priory kitchen of rodents. With the coming of winter, he often burrowed into the blanket that covered Eleanor's bed in her private room.

"At least this time my bed will remain dry," the prioress said to her friend, as she glanced at the wet spot left on her robe by her beloved cat.

Sister Anne laughed as she watched the splendid feline trot with single-minded purpose into the private chamber.

Eleanor sought the ewer of wine, poured two small mazers, and handed one to her friend. "This is Master Durant's latest discovery which he sent last month as a gift to the priory. His message included the ardent hope that it be served to our religious here. Prior Andrew confirms that it adds efficacy to the fire in chasing away the chill."

The sub-infirmarian sipped, and a look of appreciation brightened her expression. "A gift to God that truly brings much joy to mere mortals."

"From your cheerful mood, I suspect you have brought good news. What have you discovered?"

Sister Anne sipped again, and then put her cup on the nearby table. "I hope I have. Once we decided that all the deaths must be the result of poison, I narrowed my study when I looked through the herbals. Sister Oliva took half and I the rest to speed our search."

Eleanor finished her wine as she listened. *This may be an excellent vintage,* she thought, *but I pray that the news will be even better.*

"Monkshood was surely the method used to kill Abbot Gifre and sicken Abbot Odo." She tilted her head. "Is it wrong of me to praise gluttony in this situation? Abbot Odo's insistence on a larger portion of a food more acceptable to him saved his life."

The prioress stared into the fire. "Your remark holds no malice. As for any accusation against the Abbot of Caldwell, you have the right. You have known him longer than anyone except Ralf. Indeed, I have not yet found any reason to like the man myself. Please continue!"

"I now suspect that Abbot Tristram was killed with a death cap mushroom. For a noxious thing, it reputably has a pleasant taste. The initial symptoms resolve but subsequently return with a fatal conclusion. His early sufferings, as described to me, matched the ones listed in the herbal. His later ones do most certainly."

"Where might he have eaten the mushroom?"

"At the inn. I sent a lay brother to ask his servant who confirmed that the bowl of stew he was given to take to the abbot was topped with sliced mushrooms, a food of which his master was especially fond."

"Which means the killer knew his preferences. Did the other abbots have mushrooms in their bowls?"

"I asked about that as well. It seems Abbot Ilbert's servant noticed that his master did not receive any mushrooms. Abbot Mordredus did and objected, spooning the offending item out. Abbot Didier did not but hates the things, calling the taste akin to the Devil's midden. Abbot Odo is not fond of them but will eat the food during Lent. He got none, nor were Abbots Gifre and Ancell served mushrooms in their portions."

Eleanor sat still for a moment, pondering the information that brought her assumption about the murderer's identity into question. "I pray that Brother Thomas has found this mysterious servant who so eagerly offered to help in the abbots' service. Why did he choose these men?" She looked over at her friend. "You say that Mordredus was served the poisonous mushroom, yet he avoided death by removing them? That suggests he was another intended victim along with Tristram."

"Apparently not," Anne replied. "Abbot Gifre's servant was ravenous so begged to be given the discarded mushrooms when they were removed from the table and ate them with no fatal results."

"Which makes this inn supper even more curious." Once again, Eleanor was reminded of what Abbot Ancell had said. The evidence still suggested Abbot Mordredus, who might have done something to indicate he was a victim while avoiding a fatal end.

"As for Abbot Ilbert, Brother Thomas remembered he had been told the man had complained of flatulence." Sister Anne reached out for her mazer and finished her wine. "This is the most interesting part. One cure for the problem is tansy, an herb that is most efficacious in small quantities but is fatal in large amounts. Handling it in any significant amount also produces a rash."

Eleanor flinched as if struck. "A rash?"

"Brother Thomas mentioned that a man at the inn suffered just such a condition on his hands. I sent a salve with him to treat the problem."

"One of the abbots said that Abbot Ilbert had been advised to ask Abbot Odo for a remedy. The latter vehemently denied the story."

"Perhaps because tansy, if fatal, would be linked to him?"

"Or he never suggested it," Eleanor replied.

"Where is Brother Thomas?"

"Still at the inn, asking questions about those who had traveled with the abbots." Eleanor walked over to her window, cautiously opened the shutters enough to peek through, and stared down at the path leading to the village.

No one was on it.

"He should be back here soon," the prioress said, "but I had best send for Ralf. I think this man with the rash may be our suspect, and the crowner would want to question him further." What she chose not to mention was her sudden fear that Brother Thomas might come to some harm if the man was the murderer.

"And I should examine his hands. I know the look of a rash caused by tansy."

"If he is the servant, he must answer the question of whether he acted alone or at the behest of another. I still believe most strongly it is the latter."

"And let us pray that this man is the servant we seek and has not already fled," Sister Anne replied.

While Eleanor went to the door to summon a messenger to be sent to the Crowner, the sub-infirmarian poured them both a little more of the wine from Master Durant.

Chapter Thirty-one

The still-healthy abbots warily eyed each other as they huddled over their midday meal. They sniffed the ale before drinking and had not spoken beyond the obligatory prayers. Despite the reassurances of Prior Andrew that every precaution was taken, no one had even added salt, shunning anything that was not cooked into the food.

Dinner was as dreary as their expressions. Sister Matilda, alternating between worry and fear, had not tried any culinary miracles with the pale slabs of dried fish or the potage of beans and carrots flavored only with onions and desiccated parsley. Since a recent meal had killed one of them, she assumed they would eat only because they must and not to seek the pleasure of finely seasoned dishes. Indeed, they might be suspicious of them after the mushroom tart.

Brother Anthony stood by the door to the dining chamber. Since Brother Thomas had not yet come back from his errand to the village, the young lay brother had taken it upon himself to watch over the final preparation of the food in the new kitchen.

Ashen with terror and praying God would protect him, he had even tasted everything from the potage reheated in an iron pot, hanging by a hook over the fire, to the salty, tough fish kept warm near the hearth. He did not want to wait for the verdict of the caged mice before he let the meal be delivered to the abbots.

Then he insisted the entire meal be served at the same time and watched as the abbots were given their portions before sending the lay brothers back to the kitchen. Extra loaves of barley bread, a bowl of dried fruit, and ewers of ale were placed on a nearby table for him to offer as needed. He also made sure no one entered the hall while the three men ate.

Mordredus looked around. "Is there anything more to drink? This fish is as tough as a badly tanned cow hide and tastes little better."

Brother Anthony quickly poured a mazer of ale from a ewer he had already sampled. "The fish is from our own ponds, my lord, but it has been air-dried to last through the winter season."

"In comparison, the potage has no flavor at all, although acceptable enough for Lent, were it the season, which it most certainly is not," Didier said. "Our brother, Odo, is correct. A little meat is needed in winter. Such is necessary to warm the blood and chase away the cold." Reaching out politely with three fingers to take another small morsel of fish, he carefully took a bite, grimaced, and rudely spat it out.

Ancell looked at him with disgust.

Didier wiped his mouth with his napkin and ignored the silent rebuke.

One of the kitchen lay brothers knocked at the door and asked if Brother Anthony wished to be relieved. Since Brother Beorn had confirmed him to be a reliable man, the youth agreed. The meal was almost done, and there was only the dried fruit, should the abbots desire it. Brother Anthony did need to visit the garderobe.

Stepping outside the dining hall, he wondered what had caused Brother Thomas this long delay, then hoped it meant he had found an answer to the deaths. But he knew he would regret the resolution to the crimes. Sinful though the thought was, he dreaded returning to the tedious tasks Brother Beorn assigned to the youngest lay brothers.

He had enjoyed working in the new kitchen as well as watching Sister Oliva and Sister Anne in the apothecary, but he had skills in neither task. He sighed as he thought of the many days he would have to spend sweeping walks and, later in the year, pulling weeds. Did God truly believe it was a virtue to be bored?

Trudging off to the garderobe, he relieved himself and then decided to make sure the place was free of danger. It did not take him long to prowl through the latrines, checking for hidden caches of questionable mushrooms or secreted daggers. He regretted that he could not examine the abbots' individual quarters and prayed that none of their attendants was the killer. Before the dinner was served to their masters, he had seen the servants led off to the church, ordered by the abbots to pray for the souls of the dead men. Soon the men would trudge back for the brief and even more austere dinners they were permitted.

"What are you doing here?" Abbot Didier stood at the entrance to the latrine with his hands on his hips. His expression was grim.

"Making sure the supply of moss is adequate, my lord." Brother Anthony was surprised he had thought to say that and quickly gestured at the small piles of the essential article near each hole.

The abbot approached one of the holes and looked into it as if expecting to find a hidden spear ready to stab him should he sit.

"I am leaving," Brother Anthony said and hurried out the door.

Abbot Mordredus greeted him just outside. "Is Didier in the garderobe by himself?"

"He is, my lord."

"How long has he been alone?"

"I just left him." Brother Anthony was beginning to wish his bladder had been stronger and he had remained in the dining hall.

"And why were you there?"

"Moss, my lord. I was checking to make sure…"

Mordredus pushed past the youth and hurried into the latrine.

With relief, Brother Anthony went back to the dining hall. The lay brother, who had replaced him, quickly fled with an armload of items to the kitchen.

The table had been cleared of trenchers and platters. The bowl of dried fruit sat in the middle. No one, it seemed, had eaten any. Two ewers of ale had been placed on the table as well. One was empty and the other almost so.

Ancell was staring out the window, a mazer in hand. His expression was pensive.

Compared to the other two, Brother Anthony thought, he seems so calm. Looking outside as well, he saw the line of servants walking slowly from the church. The lay brother bowed his head and backed away from the window to await any requests.

Didier entered the dining hall, went directly to the ale, and poured himself another cup. Looking over his shoulder, he glared at Mordredus, who had just marched in from the garderobe.

Mordredus looked into the ewer. "Greed is a sin," he muttered. "Of course, Didier took the last of this."

Abbot Didier walked into his chambers with his cup and slammed the door shut.

Just as he did, a servant of one of the abbots peered cautiously into the hall, his face bright pink from the chill. His expression suggested he hoped none of those men would have any demands so he could eat his meal.

Suddenly, there was a scream of rage. Didier emerged from his room, holding a parchment in his hand. His face was apoplectic red.

"You!" He pointed at Mordredus. "You have done this!" Dropping the item, he raced to the abbot and began striking him with the palm of his hand. "You are the killer! Only you could have committed this blasphemy!"

His contemplations shattered, Ancell spun around and grew pale with either shock or indignation.

Brother Anthony shouted at the two men, begging them to stop the violence.

They had fallen to the floor, kicking and scrabbling at each other.

The young man picked up the parchment and ran to the door, summoning servants to separate the two fighting men while sending another to Prioress Eleanor with word of the fray.

As the servants fought to restrain the enraged men, Brother Anthony looked at the object he held.

On the parchment was a crude drawing of a man in an abbot's outfit, holding up his robes and standing before a kneeling, naked woman who was reaching out for his grotesquely engorged penis.

Stunned by what he saw, the youth squeezed his eyes shut and tried very hard to pray.

Chapter Thirty-two

The offending parchment lay on the table in Prioress Eleanor's audience chamber.

With a wry smile, Brother Thomas stepped back from viewing it. "I have seen better drawings etched into the walls of churches by bored young clerics," he said. "But the message is clear enough, and I doubt the one who did this cared about his reputation as an artist."

Eleanor might have laughed if the situation had been less fraught with danger. "Abbot Didier has been accused of having a mistress and fathering children," she said. "Abbot Mordredus wrote a letter to Rome in which he revealed his brother abbot's sins in much detail. If he is the one who left this in Didier's chamber, what more did he think his act would accomplish?"

Sister Anne's eyes twinkled with the hint of amusement. "Surely one does not willfully ravage good parchment without excellent cause."

"Maybe Mordredus is obsessed and considers lust to be the greatest of the seven deadly sins? He wants Didier to suffer even greater humiliation because he so blatantly flaunts his vow of chastity?" Thomas face suggested he had doubts about this suggestion.

"Yet he denies he is culpable and claims he is equally outraged by the insult to his brother in God." Eleanor looked at Gracia, who was standing with head bowed by the chamber door, and asked her to serve them all something to drink. Then she quickly flipped the parchment over to hide the drawing. In a rural world where farm animals openly rutted, the sexual act was not shocking. Yet Gracia had been raped, and that was reason enough for the prioress to keep the young woman from seeing something that might remind her of the violation.

Sister Anne was surprised when Eleanor did this, glanced at the young woman, and then nodded to the prioress with understanding.

"Prioress Eleanor and I questioned Mordredus after he was taken to our small priory cell," Thomas explained to the sub-infirmarian who had not been present.

"Since the attack by Didier was vicious, he did not protest the indignity of his incarceration," the prioress said. "After his wounds were cleaned and treated by the hospital lay brother, I explained that he would be made as comfortable as possible and that the decision to place him in a guarded cell was as much to protect him as anything else."

"And Abbot Didier?" Sister Anne thanked Gracia for the cup but noticed the hesitant glance the young woman gave the parchment on the table. Had the prioress not hidden the drawing quickly enough?

"He is satisfied that the man he thinks is a murderer is locked away and under guard."

"What of Abbot Ancell?" Sister Anne regretted she could not have been there for the interrogation but understood that the abbots would have objected. It must have been hard enough to tolerate the presence of Prioress Eleanor.

"He saw nothing. After Didier left for the garderobe, Ancell went into his own chambers to escape Mordredus, a man whom he dislikes. When he heard that man leave the dining chamber as well, he came out and went to the window where he fell into a musing on the definition of virtue. According to him, that is a debate he enjoys having with himself." Prioress Eleanor hesitated. "He said Abbot Didier returned to the dining hall shortly after but had the courtesy not to interrupt his contemplations. Mordredus was not far behind. Ancell chose to ignore them both and continue with his thoughts until Didier screamed and the fight began."

"Brother Anthony confirmed that. When he arrived back, the abbot was standing by a window, clearly deep in thought, and Didier did arrive as claimed," Thomas said. "Then Mordredus entered and seemed bent on starting an argument over who drank the last of the ale."

Sister Anne shook her head in amazement over the petty concerns of men who ruled great abbeys.

Eleanor sighed. "Abbots Ancell, Didier, and Odo have been assigned guards. To watch over them, Brother Beorn picked a former blacksmith, a well-scarred crusader, and a brawny fisherman from among the lay brothers. No abbot has any wish to venture from his quarters. Their servants will accompany the food from the new kitchen and serve their masters' meals under the vigilant eyes of our lay brothers."

"Do you think Abbot Mordredus is telling the truth?" Sister Anne looked at the floor where the great orange cat was patiently waiting for her to pet him. She willingly bent to do so.

"Before I express any opinion on this or who might even be the killer, Brother Thomas has news which you must hear first." Eleanor gave permission to the monk to speak.

Thomas repeated his discussions with the elderly couple and the man who had benefited from the salve for his rash. "Two men have escaped, however. One may not be the man we want, but I have my doubts about the other. We could have lost the killer."

"I pray not, Brother, but I discovered some information in my herbals which suggests hope. I believe that tansy may well have been used to kill Abbot Ilbert. If he suffered from attacks of wind, tansy in a small dose can bring ease. In a much larger amount, it is fatal. The symptoms he exhibited match those of one suffering a surfeit of the herb."

"Tansy? You have prescribed that for Sister Ruth," he said.

"And for that ailment. I blame myself for not realizing the significance of one special problem with the remedy. If handled without caution, it produces a rash."

Thomas gasped. "The man to whom I gave the salve…"

"He suffers from just such an affliction on his hands," Eleanor said.

"And the treatment has not yet caused the symptoms to disappear, although it has lessened the redness." Thomas hesitated as he saw his prioress about to speak.

"I have already sent for Ralf and his sergeant," she said. "You and Sister Anne must accompany them to examine the man's hands."

"My question about Abbot Mordredus shall wait," the sub-infirmarian said. "If this man at the inn is the one we seek, he may well name the one who ordered the killings, unless he himself is the sole murderer."

There was a knock at the audience chamber door, and Gracia rushed to open it.

Ralf and his sergeant, Cuthbert, stood outside.

Chapter Thirty-three

Brother Thomas waited outside the inn with Sister Anne and her lay sister attendant.

Standing away from the entrance, the trio was discreetly hidden from view. Although the sub-infirmarian had occasionally come to the village, those instances had involved violent death or an illness that might cause terrified villagers to wonder if God had sent a fatal plague to destroy them like Sodom and Gomorrah. Neither was something the monastics wished to suggest lest it cause panic.

Ralf and Cuthbert had just walked into the inn with cheerful demeanors, suggesting that their visit was a casual one. The village locals were accustomed to seeing the men stop by for a companionable cup of ale. To avoid frightening Signy's good customers away with any suggestion of coming violence, the two greeted particular friends and soon sought the innkeeper to quietly explain why they were there.

Skillfully feigning cheerfulness, Signy described in a low voice where the wanted man lay, suggested they remove him through the kitchen, and offered her house across the road for the interrogation.

Cuthbert used the kitchen entrance to slip outside and alert the religious to the plan, then the sergeant went back to join the crowner.

The three monastics hurried to Signy's home.

As she opened the door, Sister Anne was relieved to see that the innkeeper's foster children were not there, although a poppet was seated on a small stool, snuggly wrapped up in a colorful scrap of wool. A heavy slingshot hung from a peg in the wall. She smiled, remembering when Ralf had given it to Nute.

In silence, they waited for the crowner and Cuthbert to bring them the man they sought for examination.

Ned was sleeping on his straw mat, the cheapest lodging available at Signy's inn. When Cuthbert shook him awake, and the man saw the scowling visage of the crowner above him, he paled but offered no resistance. With little effort, the king's men led him down the stairs, through the kitchen door, and into the house where Sister Anne awaited.

"Stretch forth your hand," she said, her voice firm but not unkind. Brother Thomas gripped one arm and held it steady so she could carefully examine the irritation. It may have faded in color but oozing blisters and thickened skin remained. "When did you last handle the tansy?" Her expression was now as frosty as the outside air.

Ned looked first at the two men standing by the house entrance and next at the tall, muscular monk holding his arm.

Thomas grasped him with slightly greater firmness to emphasize that the man might find cooperation more reasonable.

"Tansy? How did you...?" The suspect began to tremble.

Ralf put his hand on his sword hilt and walked up to the man. "You are the one who offered to help the abbots at the inn where they stayed the night before they came to the priory here." He clasped Ned's shoulder and squeezed it hard. "You helped their servants with the meals. Then you accompanied them here."

"I did, my lord. No law prevents me from doing any of that."

"Has some imp changed you into an autumn leaf? You shake like one in the wind." Ralf crouched to stare into the man's widening eyes.

Despite emitting a strong reek of terror, the trapped suspect tried to stare boldly at his inquisitor. "If you were not the king's man, would you not do the same if a man with a sword shook you awake and asked you about an innocent act as if it were a treasonous thing?"

"I think you know you committed a crime and fear hanging."

Ned paled. "I have done nothing to warrant that, my lord! Of what do you accuse me?"

Ralf raised an eyebrow that was halved by a scar from a long ago battle.

"I swear an oath of innocence on my soul's hope of heaven!"

"Tell us the tale of how you came to meet the abbots at the inn and begged to serve them." The crowner sat back on his haunches but made sure he could still easily draw the dagger at his waist if not his sword.

Looking at the sub-infirmarian and monk, the man's eyes begged for mercy but found none reflected back at him from their gazes.

The lay sister had bent her head and ignored him.

"I am not a patient man, knave," the crowner warned, "nor do I find your stinking company worth more than a brief moment. You are a thief, stealing me away from the attention I should be spending on the king's more pressing duties. A dank cell with a few hungry rats can hold obstinate criminals who waste a crowner's time."

"Nay, my lord! I am willing enough to tell my tale. My cousin, who serves Abbot Didier, sent word that I should meet the abbots at that particular inn. The message said that Abbot Mordredus might have some work for me." He looked pitiful. "I needed money, my lord. The winter is hard, and I have no master." He coughed and looked around. "A drink for my dry throat, my lord? Out of charity?"

Ralf ignored his plea. "How did your cousin know that the abbots would arrive at the inn when they did? Travel is never certain in winter."

"I do not know. You must ask him. Perhaps a horse lost a shoe...."

"And where were you?"

The man turned pale. "Ale, my good lord?"

"Continue with your story, knave. Then I shall decide if you have been honest enough to deserve that munificence, but also do not forget that men who live with outlaws in the forest are due little mercy. I have no doubt you know such men well."

Ned gulped and went on in a voice made hoarse from terror. "I am no kin to outlaws! It was honest work I sought. My cousin told me to suggest I worked at the inn and must appear desirous of employment in a more righteous place. Since it was a remote area, he assumed there would at least be whoring. If I offered to help with the serving of the meal to ensure none of the abbatial party would be contaminated by sin, Abbot Mordredus would look even more favorably upon my plight." He stared at his feet.

Ralf bent closer and hissed into his ear. "I am swiftly losing patience."

The man wiped sweat from his eyes. "I did as I was advised, spoke to the abbot, and was greeted kindly. He asked me what I might do about the serving of the meal, and when I replied, he agreed to the plan. In the kitchen, I spoke with each servant and tried to accommodate the desires of each abbot. When I conveyed the demands to the cook, she was furious because they made more work for her. But I did my best." He tried to puff out his chest. "I was very forceful."

Brother Thomas whispered to the crowner who nodded.

"I have heard that the meal at the inn included mushrooms," the monk said. "Were there other differences in the food served?"

The man seemed bewildered. "It was a stew made from ox meat, to which I added some additional slices. My cousin also found a moment to whisper to me that it would be more palatable to Abbot Tristram if mushrooms were added, a food to which he was especially partial. Abbot Mordredus was also fond of them but liked them whole, not sliced as did Abbot Tristram. The other abbots either hated or were indifferent to mushrooms so I should not add them to the stew. He gave me a handful of sliced mushrooms for Abbot Tristram's stew and whole ones for Abbot Mordredus. I added them as requested."

"I have heard that Mordredus saw the offending item and spooned them all out," Thomas said. "When you learned of this, what did you think or do?"

The man looked confused. "I was not told, Brother. I can only repeat my truthful account. I did what I was asked to do and nothing more."

"After the serving of the meal, what happened?"

"I sat with the cook and listened to her complaints before taking my meal with the abbots' servants. The cook was angry but no longer blamed me for what the holy men had demanded. She let me sleep in the kitchen until morning light when I rose and spoke with Abbot Mordredus. He was willing to take me on until they reached Norwich." He fell silent, looking anxiously for some reaction or word from the king's man.

Expecting him to continue, the crowner and the monk said nothing.

Sister Anne stood and walked away, ostensibly to examine the fine stitching on a youth's robe that Mistress Signy was sewing.

Cuthbert remained by the door.

"The tansy," Thomas finally said. "Tell me why you handled the tansy that gave you this rash."

"It did?" He blinked. "My cousin told me that Abbot Ilbert was suffering from the wind after the meal and needed relief. He handed me a packet of tansy, told me how to prepare it and, when I was done, he took the remedy to the abbot." Ned shrugged. "I know nothing of the herb. If I had, would I not have refused or at least taken precautions against this painful affliction?"

The monk frowned as he tried to decide how much truth the man spoke. Finally, Thomas looked at Ralf and said, "I think that is honest enough, Crowner. It is Didier's servant we need to question."

Ned threw up his hands. "Why would it not be true? What reason would I have to lie?"

Ralf and Thomas glanced at each other and back at the quivering man.

The crowner tilted his head to one side, his expression similar to a hungry bear contemplating a floundering salmon in a shallow stream. "Abbot Mordredus agreed to let you travel with them until Norwich. Why did you not accompany the party to the priory?"

"When the abbots decided to change their destination, my cousin came to me with a bag full of coin. He said my services were no longer needed, and this was my compensation. It was far more generous than I had imagined and much more than any other man would have earned for the small things I had done. Of course, I was content to depart, thinking I would immediately travel with another party on to Norwich—until I discovered the road was impassable."

"You did not wonder at the impressive largesse for so little effort?" Ralf looked incredulous.

"These were abbots, my lord! Men of God. I assumed my cousin had told them of my plight, and God moved their hearts. He said he had been given a fine gift as well for finding a man to protect their virtue on the road. Since he had been amply rewarded, why would I question their charity to me, a poor man?"

Sister Anne looked over her shoulder. "Why go to Norwich?"

"My brother lives there. I thought he might give me shelter and food until I could find work."

"Give me his name," Ralf said.

The man also gave his brother's occupation and described where he lived.

"Have you had any further word from your cousin in the priory?" Anne asked.

"Why should I? My services were ended." Ned shrugged in an attempt to show confidence, but the stench of his sweat betrayed him.

"Have you gone to the nearby priory since you arrived at this inn?"

The man shook his head with evident bewilderment at the query.

Thomas first glanced at the stern Ralf and then forced all gentleness from his voice as he asked, "You have heard no news of the abbots while you waited here?"

"My hands were painful, which put me in bad temper. Why would I talk to people who annoyed me or who seemed to have cares I did not share? Lest you think me uncharitable, Brother, let me remind you that I could barely feed myself with the pain in my hands. Was it not a kindness to avoid adding to the burdens of others like the young couple or the man with the rotting leg?" He raised his one free hand. "And I, too, have the right to ask questions! Although you helped me with the salve, why have you brought the king's man to accuse me of some unnamed but clearly despicable crime?"

"You do not know of any reason why I should be asking you about your time with the abbots or have your hands examined by the priory sub-infirmarian?" For the first time, Ralf's question was asked in a neutral tone, his eyes unusually sad for a man who thought he was confronting a killer.

"My lord, I do not. I can only assume you have confused me with another if you think I committed some crime."

The crowner looked at his sergeant and signaled to him. "Cuthbert, take this man away and lock him up."

"But I have done nothing!" Ned shouted as the sergeant pulled him to his feet, then squealed in pain when his wrists were tied.

"Nothing except kill at least two men," Ralf said.

The man screamed and struggled, but he was held fast by Cuthbert.

Gesturing with his head to drag the howling man away, the crowner added, "But don't beat him until you hear from me." Ralf was not inclined to torture or to violence, but it never hurt to let a suspect believe otherwise.

After Cuthbert departed with his prisoner, Brother Thomas shut the door.

Sister Anne rejoined the two men. "I do not think him guilty," she said.

"Not willingly," the monk said, "but he did the killing, even if he did not mean to do so."

"Now we have Abbot Didier's servant to catch." Ralf looked frustrated. "What possible cause had he to kill these men?"

"Or did he do so on the orders of his master?" Thomas was equally baffled.

"And yet it is Abbot Mordredus who is locked in a cell," Sister Anne said. "Didier is free, and both Abbot Ancell and Abbot Odo remain alive. Guarded though they may be, Abbot Didier has proven to be a very clever man."

The crowner paled and ran from the house. The three religious were close behind. Stumbling through the snow, all prayed that they would be able to reach the priory before another death occurred.

Chapter Thirty-four

Winter is not kind to stone, but maintenance on priory walls and roofs is often dangerous or impossible between the harvest season and Easter.

Prior Andrew had taken his prioress on a tour of the damage done so far by ice and storms to the structures in Tyndal. As he showed her each crack, leak, and broken stone, they discussed whether the damage was too hazardous to leave until spring and in what order the repairs should be made.

"We are fortunate that you have found good workmen," Eleanor said to her prior. "The last repairs have all held. These are new defects, and you have gotten the most serious leak fixed."

"I claim no credit, my lady. It is Tostig who found the men for us." Prior Andrew leaned heavily on his stick, his face taut from the pain of his old wound sharpened by the pervasive cold.

She agreed in part. Tostig, Gytha's brother, was a man of many talents who had taken over the priory brewery to the great profit of Tyndal and was also gaining much wealth in his other business endeavors. A man of quiet faith and much gratitude, he did all he could for the benefit of the priory in appreciation for God's kindness to him in his ventures.

"You still deserve praise. Tostig may have sent the men to us, but it is you who have made sure the work was well done," she said, then suggested they quickly seek the warmth of a fire.

Prior Andrew was a humble man, but her comment made him blush with happiness.

As they approached the path that led to her chambers, they heard a man cry out, begging them to stop.

Abbot Didier was running toward them, his arms waving frantically. The priory lay brother assigned to guard him was valiantly trying to keep up.

"My lady, please!"

"Calm yourself," the prioress said to the sweating, wheezing abbot.

He took a deep breath and gasped the words: "You must come immediately! My servant is dead!"

Eleanor was horrified. How could this happen? She turned to Prior Andrew. "Quickly send a messenger to the village. Crowner Ralf, Brother Thomas, and Sister Anne are at the inn. They must return immediately."

The prior hobbled away as quickly as he could until he disappeared into the icy mist that presaged the next snowstorm.

"Take me to see the corpse," she said to Didier, and they hurried to the guest quarters. The red-faced guardian, a man of significant size, puffed steadily behind.

◇◇◇

The body lay near the dining table. As Eleanor knelt beside it, she saw the cup which had fallen from his hand, the contents seeping into the cracks of the wooden floor. Bending close to examine the liquid, she saw bits of herbs, a few with the spiked appearance indicative of monkshood. The man had vomited, and his mouth was frozen open in an expression of horror. His face still glistened with sweat, and when she touched his neck, the flesh was warm. He had died recently.

She stood and looked at the trembling abbot. "Tell me what happened."

Didier opened and shut his mouth, but he had lost all power of speech.

"If I may, my lady, I shall speak for him." The sturdy lay brother, recovered from the run, took the abbot's arm and led him to a chair next to the table. Gently, he pushed him into the seat.

Didier was shaking, and his face was as white as the outside snow, but he managed to nod approval.

She gave the lay brother permission.

"Abbot Didier and I went to the church to pray. After Abbot Mordredus was taken to the cell, the abbot needed to retreat to the church altar several times before his soul regained calm. This last time, we spent a long time on our knees before returning to the guest quarters, finally refreshed in spirit." He gestured at the body. "Only to find…"

"He was still alive!" Didier began to weep.

"How did you know? Forgive my questions," Eleanor said gently. "I must have answers to help me understand how this terrible crime can be solved."

"He was still convulsing like Abbot Gifre did before he died," the lay brother replied.

Didier began to hiccup with painful sobs.

The lay brother put an arm around the abbot's shoulders and whispered comfort into his ear before looking back at the prioress. "Abbot Didier and I decided we must both seek you or someone from the hospital. I was not going to leave his side out of fear for his safety."

Abbot Odo's guard opened the door to his charge's room and asked what was happening.

"Is all well with the abbot?" Eleanor asked, feeling an eerie chill spread through her.

"It is, my lady."

"What sounds have you heard recently from the dining hall?"

"Nothing," the man replied. "I have been reading to the abbot."

"Stay with him. Do not move from your chamber. Bar the door. Let no one enter unless you hear my voice or that of Brother Thomas."

He asked no questions and quickly shut the door. She heard him bolt it.

Eleanor spun around to face the chamber of Abbot Ancell. Terrified by what she might find, she ran to his door, hesitated for just a moment, and then knocked.

There was no response from within.

She knocked louder, waiting again for what felt like an eternity. Hesitating no longer, she threw open the door and stared inside.

On the floor lay two corpses: a bald lay brother and the priory man assigned to guard the abbot. After a brief examination, the prioress concluded they had both been poisoned in the same way as Didier's servant.

Abbot Ancell, however, was nowhere to be seen.

"May God forgive me," she whispered in horror. "I have been so terribly wrong."

Chapter Thirty-five

After ordering Didier and his guard to lock themselves in their room and follow the precautions she gave the man caring for Odo, Eleanor ran from the guest quarters to the stables.

Where else could the man have fled? These murders had just been committed. If God were kind, the prioress was confident she could catch up with the killer before the lay brothers in the stable had provided him with a horse to escape.

The frozen snow broke sharply under her feet, slowing her, but she was relieved to see that only one set of footprints had preceded her.

As she entered the stables, daylight was fading, and there was so little light inside she could barely see. A few horses snorted. Some shifted position.

That was the only sound.

Suddenly, she realized that it was the hour for prayer. The lay brothers she expected to find here had left for the church.

Eleanor was utterly alone.

"You are a fool to be here!" she muttered softly, then stopped and listened carefully for any noise. Cautiously watching the shadows, she began to back out of the stables before her presence was noted and she was trapped.

A hand clamped against her mouth, and she felt the sharp edge of a knife blade against her throat. She had not even heard the man's step behind her.

"You are indeed a fool," Abbot Ancell hissed into her ear, "but women can never match a man's wits."

Eleanor prayed for calm.

The abbot shoved her into an empty stall and thrust her against the wall.

For an old man, he is very strong, the prioress thought, and tried to shift her head. Her cheek was pressed against the rough wood, and she feared splinters would be lodged in her eye.

He snorted with contempt at her movement and let the knife bite her skin. A small trickle of blood from the cut rose, broke, and began to wend its way down her throat.

She willed herself not to acknowledge her pain.

"See how helpless you are, you whore. As you face death, I pray that you see how wicked it is for you to command men. Eve's daughter must never rule the sons of Adam. It is unnatural. Your Order serves only Satan."

She grunted, hoping he would interpret her sound as agreement and release his grip just enough....

He pushed her harder against the wooden planks. "To send your soul back to your dark master is a righteous act, for a virtuous man must rid the world of evil, but I never meant to kill any of my brothers in Christ."

If only she could keep him talking, she thought, she had a chance to survive if Ralf arrived in time. She chose to ignore the likelihood that Ancell would kill her anyway if the crowner tried to save her. Doing her best to sound appropriately piteous, she whined.

"Heretical and unnatural creature! Are you fearful enough of God's wrath?" He laughed. "Unlike you, my fellow six abbots were pious men, and I knew they must be given the chance to repent. They had dared to assume they were worthy of a bishopric, and God chose me to teach them each a lesson. I tried to sicken them. When a man is deathly ill, he trembles for his sins and repents. I had hoped they would hurry back to their abbeys to do penance, and then I, alone, would meet with the envoy and gain the reward I deserved. But Ilbert and Tristram were so

befouled by their wickedness that the Devil coveted their souls."
He chuckled with glee. "And since God took no action to save
them from eternal damnation, He must have been pleased when
those first two died."

Eleanor grunted in an attempt to speak, but he pressed his
hand harder against her mouth until her teeth began to hurt. If
only she could find a way to bite his hand, but he had pinched
her lips shut to prevent just that. A drop of blood slipped into
one eye from a new cut in her forehead.

Ancell's face was so close to hers that Eleanor almost gagged
from the fetid breath of his unhealthy gums. If she vomited, he
would let her choke on it, and she struggled to swallow.

"After that, I knew God wanted me to have no mercy. When it
came time to attack another, I had to kill. The victim was Gifre,
but it mattered not who died. Odo should have succumbed too,
yet God must have believed he was still able to repent. But you,
whore of the Prince of Darkness, tried to subvert God's will and
surrounded the living abbots with guards. You had one of your
wicked minions taste the food. I could not kill the rest as they
deserved." He sighed. "I almost succeeded in getting Didier
to kill Mordredus over that obscene drawing I slipped into his
chambers when both men left the dining hall." He banged her
head against the wall. "Had it not been for you and that thin-
rumped imp disguised as a lay brother, God would have been
victorious once more, aided by my hand, His most faithful
servant!"

Eleanor was dizzy from the blows but willed herself to think.
Could she kick back with her foot and strike the man's genitals?
All she needed to escape was for him to lessen his hold for an
instant. Even if he was strong for his age, surely she could still
run faster.

"Then Didier's servant demanded more money than I had
offered for his willingness to assist and remain silent. Instead of
taking joy in the virtuous deeds he had helped wreak with Ilbert
and Tristram, he fell in love with Satan and became infected
with the vice of greed. The man may not have seen me sprinkle

the monkshood on the tart, when I pretended to appreciate the hot food, but he knew it was I. He threatened to reveal all I had asked him to do unless I rewarded him more generously. God demanded that this covetous liegeman of the Devil die."

Eleanor swung her foot back, but she had miscalculated her timing and how the abbot stood. She only hit his knee.

With all his strength, Ancell slammed her repeatedly against the stall.

Her nose began to bleed, her head screamed with pain, and her knees were weak.

"You are still rebelling against God's will, whore. Your death will not be as swift as I might have offered you," he muttered into her ear. "It will not be monkshood. I promise you that."

Eleanor could not even imagine what method he would use, choosing instead to hold on to that modicum of hope that someone would find her here in time. How long had it been since the bells rang for the Office? Her next trick was to pretend she was fainting, something she was near enough to doing anyway.

She slumped.

He grabbed her and held her up against the stable wall.

Might the effort of holding my full weight up tire him enough, she wondered. If nothing else, she decided, he might kill me swiftly if it does.

"Was it you who planted that spider that bit me?"

She had forgotten that detail. If only she had known the crimes he had committed, she might have been tempted to do what he accused. Only I would have chosen a more venomous spider, she thought, then begged God to forgive her.

In reply, she tried a grunt that sounded vaguely like a denial.

"You lie!" He took a deep breath.

She knew the moment had come and began to pray for the forgiveness of all her sins.

Suddenly, he made a strange noise, and his knife slipped from her throat.

He had let her go?

Spinning around, she saw him lying unconscious in the straw. Standing over him was Crowner Ralf holding a large stick. He grinned, although his face was pale. "Do you think God will forgive me for striking an abbot, my lady?"

"You saved my life, Ralf. I shall pray that He forgive every sin you have even thought of committing."

Chapter Thirty-six

The storm had come and gone during the night, covering the hushed earth with a heavy mantle of snow. Cold though the air was, a warm sense of peace now surrounded the village and priory. As word spread of the crimes committed in that holy place, all felt a sense of relief that the violence had ended and no new plague of sickness had come to gather souls.

In the prioress' chambers, Gracia added another piece of wood to the fire before taking a fresh ewer of hippocras and heating it with a red hot poker. The steam rose, and with it the peppery scent of spices, blended by Sister Matilda, filled the air.

As Eleanor watched her maid, she saw that the young woman's look was now tranquil and suddenly knew that she had made her decision. A chill froze the prioress' heart. With determination, Eleanor banished the dread and turned back to the conversation between Sister Anne and Brother Thomas.

"At least Ralf did come to wish his brother a safe journey back to his abbey," Sister Anne said, her eyes twinkling with mirth.

"And with some joy since Abbot Odo's hopes for a bishopric died with the papal envoy." Brother Thomas smiled at Gracia who beamed in response to the monk she loved like kin.

"Some might say the timing of the envoy's death in Norwich from the lung disease was unfortunate," the sub-infirmarian replied.

"But Ralf told me that the news made him fall to his knees in gratitude that God had kept the iniquitous from gaining more power in the Church." Eleanor sipped at her wine before her eyes once again sought her maid.

"Ralf has always been wicked." Anne laughed.

"Which is why our love for him grows ever stronger," Thomas said and let Gracia fill his cup. He looked up at her and winked. "Our crowner is a good man," he said, "but I often tell him it is our friendship that saves him from himself."

"Do you think Abbot Ancell will be punished for his acts?" The sub-infirmarian refused the offer of more wine.

"Abbot Didier's servant is dead. His cousin has disappeared." Eleanor gave Brother Thomas a side glance.

The monk looked away and said nothing. He had not yet decided how he felt about the crowner's rare carelessness in letting Ned escape. Or was it intentional? He knew the crowner well enough to suspect he blamed Ancell and Didier's servant most.

The escaped man had never known that his acts might lead to murder. Ralf told the monk that Ned grew angry when he learned his cousin had used him to commit such crimes and wept to learn of how the abbots died. Apparently, his cousin had always loved bright coin and rarely questioned the source. But Ned believed his cousin would have balked at murder and may have tried for more gold from Ancell so he could escape and avoid the gallows. He did not show any grief over his cousin's murder, however, since his own neck remained at risk for the noose. Although Ned had safely vanished, Thomas doubted he would ever shed a tear for his cousin's wretched death.

"Abbot Ancell is an old man." Eleanor shook her head but regretted the motion. Her wounds, although healing, still stung. "He admits his deeds, arguing he did not intend to kill. Because the men died, he claims that God must have willed the result and thus he killed with God's blessing. He has become confident that the Church will find no crime in his acts, which he calls virtuous."

Suddenly, Gracia put the ewer on the table and asked her mistress for permission to speak.

"Of course, my child."

"Does that mean that Abbot Ancell will escape all punishment?" Gracia's expression could not have been clearer. She was outraged.

Eleanor chose to reply with caution. "Nothing escapes God's notice or judgment. The abbot assumed he was so perfect that his opinions were the equivalent of God's wisdom. Such arrogance is why pride is the worst of all the seven deadly sins. None of us can ever be the equal of God."

Gracia nodded. "How shall he be punished?"

"One of the wisest things my aunt, Sister Beatrice, taught me was that God will punish the wicked in ways that will distress them the most. You and I might wish one punishment on those who bring torment to the innocent, but we must let God respond in His own time and way. Our concept of what is justice in the situation will often fall short."

Although Gracia did not speak, her eyes revealed she was not satisfied.

"Our friend, Crowner Ralf, believes that the abbot should hang for his crimes," Thomas said, knowing that Gracia must hear Prioress Eleanor's answer.

"God might find that an inadequate penance." Eleanor smiled at her monk. "Although I will defer to those far wiser than I, it is possible that harder penance might be found for a man who has risen to the position where many serve his commands, where he has the luxury of private chambers, and where his life may be presumed austere but is far more luxurious than that of our Lord who ministered to the poor. After all, is not the intent of penance to cleanse our souls? And are we not allowed to purge our sins because God is merciful?" She suggested her monk continue.

Thomas leaned forward. "Consider this," he said to the young woman standing by the table. "Which do you think is the harder act of atonement for the crimes that have just been committed? The first is a quick hanging, even after confession but with little opportunity to ponder the full impiety of the sins committed." He waited to let her contemplate that option.

Gracia had lowered her gaze so her thoughts were unreadable. She tilted her head in reflection. "Give me the other choice if you will, Brother."

"Abbot Ancell might be striped of his rank and sent to a poor monastery where he must live like any simple monk, following the orders of others and obeying the rule of silence, eating food that is hard to chew, sleeping with only a thin blanket on straw in a dormitory, and performing hard labor as his other brothers do."

Gracia looked up with twinkling eyes. "I much prefer that to hanging him, Brother."

He gently shook a finger at her. "Remember that the punishment is intended to save his soul, my child."

"As it should if he is contrite and sees the depth of his arrogance," she replied with a more serious expression.

What her monk had described was the penalty Eleanor hoped would be Ancell's punishment. Without the testimony of Ned and his cousin, the abbot might still escape with little more than a rebuke. Yet he had confessed his crimes not just to her, when he held her captive, but later in front of Prior Andrew and Brother Thomas. She was confident he would continue to boast. Although he had originally hoped to escape detection, he now insisted that he had been God's hammer against the wicked. Such twisting of facts was typical of rampant pride.

The men he had murdered may not have been innocents, but Ancell had no right to execute them and assume God willed it. As for overweening ambition, from which they all suffered, the sudden death of the papal envoy and the loss of the chance for a bishopric should have made some ponder the frailty of their worldly desires. Eleanor suspected Odo would not be deterred, but Didier might. One lethally covetous servant was bad enough. How many more might surround a bishop who had an ever-growing brood?

Brother Thomas and Sister Anne looked at Gracia, then at each other.

"I must go to the hospital," the sub-infirmarian said.

"And I to consult with Prior Andrew," Thomas said. "Brother Beorn seeks advice about the young lay brother who showed such skill and courage in dealing with the abbots after my return was delayed."

Gracia brightened. "Brother Anthony? Oh, he is a clever youth!"

Eleanor tried not to gasp.

"He is that," Thomas replied as he handed her his empty cup. "Prior Andrew may find a use for such a man."

Glowing with joy, Gracia followed the two religious to the outer chamber door.

Eleanor ran a hand over her eyes. The time had come, and she was numb with foreboding.

If Gracia wished to leave Tyndal Priory for the world and a husband, the prioress would never let her see tears. The young woman's evident joy over the mention of the lay brother suggested strongly that she had found the companionship of men pleasing. Not that Eleanor failed to do so, but she had been determined to take vows from a far earlier age, and her fondness for most of the sons of Adam was chaste.

Well, most. The thought of the handsome Brother Thomas made her face grow hot. Lust for the monk and pride were her greatest sins, and she asked God once again to give her more strength in banishing them than either Abbot Didier or Ancell had shown.

"Are you ill, my lady?" Gracia was standing by the chair where the prioress still sat.

"I am sitting too close to the fire. That is all, my child." Eleanor stood and walked to the window overlooking priory land. The soft white mounds were dotted by blackened trees with limbs like clawed hands rising heavenward. Her heart ached, and she wanted to weep.

But she realized that Gracia had just slipped up behind her. I shall regain control of myself, she vowed, for my wishes may not be the same as God's.

Thy will be done, she silently prayed.

"May I beseech a favor, my lady?" The maid's tone was soft but resolute.

Eleanor forced her expression into one of calm gentleness and faced the child who had become a woman even though she had never grown much taller. "Always," she murmured. The look she presented Gracia was filled with maternal love.

The young woman knelt and folded her hands prayerfully. "I have thought about this for over a year, my lady, and now beg to be admitted to Tyndal Priory where I long to take vows. I am a flawed creature and the world may tempt with its delights and comforts, but I have found greater pleasures here. Both you and Brother Thomas, by your words and examples, have taught me that no earthly joy can ever match the fulfillment of serving God."

Throwing aside all attempts to rein in her emotions, Eleanor fell to her knees, embraced Gracia, and freely wept.

"Of course, you have my permission!"

Outside in the silence of a bitter cold and snow-burdened world, a bird called out, proclaiming to all that it had found the courage to survive.

Brother Thomas heard it and felt optimism slip into his heart. It was only a bit of hope, but the feeling was a balm and just enough to chase away the melancholy he had been suffering.

As he entered the monk's cloister on his way to Prior Andrew's chambers, Thomas decided how best to reply to Master Durant's last and very painful missive. He vowed not to part from the man. Somehow he and the wine merchant must find a way to love each other without offending God, and he swore to promise Durant just that.

No lightning bolt struck him. The peace he felt grew. The words he would use to the man he loved began to flow into his heart.

Author's Notes

The period between the end of the last war with the Welsh in late 1277 and the beginning of the next in 1282 was a comparatively quiet one. King Edward used the time to resolve his debt problems as well as build stronger bonds with his barons and the Church. In this, he proved he had learned a lesson from his father's bad decisions.

Parliaments were regularly held, allowing grievances to be heard and addressed before they festered beyond solving. This succeeded in keeping his barons reasonably quiescent.

But on the Church side, Archbishop Pecham, with his passion for reform on such issues as pluralism, was a thorn in the king's side. Pluralism was a practice especially favored by the king to reward his clerks with multiple church benefices for services rendered. But the two men remained friendly, and concessions were made on both sides. In 1280, Pecham even allowed the king to collect a tax on the clergy, a grant Edward had been trying to obtain since the beginning of his reign.

Now in his forties, Edward enjoyed time with his queen in their favored pursuits of hunting, pilgrimages (a tour of East Anglia in 1281 could have impacted a certain fictional priory), visiting with their children more than they previously had, renovating castles (a bath was built in Leeds Castle), and redesigning gardens with fountains or plantings to remind the queen of Castile. All this came to a dramatic end in March 1282.

That, however, is for another book.

To the best of my knowledge, there was no special papal representative (as opposed to the usual resident one) visiting or dying in England during the winter of 1281/82. The premise that one might have been sent with the particular goal of urging the king and his nobles to donate money, soldiers, and themselves to snatch Jerusalem and the Holy Land from the Muslims is reasonable. Such visits were frequent in Christian Europe.

Most of the crusades were pretty much failures for Christians, but that didn't stop the West from pouring money and blood into the efforts. The king, a former crusader himself, longed to return to Outremer and encouraged the effort, although he was too busy with the Welsh and the Scots to go back personally. The concept that abbots of important abbeys might want to meet with the envoy to prove their ability to get money for the cause, while preening or offering bribes for the next available bishopric, is also plausible.

In this book, Prioress Eleanor mentions that Pope Martin IV was known to have his faults. Popes may be popes, but no one dealing with the intricacies of power, secular or religious, was unaware that politics was played in the Church as well as the king's court.

And politics made the atmosphere toxic at the time in Rome. Part of the problem lay in the lack of stability. Pope Martin IV was the sixth occupant of the throne of Saint Peter during a twelve-year period. He rested firmly in the pocket of Charles of Sicily to whom he essentially handed over the papal State. Martin IV was often described as excessively mild-mannered, a terrible businessman, lacking in political judgment, and utterly obedient to Charles. (*The Sicilian Vespers: A History of the Mediterranean World in the Later Thirteenth Century* by Steven Runciman not only describes the problems but also gives the background to Dante's *Divine Comedy*.) Apparently, this pope's number was even wrong, thanks to errors in the thirteenth-century papal lists. He was really Martin II, but since he himself only lasted four years (and appropriately died a few weeks after Charles of Sicily), this little discrepancy was probably never considered important.

Let me assure you that the discussion in Chapter Thirty-six is not a thinly disguised authorial rant (heaven forfend!) to end the death penalty in modern-day America. It was a common stance of the Church for its clerics at that time. If the reader wants the other point of view, listen to Crowner Ralf who passionately believes in capital punishment for all murderers, clerical or secular. His opinion is scattered throughout all my books.

The term *penitentiary* was a Church concept, suggesting a place to serve penance for sins, after which the *sinner* (AKA *criminal*) was deemed to have cleansed himself of his sins and could be released as a full societal participant. We retain this concept with our modern penal system, at least in part.

Church history certainly provides enough examples of those deemed heretics, or otherwise offensive, suffering grisly executions after a Church trial. The actual mutilations, burnings, or quarterings were usually given to the seculars to perform. There remained a general prohibition against clericals performing executions.

Brother Thomas mentions that King Alfonso X of Castile and León (Queen Eleanor's half-brother) had his brother, Don Fadrique, strangled and Don Simon Ruiz de los Cameros burned at the stake for homosexuality. This was one belief, current at the time.

There is much debate over why these death sentences were given without any trial and carried out so swiftly. The myriad claims include allegations that the two men were involved in treason, an assassination attempt, were caught in bed together, perhaps guilty of a religious heresy, or that Alfonso was suffering the effects of a major health issue (possibly maxillary cancer) that eventually killed him. It is interesting to note that King Alfonso's respected and apparently beloved wife also fled from him at this time, an unusual act for a medieval queen. There were stories that the king's ill health had affected his behavior and temper, often causing him to become violent and erratic.

In any case, the quick arrests and almost immediate executions are odd. Alfonso X, like Edward I, was a strong believer in the rule of law. Yet Don Fadrique and Don Simon were put to death without any trial or even an explanation. People do not always live up to their vaunted reputations (see my *Land of Shadows* on Edward I), but this was a significant departure and involved a family member whom the king apparently loved.

The *Chronicle of Alfonso X*, written some sixty years after the king's death, says only that the executions occurred because Alfonso X "found out some matters." The king himself never gave any reasons, another strange element in this sad tale. Since I do not have the requisite background in this area to offer a reasoned argument in defense of any firm conclusion, I will not offer one. H. Salvador Martinez has discussed all the issues in his biography of this fascinating king: *Alfonso X, the Learned.*

Brother Thomas is, however, justified in fearing that these executions might be part of a growing pattern of which he was quite aware. Legal punishments for sodomy, male homosexuality in particular, were rapidly becoming more lethal.

I have often mentioned that medieval medicine, especially in Muslim countries, was far more effective than we moderns often assume. In this book, I have chosen to point out one of those instances when a treatment was horrific.

Eda suffers from stuttering. Like any caring parents, her father and mother wanted a cure. Not only did they wish this because they loved their child but also because she would have found it difficult to find a man willing to marry her.

In Eda's situation, one of the several treatments suggested for stuttering was to place a red-hot iron on the lips. It doesn't take much to imagine what that felt like or why a parent might decide the cure was worse than the remedy and stop it. Lest we get too smug about the assumed insensitivity of a parent even contemplating the application of such a thing, we might recall that we are still faced today with a host of medical options that are less than pleasant for a child or an adult. Do we not frequently choose what we're told is the most effective, despite the side effects, because we would rather obtain a cure? Eda's parents were in the same situation.

Many in the Middle Ages with severe health and physical issues died early in life, if they even survived birth, but society generally did not greet with welcoming arms those deemed disabled. Some saw the conditions as a sign that God had cursed the child or the parents for a sin they committed, while others concluded that the suffering experienced on earth by the child must substantially shorten time in Purgatory. Although a few might choose to call the burden a blessing, society as a whole still mocked and shunned the afflicted. We are little different today, although we have at least temporarily succeeded in demanding accommodations and passing laws so more of us may function productively and get around more easily.

For one who could not speak, was forbidden to speak, or chose not to speak, a form of sign or gesturing language was used in the Middle Ages. Monastics used established non-verbal signals during meals and other obligatory periods of silence. Eda is described as using a few mentioned in the two books I added to the bibliography. But gesturing language with seculars was also common. As one example, a twelfth-century canon consulted a respected wise man, both deaf and mute, for his opinion on which schoolmaster of two was the best. The wise man's response was in a form of sign language. My favorite of his opinions was putting his hands to his mouth and blowing, thus suggesting that one of the masters was nothing but a windbag.

Medieval sign language used by monastics and other individually developed ways of expressing oneself through gestures are not the same as modern methods used by those who are hearing impaired. For one thing, medieval signs were far less complex. In the monasteries, there was as much fear of garrulous hands as gossipy mouths. Professed monks might have a larger sign vocabulary, but novices were not trusted to be disciplined enough to know more than the basics such as "pass the salt," "where is the garderobe," "the abbot is behind you," and "would you please repeat that."

I think most of us have gotten far beyond the belief that medieval manners and dining were like those bone-tossing, beer-guzzling, and leg of mutton-chomping scenes shown in the Charles Laughton film, *The Private Life of Henry VIII*.

Manners were strict. The hands of diners and those handling or serving meals were washed before, during, and after meals. Food and cups were communal, but napkins were used to wipe the cup after use, and etiquette was clear on the proper sharing of platters (fishing around for favorite parts, as Odo does, was uncouth). Some prohibitions may seem pretty basic to us (putting a partially eaten piece of food back on the communal platter was not a good thing), but how often are we shocked today by folks talking while eating with their mouths open, another pretty obvious breach of table manners.

One did not lick one's fingers. Greasy hands were washed before the next bit of food was touched. A diner used three fingers to pick up a small portion of food and never belched in the face of his neighbor. Bread was used to clean utensils and often to soak up soup or gravies, but a different bit of bread must be used for each sopping.

Utensils and dishes were limited. Hands were the primary tool. Almost everyone had a dining knife for cutting and spearing food. Spoons were provided by the host and used for liquids. Forks were rare (and only for serving) or nonexistent. Bowls were used for liquids. Trenchers (usually stale bread but sometimes wooden in more affluent halls) were plates. Platters or dishes were mostly used for serving. A salt cellar, often very elaborate, was on the table, which would have been covered with white tablecloths in Tyndal Priory or anywhere the gentry was served. Spoons and cups were valuable and often "mistakenly removed" by diners. I read that the doors at one papal court were always locked after a meal until all the utensils were retrieved and counted.

Prioress Eleanor is one of the few heads of a prosperous religious house who adheres to the Benedictine Rule on diet. Of all the rules set forth by Saint Benedict, the prohibition against eating red meat was probably the most frequently ignored. Abbot Odo said it well enough when he suggested her food was all too Lenten. Sister Matilda, with her prioress' blessing, uses spices and other legitimate culinary tricks to make mushroom tarts, cabbage chowders, and roasted vegetables a pleasure to eat. Probably quite healthy, too, since no one at Tyndal, so far, has suffered a heart attack.

At Tyndal, two daily meals were served in which the flesh of any quadruped was banned, except for the sick and in other rare situations. At each meal, two cooked dishes were presented and a third of fresh fruit or vegetables, if such were available. A monastery affluent enough to build fish ponds (Tyndal Priory has them), would salt or air-dry their own fish to eat during the winter months, although other houses might purchase fish from fish mongers if close to rivers or the coast. Chicken would likely be fresh, although a bit tough since aged birds would be killed first, or else sun-dried or smoked for preservation. A quarter liter of wine per day was allowed (ale is drunk primarily at Tyndal by the religious), and all meals must be finished before dark. It was both an inconvenience and exception when the abbots in this story ate their supper so late, but courtesy and their rank demanded that the common practice be changed for that one meal.

Research into historical weather can be fun, but looking for specific thirteenth-century data on regional storms or unique episodes is a challenge. For this book, I hoped to find a cold winter to cause travel problems as well as provide atmosphere. Luckily, I found a site that gave me information based on written descriptions. The winter of 1281/1282 was perfect, as nasty a one as I had longed for. Snow lasted from Christmas to March. The Thames froze so solidly that people could walk across it. My favorite detail was the ice damage done to five arches of the medieval London Bridge, perhaps causing collapse. This gave me confidence that East Anglia was snowy, bridges could crumble, and the road to Norwich might well have become impassable.

Unlike the Saint Skallagrim I mentioned in *Sorrow Without End,* Saint Wilgyth of Cholsey was real, and I discovered her during one of those moments of wanton browsing which often produce the most fun tidbits. Although little is known about her, she was a sixth-century Anglo-Saxon saint venerated locally in Berkshire. Legend says her father may have been a Cornish or Welsh chieftain from Glamorgan and that a few other siblings were either bishops or saints. She appears in this book because I needed a female saint with a noted facial paleness. Since Saint Wilgyth was forced to watch while her stepmother killed two of her sisters after their father died, I felt certain she would have the requisite pallor.

Bibliography

The following is a list of tempting books that discuss food, recipes, and manners in the medieval period. I also added a delightful summary of papal histories, some interesting information on monastic sign language, and yet another treasure on medieval medicine. May you enjoy!

Food in Medieval Times, by Melitta Weiss Adamson, Greenwood Press, 2004.

Monasteriales Indicia: The Anglo-Saxon Monastic Sign Language, edited and translated by Debby Banham, Anglo-Saxon Books, 1996.

The Medieval Cookbook (revised edition), by Maggie Black, Getty Publications, 2012.

Silence and Sign Language in Medieval Monasticism: The Cluniac Tradition c. 900-1200, by Scott Bruce, Cambridge University Press, 2007.

Medieval Medicine: The Art of Healing, from Head to Toe, by Luke Demaitre, Praeger, 2013.

Food and Feast in Medieval England, by P. W. Hammond, Alan Sutton Publishing Ltd, 1993.

Oxford Dictionary of Popes, by J. N. D. Kelly, Oxford University Press, 1986.

Medieval Tastes: Food, Cooking, and the Table, by Massimo Montanari (trans, Beth Archer Brombert), Columbia University Press, 2015.

Food in Medieval England: Diet and Nutrition, edited by C. M. Woolgar, D. Serjeantson, and T. Waldron, Oxford University Press, 2006.

To receive a free catalog of Poisoned Pen Press titles, please provide your name, address, and e-mail address in one of the following ways:

Phone: 1-800-421-3976
Facsimile: 1-480-949-1707
Email: info@poisonedpenpress.com
Website: www.poisonedpenpress.com

Poisoned Pen Press
6962 E. First Ave. Ste 103
Scottsdale, AZ 85251